NOAH ZARC

BOOK THREE

ZARC

DECLARATION

NOAH ZARC

BOOK THREE

DECLARATION

D. ROBERT PEASE

NOAH ZARC: DECLARATION
First Edition
Copyright © 2013 D. Robert Pease
Cover Art & Illustration Copyright © 2013 D. Robert Pease

FIRST EDITION SOFTCOVER
ISBN: 1622534085
ISBN-13: 978-1-62253-408-1

Editor: William Hampton
Chief Editor: Lane Diamond

Printed in the U.S.A.

www.EvolvedPub.com
Evolved Publishing LLC
Cartersville, Georgia

This is a work of fiction. Names, characters, places and incidents are products of the author's imagination, or the author has used them fictitiously.

Printed in Book Antiqua font.

For Dad,
You helped me understand what it
really means to be a dad myself.

CHAPTER ONE

Waiting for the drones to attack was the hardest part.

Over my shoulder, the huge, glowing planet Jupiter filled the sky. I couldn't shake the feeling the small moon I was on would be sucked into the massive red spot—a storm like none other in the solar system. And if that didn't get me, the impending battle would.

I couldn't see the soldiers below me—miners really—who hid in the craters and crevasses of Callisto, but I knew they sat waiting. Just like me.

The blackened spires of the mine itself rose toward the star-filled sky. The sun was so small at this distance, almost 780 Million kilometers, that it barely lent any light to the surface. Such a cold, dark place to eek out a living; *I'd* never want to live here, but if these miners did, I'd do my part to help them stay.

For the hundredth time I checked the systems on my mech, a machine with powerful legs for running, able to lift thousands of kilos, and armed to the teeth—every fourteen-year-old boy's dream. Everything checked out, and the biometric shielding was up, so the drones should have no clue of my presence.

At first I was leery about using a mech, which was really just a huge thermsuit—I still preferred a ship that could fly—but Hamilton had assured me this was the best tool for the job, especially in the low gravity of Callisto. Now, after several battles, I loved every minute in one of these bad-boys—seven meters of pure awesomeness.

A flash overhead caught my attention. The glow of a rocket engine approached. Another. Then another. Lights filled the sky as hundreds of attack-drones fell toward the moon's surface.

"Wait for it," I said over the comm.

The drones began to hit the surface, and a small plume of black dust rose around the one nearest me.

"Now!"

I pushed the mech out of a crouch and launched toward the drone; the key was to hit them before they had a chance to get their own robotic legs and weapons deployed. The grinding whir of the mech's legs drowned out the sounds of shouting over the comms. A quick glance left and right showed the edge of our crater filled with mechs running down toward the drones that landed around the mining colony. The mechs the miners used had been constructed as workhorses, not to fight battles, but that didn't stop the miners from signing up to fight. They would defend their home.

The drone in front of me was almost unfurled, with four legs extending from its smooth body and rotating toward the ground. I raised both arms of my mech and mentally gave the command: *Fire two x3 Stingers.*

The drone exploded in a shower of metal and burning rocket fuel. I leapt over it as it crumpled to the ground, looking for my next target.

Two more landed, one to each side of me, and I mentally pushed into the computer system of my mech. Cameras on each wrist became my eyes. I lifted both arms to pinpoint each drone, and fired two missiles before they got a chance to deploy their weapons.

"We've got a breach!" The voice on my comm belonged to Commander Russell, the leader of the mining colony on Callisto. "South perimeter. Five drones."

I swung around. It took me a moment, but I spied the drones marching toward the mining colony's south entrance. "I'm on it."

I adjusted the power to the legs of the mech, fired-up the boosters, and after a quick crouch, launched toward the drones. The strength of the mech and the boosters, coupled with the low gravity of Callisto, allowed me to leap almost five hundred meters.

Landing with a crash, I fired at the nearest drone before any of them registered my presence.

Four drones turned toward me and fired their own weapons.

"Shields!"

I pushed the mech left, but one missile caught my right shoulder. The shields held but the force caused me to spin. Throwing out the mech's left arm, I fired two missiles in the direction of the drones. A satisfactory explosion told me one, at least, met its target. I spun back around and charged forward.

Only two drones still stood, their weapons pivoting to follow me.

I barreled into one, driving a massive fist into its core, then opened the mech's hand and ripped at the drone's innards until it fell to the ground. The last drone fired, its missile connecting with the left leg of my mech. Before I had a chance to compensate, the mech was falling over. I managed to twist toward the drone and fire one last missile, and the explosion showered me with debris.

I crashed to the ground, and as soon as the mech's movement stopped, only silence remained. Hanging from my harness, I looked around at the miners battling the drones in their own mechs. It looked like most of the enemy robots had been destroyed.

We'd won the battle.

***

"You guys were amazing out there." I grinned at the weary men standing around me. "We were highly outgunned, but you took it to them."

Commander Russell sat back, his massive arms supporting his head. "It was a bit dicey for a few minutes, but we managed."

Every man and woman I'd met on Callisto had that same determination on their faces. They led a hard life, but it made them both physically and mentally strong.

A younger kid with sandy blond hair, probably around my age, asked, "Do you think they'll be back?"

"Oh, I'm sure of it." This was only a feint, to see what kind of resistance this colony would put up. "Prime Senator Sarx has decided to bring all these outlying colonies under his direct control. He can't allow you to think you're outside the government."

Commander Russell sat up. "Why now?"

I raised my eyebrows.

"Why did Sarx decide to assert his authority after all these years of leaving us alone?"

I just shook my head. How could I tell these people that it was all my fault? Ever since I learned the true identity of Sarx, and his responsibility for the Cataclysm that wiped out all life on Earth, he had been on a tear across the solar system looking for me and my family, and working to gain control of every pocket of civilization. He needed to stop us before the truth got out. The problem was that not many people believed us.

That didn't stop me from trying, just like I did with those on Ceres and Europa. I worked so hard to convince them that Sarx was the true enemy, but they didn't buy it—even with drones falling around them, even with Poligarchy troops taking their men and women prisoner.

I had to keep trying. "It's a long story. Much of it hard to believe."

The eager looks on their faces made clear that news was slow to travel all the way out here.

"You know about the ARC Project?"

A few nods.

"You know who I am? The son of Noah Zarc?" Again some nods. "I've been traveling with my family ever since I was a kid."

Commander Russell smiled. Of course, I was still a kid in his eyes.

"During one trip, back to the time right before the Great Cataclysm, we discovered that Prime Senator Sarx was, in fact, the one who caused it."

A couple of gasps. Even more snickers.

"You see, he was a very powerful man who saw it as an opportunity to gain even more power."

"But that was over a thousand years ago." The sandy-haired kid couldn't stay quiet.

"You're right." I could tell they believed my story less and less. "But as I said, *I was there*. The *ARC* can travel through time."

I sometimes wondered how many people even believed we traveled through time. If I wasn't one who actually did it, I'm not sure I would.

"Sarx orchestrated an overthrow of the colonies on Mars. He invaded with an army, and has been in control ever since."

"Impossible." Commander Russell stood as if to dismiss me. "Look, kid, I appreciate what you've done. I appreciate that your family saw fit to come out and warn me about the drones. But you expect me to believe Prime Senator Sarx is over a thousand years old? Sorry, not gonna happen."

"He's a robot." This is where I usually lost them altogether.

"And I'm a little fairy with pretty pink wings." The commander grinned, and the hardened men and women burst into laughter.

"You've got to believe me. He's been ruling the Poligarchy since it was founded, and doing everything he can to make sure the truth isn't discovered."

Commander Russell turned to leave. "Well, I don't guess he has anything to worry about there. No one in their right mind would believe a story like that." He turned to the young boy. "Andy, make sure he gets a good meal in him, then see him to his ship."

The commander glanced at me once more and left the room.

* * *

After maneuvering my mech into the hold of the *Screaming Eagle* and powering down, I smashed my fists against the controls. It took all I had to keep from screaming. You'd think I'd be used to it by now, this being the sixth or seventh colony I'd told the story to. Only about half believed at least part of the story. Mom had success with a few too, but there were still those leaders, like Commander Russell, who just could not be convinced.

Even with Sarx sending attack drones and soldiers after them, they still couldn't connect that to an event that happened over a millennia ago. They would come up with some reason, some purpose behind Sarx's actions—he'd finally snapped, or he'd gotten greedy and wanted direct control of the natural resources.

Sure the colonists got angry, and they wanted to do something, but many times, like here on Callisto, that something was to hunker down and hope Sarx left them alone.

The part that pained me most—the thing my parents forbade me to talk about with the colonists because of their fear of what might happen to me — was the fact these attacks were really our fault. Sarx wanted us silenced, and he knew we were going around to the colonies pleading our case. We'd always stayed one step ahead of him, so if he couldn't catch us, then he had to control the colonies. By any means necessary.

After locking the mech into position, I pulled myself into my magchair and headed out of the hold.

"I believe you."

I looked up and Andy stood there watching me. He'd been eager to help. It seemed like there weren't any other kids his age around.

I smiled and started my preflight check of the hull of the *Screaming Eagle*.

"What you said in there, about Sarx, about the Cataclysm — I believe you." Andy walked along beside me.

"I appreciate it," I said, though I didn't know what good it would do.

"They'll come around. You'll see."

Although Andy was much stronger than me, he was still a kid underneath all that muscle. It was strange, but after all I'd been through over the past couple of years, I was starting to forget what that was like: just being a kid.

"I hope they do before Sarx wipes this place out." I finished my circuit of the outside of the ship. "We'll try to give you another warning when his troops head your way, but you guys have to be prepared."

He stood a bit taller. "We will. No way that *robot's* gonna get the best of us."

He said the word robot with a disdain I wasn't really happy with. Some of my best friends were robots.

I stuck out my hand. "Well, take care. I hope to see you again."

"You too." He backed up as I entered the ship.

I gave him one last smile before closing the hatch. I sure hoped to see him again.

CHAPTER TWO

I rendezvoused with the ARC at the agreed upon location and time.
I was relieved to come out of warp and see her sitting there among the
huge rocks of the asteroid belt. Deck after deck twinkled with blue and
yellow lights. My heart ached at the sight of her. Here we were, the
Zarcs, caretakers of a ship built to travel through time on a mission to
save Earth's extinct species, now subjects of the solar system's largest
manhunt.

The *ARC*, parked just a few years in the past, was the base of opera-
tions for a growing resistance against the Poligarcy. After the massacre
on Venus, and my parents' first-hand experience at the hand of Sarx's
forces, we'd all agreed that our first priority was to help remove the
Prime Senator from power.

The mission to collect animals had been put on hold.

I nudged the *Screaming Eagle* toward the hangar bay doors, and within
a few minutes had her docked and powered down. Before I unbuckled
from the pilot's chair, my dog Obadiah came running into the cockpit,
followed closely by Adina. The dog jumped into my lap and started lick-
ing my face profusely.

Adina giggled. "It looks like he missed you."

"I've only been gone a few days." I tried to push him out of tongue
range. "It's the best thing about him, though. You never have to guess
what he's thinking." I looked sidelong at Adina.

"Well, I—I missed you too." She looked down at her feet.

My cheeks burned a little.

The past few months had been a blur of missions to the outer colonies, interspersed with short bursts where we had to flee Poligarchy ships. Adina and I had hardly spent a moment alone. There were moments, like now, when I thought maybe there was something more between us. Then, just when I'd get the courage up to say something, someone would interrupt us, or she'd change the subject.

"Your dad wants you on the bridge right away. He wants to know if Callisto is on board."

I frowned.

"They didn't believe you?"

I shook my head. "No. Just like the rest." I pulled myself into my mag-chair and turned toward the door. "There will come a time when they find out the truth."

Adina reached out and touched my shoulder. "I'm sorry, Noah."

"Yeah," I mumbled. "Me too."

* * *

Mom, Dad and Hamilton were all on the bridge when Adina and I entered. Mom was visibly relieved and rushed over to give me a hug.

"I'm okay, Mom." I glanced at Adina as Mom smothered me.

"You've got to let me worry. It's my job." She pulled back and looked me over. "You're not hurt?"

"Of course not. That mech is a beast." I glanced at Hamilton and grinned. "The new shielding was amazing. I took a direct hit and it barely scratched it."

Mom's face filled with horror.

Man, why'd I have to say that?

Hamilton cracked a smile, but immediately suppressed it when he saw Mom.

"Noah, we only allowed you to go on these missions with the understanding that you'd be careful and stay out of danger."

"It's a war, Mom!" *Why does she keep treating me like a baby?*

Dad took a step toward me. "Don't speak to your mother that way." He spoke calmly, but he meant business.

"I—I'm sorry." What did they expect? "The good news is I got there in time. We stopped the drone attack, and I warned them Sarx would be back."

Dad brushed aside my obvious attempt to change the subject. "We've had this discussion."

A million times.

"Your mother and I understand things have changed. We are on the *cusp* of war, and you aren't a baby anymore, but you are still only thirteen years old—"

"Almost fourteen."

Dad put up his hand to silence my protest. "You are still a child."

Ugh, I hate that word.

"But you're also the best pilot in the solar system. You've got a good head on your shoulders, and our resources are thin. And...." He glanced at Mom. "We realize you're going to put yourself in danger with or without our knowledge, so please, at least try to be the adult you so desperately want to be. Don't put yourself in harm's way needlessly." He watched me, waiting for a response.

I sighed. "Got it."

"You don't sound too convincing," Mom said.

"No, you're right. What good would I be to anyone if I ended up dead?"

"Not exactly the way I'd put it." Dad smiled. "But well said."

He glanced over at the clock on the main console. "Now, get yourself cleaned up. I'm going to be addressing my contacts in the Poligarchy in one hour. I want you here, and in your best uniform."

I gave a mock salute. "Yes sir."

He grinned. "Dismissed."

I spun my chair around, glanced at Adina, and headed for the door.

* * *

Back in my room—well, the messy half of the room I shared with Hamilton—I glanced in the mirror. I was covered in black grime from Callisto.

Oh man, I let Adina see me this way!

I worked myself into the shower. Simple tasks like this brought back the reality that my legs didn't work, but I was coming to realize there were more important things in life than being able to walk. I sighed and let the warm water run over me, and the thrill of the battle on Callisto started to fade away, replaced by exhaustion.

Noah?

I opened my eyes for a second and looked around the bathroom, then realized I'd heard the voice in my head. After almost a year, I still wasn't used to it.

Closing my eyes, I found myself back in my room; well, James's room, on Mars. "Hi, James."

'How'd Callisto go?'

"Great! You should have been there. The mech was awesome!" It didn't take me long to forget about Dad's little talk.

'That's good to hear.'

I could tell something was bothering him. Not only could we talk via his link to my neuro-processor, I could also get a pretty good sense of his emotions too.

"What's going on? Is Gramps okay?"

'He's fine.' He paused. *'But I'm a bit worried. For the past few days there's been someone watching us from across the street.'*

"The Poligarchy?"

'I don't know. Probably.'

"Well, that doesn't surprise me. They have to wonder about you. I mean, you look just like me, except you can walk. They know Gramps is – "

'But it's not me.'

James glanced around the room. I smiled upon seeing how messy it was.

'They're following Gramps. He left earlier today to go to the market, and the guy across the street took off after him. When Gramps is gone, there's no one watching the apartment.'

"What do they want with him?"

I'd thought a few times about whether it was safe for Gramps to stay on Mars. Dad had even tried to convince him to leave.

It was the main reason James had remained there, and he was worried too. The other reason for staying was that he and Draben were our 'eyes on the inside.' They kept us up-to-date on the goings on with the Poligarchy, stuff we may not catch on the SolWeb.

'I don't know, but I don't like it.' He stood and headed for the door. *'I'm going to head out and see if I can find out what's going on. Maybe Draben has some intel.'*

"Okay. Keep me in the loop."

'Will do.' He severed the connection.

CHAPTER THREE

I thought it was funny we had these fancy uniforms. Mom and Dad weren't in the military, and we didn't have a *crew* to speak of, but Dad said that sometimes we needed to look official: like when we did any kind of fundraising for the *ARC 3000 Project,* or showed dignitaries around the ship. Most of the time though, they stayed in our closets collecting dust.

I had to admit, looking around the cockpit at my whole family dressed in bright white uniforms, and at Dad with his captain's hat on, we did look impressive. We all wore jackets with gold buttons down the front. The men wore pants, and the women skirts. Sam *never* wore skirts and didn't look too comfortable, and this was the first time I'd ever seen Adina in one. She had her dark hair up in a fancy series of braids, and her chocolate-colored skin looked amazing against the white of the uniform.

She glanced at me and smiled.

I quickly looked away as Dad moved to stand in front of us. "This is a very important call. I don't need you to say anything." He looked directly at me. "Just stand behind so they can see we are united."

We all stood — well, I sat — at attention. Dad continued to look at me until I nodded. *Why does he think I'd say something?*

"Okay then." He turned and faced the center of the bridge. "Computer, please open a connection to Senator Billingsworth."

"One moment please."

We waited for a minute or so, and as I fidgeted in my chair the computer chimed in, "Connection established."

Three men shimmered into view. Senator Billingsworth sat in an old Victorian chair. I'd met him once, back when we released the elephants on Earth. The other two men stood behind him.

"Senator, it is good to see you are well." Dad stood as straight as his old body would allow him.

"It's good to see you too, Noah." Senator Billingsworth was a small man, and looked to be in his early hundreds, not quite as old as Dad but older than Gramps. He had gray hair and sported a neatly trimmed mustache.

He nodded over his shoulder. "Of course, you know Senators Kline and Fisher."

Dad nodded. "Gentlemen." He gestured to the side. "And you've met my family as well."

Senator Billingsworth looked at Adina. "The girl's new."

"Ah yes," Dad said. "She joined our family a year or so ago. A fine young lady."

The senator nodded, and the room grew uncomfortably quiet.

Finally, Dad cleared his throat. "Thank you for taking time out of your busy schedules to meet with me."

Billingsworth just nodded again.

"I'm sure, by now, you've heard rumors of activity out in the far colonies."

Again, just a nod.

"There have been a number of attacks by drones, and even a few battalions of the Guard."

Senator Kline sighed. "We *are* members of the Senate. Of course we know about the—"

Billingsworth waved to cut him off. Apparently we weren't the only ones who were supposed to keep quiet.

"Continue please," Senator Billingsworth said.

"I don't deem to question the reason behind these attacks. The Poligarchy has their reasons, but—" Dad paused. He'd probably rehearsed this conversation a million times so it wasn't for loss of words. "I question the timing."

Billingsworth raised his eyebrows.

"You see, this all began immediately after we heard some disturbing news. After my son—" He gestured in my direction. "—witnessed some disturbing events, involving our Prime Senator."

"Do tell." It seemed Senator Billingsworth already grew tired.

"During a mission, back in time, my son met the Prime Senator."

"I imagine you meet all kinds of people in the past."

"But this was over one thousand years ago."

The senator's eyebrows shot up again. "Obviously, he's mistaken."

"Hear me out."

The senator nodded.

"During this mission, my son determined that it was indeed the Prime Senator, and that he was involved in some rather heinous acts, namely, the overthrow of the newly formed colonies on Mars, and the destruction of Earth."

"Please!" Senator Kline interrupted again. "You mean to say that Prime Senator Sarx was responsible for the Great Cataclysm."

"That is exactly what I'm saying." Dad paused to let that sink in.

"That's ludicrous—"

Again, Senator Billingsworth waved off Senator Kline. "And do you have proof for such an extraordinary claim?"

"I have my son's eyewitness account, and the testimony of...." Dad trailed off.

"Of who?"

Dad clenched his jaw as if he'd made a mistake.

"Who else? Who witnessed the Prime Senator partaking in these heinous acts?" Billingsworth sounded more bored than interested.

Dad sighed then said, "Benjamin Zarc."

"You're brother? Haon?" Billingsworth scoffed.

Senators Kline and Fisher laughed.

"You realize, don't you, that Haon has been imprisoned on Deimos since you captured him two years ago?"

"But he figured out a way to escape."

"Wouldn't we know if the greatest criminal of all time had escaped?"

"But—"

The senator was growing weary of the discussion. "I'm sorry, Noah. We've been friends for a very long time, but you are really starting to make me question your sanity. Still, for the sake of argument, let's say what you are proposing is true."

Billingsworth held up his hand and counted on his fingers. "One, Haon escaped an unescapable prison. Two, your son, and Haon, traveled back in time, one thousand years, where they witnessed Prime Senator Sarx carry off an invasion of Mars. And, three, they also saw him enact some event that caused the Great Cataclysm. All of this would imply that our Prime Senator then traveled back to the future where he is now in fact Prime Senator of the descendants of those he conquered a millennia ago."

"No," Dad said. "He did not have the capability of time-travel. Sarx has been living on Mars, as Prime Senator, for those thousand years."

"Now I know you've lost it. Sure, there has been a Sarx on the senate nearly non-stop since there have been colonists on Mars, but for you to tell me it has all been the same man, is just ludicrous. I'm sorry, Noah, but—" Senator Billingsworth paused, then licked his lips and continued. "The thing is, even if everything you say is true, even if our Prime Senator is the man you say he is, the past is the past. There's nothing we can do to change it. Even with your fancy time-traveling you can't change it, can you?"

Dad shook his head.

Billingsworth shook a finger toward Dad. "The history of mankind for thousands of years—way back to when we crawled out of the jungle—has been nothing but war and violence. Never, and I mean *never*, has there been a period of peace for longer than a few years. In fact, I would say that somewhere on Earth, there was always a war of some kind going on. For one thousand years, here on Mars, the Poligarchy has kept peace. Peace! Do you hear me? That, in my mind, is an impossibility, but somehow it has happened. That is fact, and you can't deny it. All this talk of Sarx causing the Great Cataclysm.... I say who cares if he did? Maybe it's what it took to finally get man on the right track."

Dad's shoulders slumped at every word the senator spoke. "Surely you can't—"

"I can, and I do." The Senator pushed himself out of his chair. "And the sooner you let all this nonsense go, the better." He turned as if to leave, but looked back and said, "This conversation never happened. I won't...." He looked at his fellow senators. "*We* won't let any of this get back to the Prime Senator. Return to saving the animals, and leave humanity to us."

The senator walked out of the projection and said, "Computer, disconnect." The image flickered out.

CHAPTER FOUR

"Maybe he's right." I hated the words the moment they left my lips.

Adina looked at me, her eyes wide. "Maybe he's right? Are you insane?"

"I have to go with Adina on this one." Sam paced around the dining hall.

Hamilton, Adina, and I sat at a small table. Us four kids had decided to debrief after the call with Senator Billingsworth.

"It's just he *is* right." I gripped the arms of my chair. "There *has* been peace for a thousand years."

"You call what's going on out there peace?" Adina waved in some nebulous direction. "He's attacking his own people. Drones are killing colonists, people who only want a decent chance at life."

"And don't forget what he did on Venus." Sam turned red in the face.

How could I ever forget the horror I saw on Venus?

"There is some logic to what the senator said." Hamilton sat down at the table with a cup of hot cocoa. "Maybe these actions are what it takes to keep the peace."

Adina spun toward him. "According to what I've read, there have been dictators all through history who have kept the peace. But at what price? People living in fear, the masses barely surviving while the wealthy get fat." She plopped down in a seat. "Sometimes I just wish...."

I leaned toward her. "Wish what?"

She wiped her eyes with the sleeve of her white jacket. "I wish mankind never climbed out of the Ice Age. Sure we had it tough, but we looked out for each other. Everyone in my tribe had a job to do, and if even *one* of us didn't do it the whole tribe suffered."

Somehow I think she might have had a rosier memory of life in her cave than reality, but I couldn't deny her people seemed happy.

"So where does that leave us?" I asked.

Sam stopped pacing and looked toward the door. "I don't know. I guess we wait to hear what Mom and Dad think."

Adina turned in her chair. "You don't really think they're just going to let Sarx get away with this, do you?"

I shook my head. "Knowing Mom and Dad, no way. Above all else, they believe in doing what's right, standing up for the helpless."

* * *

"What do you mean, there's nothing we can do?" I couldn't believe what I was hearing.

Dad had called us all together first thing the next morning. "Your Mother and I spent most of the night going over this. We just don't see any option."

"But he killed billions of people!" Sam obviously couldn't believe it either. "So we're supposed to just let him get away with it?"

"The only possible outcome we see is all of us either thrown in prison, or dead." Dad looked each of us in the eyes. "And we just can't be responsible for that. As your parents, we must keep you safe."

Adina dropped to the floor, devastated.

Seeing her that way made me even more upset. "Mom, you can't. We have to—"

'Noah!' James's voice in my head cut me off.

"We're kind of in the middle of something."

'It's Gramps. They've taken him!'

"What?!"

Everyone in the room stopped and looked at me. "James says Gramps has been arrested."

'The Poligarchy came to the apartment this morning and hauled him off, but not before....'

"Not before, what?"

'They tore the place up and beat him pretty badly. I don't know why they didn't take me, but they said I'd better tell the rest of my family to back off, or we'd be next.'

I relayed what James said to everyone. Dad slumped into his seat with his hands around his head.

"Don't you see?" I looked at Mom and Dad, pleading. "This is what Sarx is capable of. We have to stop him."

Dad looked up between his fingers. "This is exactly why we can't. James said we'd be next."

"I don't think we can let this go." We all looked at Mom. Her face was contorted in pain, but she swallowed and continued. "Don't you see, Noah? Sarx won't stop until we're silenced. Somehow he has kept this whole thing a secret for a thousand years. He can't let us run around telling the solar system he was the one who caused the Cataclysm."

"But he let James go free," Dad protested.

"Probably so he'd tell us, and we'd go after Gramps."

"It's a trap," Adina said.

Mom nodded. "Most likely."

Dad didn't look convinced. "So if it is a trap, we have to stay as far away from Mars as we can."

"Noah." Mom reached out and grabbed Dad's hand. "This is your father we're talking about. We can't let something happen to him because of what we have done."

Something I've *done she means.* "Let me go," I said. "Even if I'm caught, surely they wouldn't hurt a kid." Even as I said it, memories returned of the dead children on Venus, of Sarx trying to shoot me back on Earth. "You have to let me—"

'I'll go after him.' James cut me off.

"What? No."

'I'm not really asking, Noah. By the time you get here they'll be long gone anyway.'

Everyone in the room watched me, knowing by my expression that I was talking with my robot twin.

"James says he'll go after Gramps."

"You can't go alone."

'I'll talk to Draben. I'm sure he'll be up for another adventure.'

I didn't like the sound of that, either. I'd already put him in too much danger.

Dad interrupted my thoughts. "Tell him we can't ask him to do that."

'He's my grandpa too.' I could feel the pain in James's words.

"James says he's doing it, and there's nothing we can say to stop him."

Dad still didn't know how to react around James. Mom seemed to adopt him as her own almost immediately, but Dad struggled with the whole idea that James was a machine — as if he were nothing more than a glorified vacuum cleaner that could talk.

"I guess it's settled then," Dad said. "Tell James we'll head toward Mars. If he's able to get Gramps free, we'll pick them both up."

"He can hear you just fine," I said.

Dad just couldn't understand the concept that James could hear what I heard, see what I saw — at least when I let him.

'Thank you, Noah.'

"You just be careful."

'As careful as you would be.' His laughed echoed in my head.

CHAPTER **FIVE**

"I'm not ready to give up on the diplomatic option." Dad rubbed his temples;
the news of his father had hit him hard. "But I suppose we should be
prepared. Hamilton and Sam, why don't you see what kinds of weapons
systems we can piece together. We've got those J-3500s in the hold, but
I don't want you dismantling them. Just make sure they're in working
order. Also, continue your work on those mechs. Noah has obviously
shown they can be effective in a ground assault."

It was so strange hearing my dad talk of weapons and ground assaults.
He was a scientist, not a soldier.

"Noah, I think maybe you and I should pay a visit to Mars—"

"I thought that's where we were headed," I said.

"Not Mars of the present. I want to see this invasion Sarx pulled
off. Maybe if we can get proof it was in fact him, we can convince the
Senate."

I couldn't help but grin. It sounded like my kind of mission.

"Hannah," Dad turned to Mom. "I want you and Adina to work on
that project we talked about. If the Senate doesn't see the truth, then we
may have no choice."

Mom nodded.

Adina looked at me, scrunched her eyebrows together and mouthed,
"Project?"

I just shrugged my shoulders.

***

I wasn't happy about leaving the mech behind, but Hamilton said he needed it if he was going to build more of them. Once we got the hatch closed on the *Screaming Eagle*, I headed for the cockpit. It was strange going on a mission with Dad; I'd almost started to think of him as too old for this kind of thing.

He was in a lot of pain at times, and some mornings needed the aid of his exoskeleton to move around. He never complained, though.

I'd have been whining up a storm.

Mom and Dad both stood on the bridge, off to the side whispering when I came in. I buckled in as Mom gave Dad a kiss.

She turned to go. "Take care, boys."

"Yes, Mom," we both said. Dad looked at me and grinned.

Moments later we were rocketing through the asteroid belt. Once clear, I set the coordinates: Mars in the year 2099—more precisely, September 15th, just a few months after we'd been there before. We'd thought about going back to before the invasion took place, but all of us were finally convinced time couldn't be changed. Haon and I had spent enough time trying, and every attempt failed.

"Engage." Dad did his best impression of the captain from some old movie of his that we loved to watch.

I smiled and hit the button on my monitor for the warp manifold.

Going back a thousand years took several jumps, but at last we flew out into open space. As soon as the energy dissipated from around the ship, I searched the space around the red planet that had appeared in front of us.

"No sign of any ships. Maybe we got here too soon." I brought up long range sensors and searched for any ships between Mars and Earth. A couple appeared headed our way, but they were too small and too few to be the invasion fleet I had seen leaving Earth.

I reoriented the scanners and took a look at the Martian surface, and noticed right off the bat how sparsely populated it was.

"Take a look at Capital City," Dad said.

Pushing my fingers through the image from my holo-display, I located the capital. Again, it was a much smaller place than I'd visited in the past.

"Bring it up on the big projectors."

I flicked the three-dimensional image toward the middle of the cockpit between our chairs, then zoomed in so we were inside the dome, looking down on the city below us.

Dad sat back and studied the display. It was utterly empty — no people moved about the streets, no cabs, nothing. Then the destruction came into focus. The roofs of some buildings had collapsed, and wisps of smoke curled up from the windows of others. Piles of rubble and burned-out vehicles filled the streets.

"There's definitely been a battle here." Dad grabbed areas of the display and pulled them into tighter focus. He moved toward the city-center.

"There." I pointed to a column of smoke rising from the Capitol building itself.

He zoomed in. "It looks like we may have gotten here just in time to see the last push of the invasion."

Columns of armored vehicles surrounded the Capitol. Great guns mounted on the tops of some belched forth smoke and fire, and explosions rocked the buildings in front of them. Behind the vehicles, men marched slowly forward.

Dad zoomed in closer, and we could see little puffs of dust from small arms fire coming from the Capitol, which was outgunned. The remaining defenders could do nothing to stop the devastation.

"Let's get down there." Dad turned back in his seat and brought up a schematic of the Capitol Building.

"On it." I pushed the Screaming Eagle toward the Martian atmosphere and let gravity pull us in. "Cloaking shields up."

"Good idea. Computer, monitor all frequencies using voice and visual profiles of Prime Senator Sarx. Let me know if you locate him."

"Acknowledged."

"While the computer looks for the proof we need that Sarx is behind this, let's see if we can be of some help." He looked over and saw the smile on my face. "There's nothing we can do to stop the invasion, but perhaps we can save some lives."

I dropped toward Capital City, looking for an entrance to the main protective dome. It wasn't hard to find: a whole section of the dome had been destroyed along the northwest wall. It must have been where the invasion started. As we swooped down, I slowed and squeezed the ship through the opening, then immediately pulled back up and skimmed along the underside of the dome roof.

As we drew closer to the Capitol building, it became apparent Dad was right. With holes in the sides, the domed roof of the building looked about to collapse in.

I flipped on the external mic and the explosions of guns pounding the building echoed around us.

"Bring us in, but not too close," Dad said.

I spiraled down toward the Capitol dome, all the while keeping an eye on the tanks. "Switching to external cameras."

An image from directly below the ship came onscreen. Through the smoke and dust, I could see a fire burning within the building. A huge, gaping hole cut through the top of the dome. Several figures ducked in and out of the rubble inside, firing at the tanks with hand-held rifles and rocket launchers.

"Dad, how much do you think the ship's shields can take?"

"How much... what?" He looked at me with an expression that said he knew exactly what I was talking about, but didn't like it one bit.

"Fire from those tanks. I mean, they're thousand-year-old technology."

"A bomb's a bomb." But he cocked his head and watched the image. "We could probably withstand a few hits."

He watched me for a few moments and then nodded. "We've got to give it a try. Wait until I'm in place down in the hold."

I smiled, not sure if I was happy he agreed we needed to do something, or not. For the next few minutes, I sat nervously watching the building being pounded. *Hurry up, Dad.*

"I'm here."

"Okay, hold on."

Several tanks fired. The moment the ones on the side of the hole in the roof fired, I took *Screaming Eagle* down. I'd noticed a pattern. First one side would fire, then the other.

"Shields at maximum." I caught a dull shimmer outside our ship as the magnetic field surrounded it.

After spinning the ship around, I headed straight for the breach in the roof of the Capitol. The ship wouldn't fit through clean, but I counted on the shields keeping us safe. A huge shockwave hit as we collided with the dome—not pretty, but the quickest way in. I gave it a little more power and the ship widened the hole in the roof, pushing concrete and debris outward. I hoped not too much would fall on the defenders inside.

The magnetic field actually worked to repel the steel reinforcement in the concrete and the farther in we went, the wider the hole got. Finally, I pushed the *Screaming Eagle* all the way in, a tight squeeze, but the ship actually fit inside the giant hall that served as the main atrium to the Capitol.

I leveled off and descended toward the floor. "Just a few more seconds, Dad." A quick scan of the exterior monitors showed several men ducking for cover from the debris that fell from the dome. It actually helped keep them away as I landed. I had to turn just right to keep the wings of the *Screaming Eagle* from clipping some massive chunks of ceiling that littered the floor, but she settled down nicely.

"Okay, open the doors." I unbuckled and pushed myself into my chair.

Dad had a gas mask on and handed me one when I entered the hold. "The atmosphere is pretty bad in here."

Of course; a huge hole had opened the shield that covered the city to the thin atmosphere beyond. I nodded and slipped the mask over my head and face.

We headed down the ramp into the smoke. An explosion rocked the building, and Dad covered my head with his body. The rumble subsided and we looked around. A soldier, with a gas mask of his own, lunged from behind a fractured column, his weapon aimed right at us.

Dad thrust his hands in the air, and I did the same. "We're here to help!" yelled Dad.

Even through the mask, I could see the surprise on the soldier's face. He waved his rifle to call us over. Dad glanced at me and walked toward him, his hands still up. I followed as two more soldiers appeared on either side of us and leveled their guns in our direction.

"There's no time for this." Dad nodded over his shoulder. "We've got a ship. We can get you out of here."

The first soldier hesitated for a moment, then nodded. "This way."

He turned and dashed between two columns, and Dad and I followed. The soldier yelled something over the noise of explosions, but I couldn't make out the words. He came to a huge steel door, and knocked three times with the butt of his rifle. The door opened and he pushed through, motioning for us to follow. Once inside, the door slammed behind us and the sound of the bombardment quieted slightly.

"This way," the soldier said, and started down a flight of marble stairs.

At the bottom we found a huge, round door standing open, like an old bank vault. Inside a single light hung swaying from the ceiling. A man sat on the corner of a desk with a paper schematic laid out on it of the Capitol and surrounding buildings. He had a rifle on his shoulder, and a gas mask hanging at the side of his face. He looked up when we entered, his face covered in soot and filled with worry.

The soldier snapped his heels in attention. "General Roosevelt, sir."

"Who are these?" he barked.

"They just—landed a ship inside the building."

He jumped to his feet. "You what?" He towered over Dad.

Dad didn't shrink away. "We've come to rescue you."

"How's this possible?"

"I'm not sure we have time to explain. It looks like the building is going to fall around us at any moment." As if to emphasize the point, a blast shook the walls, and dust fell from the cracked ceiling.

The general slumped in thought for a moment, but then snapped up straight. "Agreed. How many men can you carry?" He started moving toward the door.

"If we squeezed, probably fifty or sixty." Dad stepped aside to let the general pass.

"Well, we don't have that many left, at least not here." He looked at the soldier still standing at attention. "Sergeant, get everyone moving. We need to get the wounded loaded up first."

"Yes sir." He saluted and ran back up the stairs.

General Roosevelt snatched the schematic off the table and a backpack sitting on the floor. "Let's go." He took the stairs two at a time.

Dad followed more slowly behind.

By the time we made it back out into the atrium, dozens of soldiers with loaded packs on their backs had gathered. Six wounded were carried on stretchers.

"This way." I hovered toward the open hold.

It must have been a strange sight for them. The inside of the ship was readily visible, but the cloaking shield hid the outside still. Although dust and debris made it so you could see the basic shape of the *Screaming Eagle*.

The soldiers, though, didn't hesitate and ran up the ramp, the ones carrying the wounded first, followed by about a dozen others. General Roosevelt stood barking orders and directing soldiers inside, while Dad stood beside him.

A whistling sound approached, followed by a flash and explosion. The wall behind Dad and the general exploded in a ball of fire and shower of concrete. The two men, along with several soldiers, were thrown to the ground.

General Roosevelt shook his head and climbed to his feet, but Dad didn't move.

I shoved my chair down the ramp, but a huge soldier with tattoos covering his muscled forearms stood in front of me. "We'll get your grandpa for you. Stay put."

I looked past him to see the general leaning over Dad. I nodded and tattooed arms guy turned and ran back down the ramp. He helped the general get Dad to his feet and they brought him onboard.

Dad smiled as they carried him past. "That was a close one. Perhaps we should get out of here."

"Do we have everyone?" I asked.

General Roosevelt glanced back at the destruction behind him and nodded sadly.

CHAPTER SIX

When I pulled the Screaming Eagle up through the roof of the Capitol, the walls and dome crumbled around it. A faint cheer rose from Sarx's soldiers outside as the building collapsed on itself. The invasion was over.

I sat alone in the cockpit. Dad had gone to the bunkroom to lie down, and the general and his men stayed in the hold; there wasn't much room for them anywhere else. I pushed the ship back along the way we had come and exited the city's protective dome by the same hole.

"Computer, have you located Prime Senator Sarx."

"Unable to determine his exact location."

My heart skipped a beat. "But you do have confirmation he's here?"

"Affirmative. I've recorded several audio samples."

"Play back from the beginning—"

"Permission to enter the bridge." General Roosevelt stood in the doorway.

"Computer, belay that request."

I nodded at the general. "Of course. Have a seat." I motioned toward the chair next to me.

He sat. "I had my medic check in on your....?"

"Dad," I said.

"He's resting comfortably." He studied me for a moment. "There are a great many questions that need to be answered."

I laughed. "I'm sure there are, but the first one is, what next?"

He shook his head. "I just don't know. I'm still a bit baffled by what happened."

"It was the Chinese," I said.

"Well that much was apparent, but why?"

"That's pretty complicated."

He raised his eyebrows. "You know?"

"I know some of it, but it's going to be hard to explain, and even harder to believe."

He snickered. "After everything that's happened these past few days, culminating with some kid and his grandfather—I mean father—landing a ship, the likes of which I've never seen, in the middle of the Capitol building... I may just believe you."

I put the *Screaming Eagle* in a holding pattern at twenty thousand meters. "I was there when the Chinese launched the invasion from Earth. They were led by a man named Sarx. Have you heard that name?"

The general shook his head. "We never heard anything. They just landed and began attacking us—no warning, no attempts to negotiate."

"That sounds about right." I tried to control my anger thinking about Sarx. "We actually tried to stop the ships as they left Earth orbit, but then I...." How could I tell him I had to let the invasion happen so I could rescue my family? "I was attacked."

"I'm surprised they had any kinds of weapons that worked in space. The ships we saw were nothing more than freighters."

"You're right. The ships that attacked me weren't from Earth."

His eyebrows went up again, but he kept quiet.

"I know this is going to be nearly impossible to believe."

He inclined his head toward me. "I'll try."

"The ships were from Mars, but not the Mars of today. They were from the thirty-first century."

The general just stared at me, trying to process my words.

"I'm from that time too."

He looked around the ship again, then back at me. "I—I guess that would explain a few things."

I watched him take it in. He actually looked like he might believe it, partially.

"You see, I only recently learned about the invasion at all. In the future there's no mention of the Chinese taking over. At least not publicly."

"So this Sarx, he — ?"

"Well, that's even more complicated."

"Lay it on me, kid."

I told him the whole story of how Sarx had tricked the Chinese Emperor, how he got Haon to make him a robot body so he could live practically forever, and how he was still ruling Mars almost a thousand years in the future.

"What about Earth? Why did the governments of all the member-states allow him to rule for so long after what he did here?"

I had avoided telling him, even hoped that maybe Dad could do it. "They—" I just couldn't bring myself to say it.

"They... what?" His face was deadly serious. He could tell it was something bad.

"They don't exist anymore. At least in the future."

"What? The governments. Is it the Chinese? Do they take over?"

"No." I swallowed. "They're all dead. Everyone."

He just stared at me, working his mouth.

"In the not-too-distant future, about four or five years from now, there's an event we call the Great Cataclysm. Everyone on Earth is killed."

"H—how?"

"Sarx, again. He created a virus, a biological weapon for the Chinese in exchange for control of Mars. What the Chinese don't know is that, once unleashed, it will destroy all living life on the planet—humans, animals, insects, everything."

The general sat, dumbfounded. His shoulders slumped forward as he tried to process it all.

"Everyone," he mumbled. I could imagine him picturing those he loved who were still back on Earth. Then his face brightened.

"But, if we know it's going to happen, we can stop it."

I shook my head. "No. We've tried. Time-travel is a strange thing. Once something has happened, it can't be stopped. No matter what we do, the Cataclysm will still take place."

"Surely—"

"I'm sorry."

"But you rescued us."

"Yeah, I know it's hard to get your mind around, but you were always rescued. We didn't change your future."

General Roosevelt stared blankly at the floor.

I tried to give him time to process it all, but I still didn't know what we were going to do next.

He looked up at me, with tears pooled in his eyes. "You know, I'm descended from a president of the United States of America, the most powerful country on Earth, at least it used to be. His name was Theodore Roosevelt Jr. — most people called him T.R. or Teddy."

I knew the name, having studied U. S. Presidents in Earth History.

"I'm Theodore Roosevelt the eighth. All my life I've lived under the shadow of that legacy. Roosevelts have been doing great things for generations. This was to be my big achievement." He waved toward the surface below. "I volunteered to oversee the security of the planet. Can you imagine the hubris I had, to think I could protect a whole planet?"

He just shook his head sadly. "Teddy Roosevelt pulled the country out of a great recession, putting people back to work. His son, in my mind, was an even greater hero. There was this huge war, back in the 1940s. They called it World War II. Theodore Roosevelt III was a general for the army. He led the first wave of soldiers who invaded enemy-held territory. It was called D-Day. Everyone knew it was suicide, but Ted Roosevelt. volunteered anyway. He didn't want to stand on the sidelines and send the younger men in to die. He would be there, on the front lines, giving encouragement, sending back vital information to the troops landing behind him."

He wiped his grimy sleeve across his eyes. "I always dreamed of having a chance to be that brave, but what happens when given the chance? I can barely hold out for three days."

"It's not your fault. The colonies on Mars were mostly scientists and families looking for a fresh start. Who could fathom someone would decide to invade?"

"I should have. That was my job. If only —"

"If only what?"

He glanced at the window. "If only I had more men. We were outmatched the moment those troops landed. I only had about two hundred soldiers total, and all we had were small arms."

As he beat himself up, I wished there was something I could say to help him. Then an idea hit me. "What if there *was* something you could do?"

"You told me we can't change what's already happened."

"True, but what if you could set things right? Bring those responsible to justice?"

"This *Sarx* character?" He looked at me, a small hope filling his face.

"Yes. I told you he's still in power. Dad and I came here to see if we could find proof of what he'd done, so we could convince those living in our time that Sarx was who we said he was. What better proof than an eyewitness?"

"But I've never heard of Sarx."

"Yeah, but you saw the invasion. And just before you came in, the computer told me it had recorded Sarx giving orders to attack the Capitol."

The general's face lit up. "So you think I should go with you? To the future?"

I nodded. "Why not? What do you have to lose?"

He thought a moment. "Apparently I've already lost it all." He glanced toward the door. "What about my men?"

"They can come too. We need all the help we can get. But... I do need to tell you that all the proof in the solar system probably isn't going to be enough to remove Sarx from power. We're most likely headed toward war."

A gleam entered the general's eye. "All the more reason for us to go with you."

"We need to talk to my Dad."

He stood. "What are we waiting for then?"

CHAPTER SEVEN

We entered the thirty-first century just outside the leading edge of the asteroid belt. I immediately scanned for any ships nearby and found none.

Dad looked up from his holo-pad. "Find us a good hiding place, Noah." He went back to his work. He and General Roosevelt were working on some kind of "battle plan."

I didn't like the sound of that.

I located a nice big asteroid and took the *Screaming Eagle* in. After gently setting her down, I reached out to James. *"Can you hear me?"*

'I'm here, Noah.'

"Any news on Gramps?" I knew it wouldn't be good, because his emotions were all twisted up in a ball of fear, anxiety, and sadness.

'They took him to Deimos.'

"What? No!"

His anger felt ready to bubble over. *'They deny it, saying he's being held downtown, but Draben did some digging. They transferred him last night to the moon.'*

Deimos was an inescapable prison. The atmosphere inside the prison itself was filled with a nano-virus of some kind. As soon as anyone set foot on the surface, they became infected. If they stayed on the moon, everything was peachy, but if they tried to leave the nano-virus attacked them from the inside, killing them almost immediately—nasty, but effective.

Of course, Haon had figured out a way around it, but now he was back there. And so was Gramps.

My emotions ran wild and I started to tear up.

'I'm sorry, Noah.'

"I'm sorry, too."

Dad heard me sniffle and looked up. "What is it?"

"Gramps."

He stiffened. "Is he — ?"

"No, he's alive, as far as I know, but James said they took him to Deimos."

"How could they — ?" He clenched his jaw shut and his temples throbbed.

'Why doesn't he just let it out?' James had the same thought I did.

"What are we going to do?"

Dad shook his head. "What *can* we do?" He was quiet for a few minutes, then looked at me. "Tell James we're coming to get him."

I smiled. It was something, at least.

'You can't do that.'

"Why not?"

'Because.' James was obviously fighting his desire to get off the planet with his concern for us. *'It's not safe. They want you to come. That's the whole reason for taking Gramps.'*

"We'll have to chance it." I wasn't about to let him get taken to Deimos too.

'No way. I'll find another way. Draben should be able to help. Maybe Sastra — '

I'd rather be the one flying in to rescue him, but he had a point. "James said he'd figure a way off the planet. He doesn't want to put us in any more danger."

Dad looked at me for a moment, then nodded.

'Okay, James. Be careful, and let me know the moment you're in space.'

"Will do, Noah."

Dad leaned back in and started talking with General Roosevelt in whispers.

"How can you go on like nothing happened?" I said.

He looked up, his eyes full of pain. "That's all I *can* do."

"But Gramps is in prison, one of the worst places in the Solar System, and you're plotting a war. I'm not even sure we should be fighting."

"How can you say that?" He looked genuinely puzzled.

"There hasn't been a war for a thousand years. Did you tell the general that?"

"Of course, we've talked about it."

"So, we're going to start one... for the first time in a millennia?"

His face softened. "Oh, Noah, we aren't starting a war. Sarx did that a thousand years ago. We're standing up for the helpless, delivering justice for those billions that died at his hands during the Cataclysm. We're defending those he's marching against now: the people of Venus, the colonists on the outer planets and moons. Don't you see? War is here whether we like it or not."

He gave me a smile. "Gramps understands this. He might be a crotchety old man, but he knows when to stand up and when to run. He knew they were probably going to come after him, but he didn't back down.

"Please understand, war is not my first choice. Even now I still have hope we can end this peacefully. You'll see when we rendezvous with the *ARC*. Your mother and Adina are working on something—a proclamation to the Poligarchy. It will probably still lead to war, but the blood won't be on our hands. They'll have a chance to step up and do the right thing, to be remembered through history as the ones who helped keep us from the brink."

"Okay, Dad, I'll give it a chance."

"And Noah...." He held my gaze with his brown eyes. "I'll do everything in my power to see Gramps free. There has to be a way. He's my father and he won't be forgotten." Some of the youth returned to Dad's face, and a determination I hadn't seen in a while.

***

I was still trying to wrap my mind around what was happening when the computer chimed, "Ship approaching."

I held my breath until the *ARC* came up on the screen.

Dad looked up and smiled. "Excellent. Computer, open a channel to the *ARC*."

"Channel open."

"Hannah, are you there?"

"I'm here, Noah." An image of Mom appeared on the screen. I pushed her to the center of the room.

"Were you successful?" Dad asked.

"Good to see you too." Mom feigned annoyance.

"Sorry. It's good to see you. So were you successful?"

She kept her mouth shut a second then smiled. "Yes, a complete success." A frown tugged at the bridge of her nose. "Well, almost complete."

"Great!" Dad seemed to miss the last statement. "We have a lot to discuss."

Mom looked at General Roosevelt. "I can see that."

"Oh, sorry again." Dad gestured toward the man sitting to his left. "This is General Roosevelt. He has—um—joined the cause."

"Good to meet you."

"And you, ma'am." The general tipped his head.

"Please, call me Hannah."

I fired up the engines and pushed away from the asteroid.

Minutes later we were all on board. Mom, Sam, and Adina met us when we came out of the *Screaming Eagle*.

Dad gave Mom a kiss and then turned toward the back of the ship. "We've got wounded we need to get to the infirmary."

Mom's face filled with concern. "Wounded?"

"From the invasion of Mars."

She glanced at Dad and I, searching for any wounds.

"We're fine," Dad said. "But there are some soldiers that need medical attention."

I hovered around and opened the gangplank to the hold, and soldiers climbed out of the ship, looking around warily holding their rifles at the ready.

General Roosevelt waved a hand toward them. "Stand down, men. We're safe." Then he whistled. "This is a ship?"

I glanced at the hangar bay. Looking through his eyes, I saw it was almost unimaginably big. The far side of the sphere that spun around us was almost lost in a blue haze.

"This is actually only a small part of it," I said.

He just shook his head as Mom went onboard the *Screaming Eagle* and quickly assessed the wounded. "Sam, help me get these men to the infirmary."

A pair of soldiers picked up each wounded man and followed Sam down the gangplank.

I moved over to where Adina stood watching with her arms folded, holding a tube about half a meter long. "Good to see you." I wasn't going to make the same mistakes as Dad.

She smiled. "You too."

"So...." I waited for her to tell me what she'd been up to.

She just stood with a mischievous grin on her face.

"Dad said you guys were up to something important. What's going on?" I turned briefly as Dad and General Roosevelt led the remainder of the men from the hangar.

Adina laughed and I turned back.

"It's fun messing with you." She conked me on the head with the tube. "Your Mom and I have been meeting with the leaders of all the various colonies, out in the outer planets, and even Earthome. We have a majority agreement."

"Agreement to do what?"

"This." She popped a cap off the end of the tube and tapped it against the palm of her hand, and a rolled-up piece of thin plastic slid out. She dropped the tube to the floor and unrolled the plastic. There was writing on it. At the very top it read: *The Unanimous Declaration of the United Colonies of the Solar System.*

"Is that—?"

"Yes." She beamed. "It's a Declaration of Independence. We're presenting it to the Poligarchy tomorrow." She pointed to the bottom of the page, at several dozen signatures. "Nearly all the colonies signed it. Look." She pointed to one signature: *Oliver Wolcott.*

"Ollie?"

"Yup. He says hi, by the way."

"So this is really happening?" I wasn't sure how I felt about it, but Prime Senator Sarx would be furious.

"Your Mom and Dad think it's the only way. Put it all out there and let the Poligarchy decide. Maybe when they see the overwhelming support we've gained, they'll listen to reason."

Don't hold your breath. "How did you get them to agree? When I was on Callisto it seemed there'd be no way they'd sign something like this."

She frowned. "Well, Callisto didn't sign. They still think they're far enough away that the Poligarchy will forget about them."

"The Poligarchy attacked them!" I just couldn't understand their thinking.

Adina shook her head. "I know, but the good news is that all the other colonies signed up. They know it's just a matter of time before Sarx takes over completely."

"Venus too?"

"Well, your mom said there's definitely a group of people on Venus that oppose the Poligarchy, but she has no way of contacting them. Sarx has too much control of the planet."

I thought about all I'd seen on Venus—the people Sarx had killed. They, more than anyone, had a right to declare independence from the Poligarchy. "So who wrote this?"

She smiled. "Well, much of it was written by Thomas Jefferson."

I laughed.

"But I adapted it to our needs." She rolled the plastic, picked up the tube, and slide it back in. Then she handed it to me.

"Why are you giving it to me?"

"Because...." She scrunched up her nose and grinned. "You need to practice. Your Dad wants you to be the one to read it to them."

"What? Me? Why?"

"He said the Zarcs are the face of the *ARC* project, and even with all this mess, it's still very popular back on Mars."

"Then why doesn't *he* read it?"

"I asked him that, and he just pointed to his own face. Apparently he thinks he'd scare everyone because he's so old."

"But he's a hero. Everyone who knows the story of what he did to stop Haon—"

"I don't know, but you've got to get working. You don't have to memorize it, but you want to make sure you don't flub up the words. I worked hard on it."

"But I'm not good at this stuff."

"You'll do just great." She bent over and kissed me on the cheek. "I have faith in you." She turned and walked away.

I just sat there rubbing my cheek, looking at the tube in my lap. How was I going to even think straight, let alone read this with any clarity, with Adina around?

I guess I'd better get studying because.... She kissed me!

CHAPTER EIGHT

Everyone congregated in the gathering hall. It was really just a big storeroom, but on special occasions — like this — we cleared it out. Once again I'd donned my dress uniform. I pulled at the scratchy collar and looked around. Adina and Sam had been working hard to make the room look official, setting up a platform with a podium on it, set to my height, with several chairs lined up behind. Each chair had its own holo-projector.

Adina adjusted a banner hanging on the back wall. She smiled when she saw me. "Are you ready?"

"No. I still don't understand why I'm doing this. Why don't you? You wrote the thing." I waved the tube at her.

"No way. I'd be way too scared." She grinned.

"You know how to make a guy feel better."

Her eyes passed over my shoulder. "Maybe you can ask him."

Dad walked in the room, dressed in his uniform and captain's hat, and strode toward me. "Are you ready?"

"Why does everyone keep asking me that?"

He smiled. "You'll do great, son."

"But why? Why me?"

He paused, then leaned over and put his hands on my shoulders. "Because, you're who this declaration is for. Your generation will inherit the solar system we're building today. If it were up to us old fogies, we'd keep everything the status quo, but not if we want a better future for you. Who better to make that point than you? You've done more to show me what's worth fighting for, these past few years, than anybody. I'm proud of who you are becoming. I'm proud of who you are right now."

He stood up, and for the first time in my life I was speechless. I'd never imagined my dad thought more of me than just a kid he needed to keep in line. Sure, he loved me, but I made it awful difficult sometimes.

"Thanks, Dad," I mumbled.

"Thank you, son." He looked around. Now, let's get this show started. "Computer, initiate connections to the delegates."

Adina took the Declaration from me, opened it, and placed it on the podium. The holo-projectors sprang to life and men and women appeared in their seats, all dressed in their finest. One seat remained empty, and I ran my gaze down the row of delegates again. Commander Russell from Callisto wasn't there. Mom must not have had any more luck convincing him than I had.

My eyes went to a small boy two seats down from the empty chair. It took me a moment before I realized who it was. "Ollie!" I pushed over to him.

"Look at you all dressed up in your uniform." Ollie's eyes sparkled.

"You too." He hadn't really changed since the last time I saw him, but he had a look on his face like he knew the gravity of what we were about to do.

"It took some major convincing by your mother to get Earthome's council to go along with this. But in the end, I believe we made the right choice."

"I guess time will tell." I lowered my voice. "Whatever happens, I'll make sure you're protected."

"Thank you, Noah. But maybe it's time we stood up for ourselves, instead of hiding away in our little bubble." He took a deep breath. "I'll do whatever it takes to protect my people, too, but it doesn't mean hiding away and hoping the rest of the Solar System leaves us alone. I can see that's a fantasy."

My dad cleared his throat behind me. "It's time."

"We'll talk again soon. Okay, Ollie?"

He nodded. "Of course. Go get 'em."

I smiled and turned toward the podium. Bright lights shone in my eyes as I stepped up. Dad took his place in a seat next to the delegates as I looked out into the empty hall. Mom, Adina, and Sam sat in chairs a few meters in front of me, while Hamilton messed with the cameras and main holo-projector. He spoke to the computer and moments later the room flickered, and the Senate chambers back on Mars appeared before me. No closed-door discussions this time; we would be projecting directly to the whole senate.

Senator Billingsworth sat alongside his two tag-alongs, Senators Kline and Fisher. The central seat, on the raised dais, remained empty.

A voice somewhere off-screen said, "All rise for the honorable Prime Senator Sarx." The senators rose from their seats. There wasn't any motion from the delegates behind me.

Prime Senator Sarx strode into the room through a door behind the dais. He glanced at his senators, and turned his eyes to me. "Please be seated." All the senators sat, as did the Prime Senator with a flourish of his robes.

"This is unprecedented." He nodded his head in our direction. "Never in the history of the Senate have we called a Gathering at the request of an outside organization, but...." He smiled a crooked smile. "I am not without compassion for the needs of my fellow constituents across the Solar System." His eyes played across the men and women seated behind me.

"And you," his gaze settled back on me, "we all know. The boy who saved Earth from that madman, Haon. Without you, there'd be nowhere to put all those animals you have onboard the ARC. I assume that's still your family's mission?"

I didn't say anything, knowing he was just trying to get me angry.

"You look like you're about to lose your lunch." The senators around him chuckled. "What have you to say to us today?"

The room grew quiet as I looked down at the page on the podium. A few people coughed.

I took a deep breath, and then began. "When in the course of human events, it becomes necessary for one people – our people – to dissolve the political bands which have connected us with another."

A murmur filled the room as the senators recognized this introduction.

"We *must* declare before the leaders of the solar system, our separate and equal standing, given to us by the laws of nature and of nature's

God. Because of our respect for *all* mankind, we are required to declare the causes which lead us to separation."

I looked away from my notes. I'd read this a hundred times last night.

"We hold these truths to be self-evident, that all men are created equal, that they are endowed by their Creator with certain unalienable rights. Among these are life, liberty and the pursuit of happiness. To secure these rights, governments are created among men, given their power by those they govern. Whenever any government goes against these truths, it is the right of the people to change or abolish that government, and to create a new one, building this new government in such a way to most effectively create safety and happiness for all."

A hush fell over the room. Many of the senators kept glancing at Sarx to gauge his reaction. For his part he simply sat with his hands bridged before him, his forefingers touched against his lips.

"Of course, no one should change governments for small or temporary reasons. But when over and over a government exercises power over its people in a cruel and harmful way, it is the right of its people — no, it is their duty — to throw off such government and to provide new protectors for their future security.

"This has been the plight of the outer colonies." I gestured toward those seated behind me. "Now it has become necessary to alter our former system of government."

I looked directly at Sarx. "The history of the Prime Senator of the Poligarchy is one of continual brutality and dominance creating an absolute tyranny over these colonies. To prove this, let the facts be submitted to the people of the solar system.

"He has imprisoned, without trial, innocent men on Deimos, from where there can be no hope of return." I had to stop for a moment as I pictured Gramps in a cold, dark cell.

"He has unlawfully deployed battleships to patrol the solar system, attacking and destroying any ship leaving its respective planet or moon.

"He has instigated an invasion of every colony, outside the asteroid belt, by highly trained soldiers or robotic drones, killing hundreds of civilians, the very people he has sworn to protect.

"He has sequestered men, women, and children to live in squalid conditions on the planet Venus, and has given them no rights or ability to petition for a better life.

"He has, in fact, murdered thousands of those very same people who, without any means of defending themselves, died by his direct orders and oversight.

"He has ruled as a tyrant, through subversion and trickery since the inception of the Poligarchy.

"And finally, Prime Senator Sarx—" I lifted my hand and pointed at him. "—has knowingly, and without remorse, caused the greatest act of horror humankind has ever witnessed, namely the Great Cataclysm, which wiped out fifteen billion people as well as all living life on planet Earth."

A gasp filled the room. Obviously the senators knew of, and were probably party to, the crimes happening today, but surely no one had ever accused the Prime Senator of causing the Cataclysm before. Sarx, for his part, only smiled and motioned for the crowd to quiet, then waved for me to continue.

I didn't like that, even now, he acted as if he were in control, but I went on. "On several occasions, we have brought these charges to the attention of this government." I looked at Senator Billingsworth. "But the only reply we have received is more attacks on our Colonies. A leader whose character is shown by such terrible acts is, by definition, a tyrant and unfit to be the ruler of a free people.

"We, therefore, the representatives of the united colonies of the solar system, gathered together in full view of the Supreme Judge of the universe, do in the Name, and by the Authority of the good people of these colonies, solemnly publish and declare, That we United Colonies are, and of right ought to be free and independent; that we are absolved from all allegiance to the Prime Senator, and that all political connection between us and the Poligarchy, is and ought to be totally dissolved; and that as free and independent colonies, we have full power to levy war, conclude peace, contract alliances, establish commerce, and to do all other acts and things which independent governments may of right do. And for the support of this Declaration, with a firm reliance on the protection of divine providence, we mutually pledge to each other our lives, our fortunes and our sacred honor. Signed and witnessed by...."

I turned and nodded to the row of men and women behind me.

The first stood. "Alexander Pavlenko, Titan."

He sat and the next stood. "Felicia Bell Livingston, Europa."

One after the next offered their support to the document.

"Fred Morton, Ganymede."

"Juan Carlos Paca, Ceres."

Prime Senator Sarx was beginning to look bored.

Callisto was listed next on the Declaration, with no name next to it. The man seated next to the empty seat stood. "William Jefferson Clark, Enceladus."

Then Ollie stood. "Oliver Wolcott, Earth."

The Prime Senator shot straight up in his seat and glared at Ollie. His glare turned into curiosity at this six-year-old boy. Then his face changed once more into recognition.

Several more stood announcing themselves until finally my dad stood last. "Noah Zarc. Sr., the Moon."

It was the last straw. Prime Senator Sarx surged to his feet, and the room erupted into chaos as the senators started shouting.

Eventually Sarx composed himself and waved for the senators to calm down. "So, this is your *Declaration*?" He spat the last word out. "You think you can just join together — a bunch of miscreants and treasonous...." Again he worked to hold in his anger. "You bring outrageous, unsubstantiated charges against me, then have the *audacity* to declare yourselves *independent!*"

There were several shouts of agreement among the senators, but I also saw some doubts. The senator from Venus, a woman named Barnes, seemed especially shaken. She glared at the senator with eyes that could melt steel.

Sarx held his fist in the air. "If it's a war you want, then it's a war you'll get." With a flourish of his robes he turned and strode out of the chambers.

A moment later, the connection was cut, and I stared at an empty room.

CHAPTER NINE

Dad paced in front of the delegates. "That went pretty much as expected."

Fred Morton, from Ganymede, stood. "I had hoped there still might be peace."

"Any hope of peace was long past." Dad smiled grimly. "We knew this document was tantamount to a declaration of war, but now it's out in the open. Perhaps some seeds of doubt were planted in the senators' minds."

Fred Morton sat back down shaking his head sadly.

Mrs. Livingston, the delegate from Europa spoke up. "Mr. Zarc is correct. We knew what we were signing. We are now at war with the Poligarchy. It may not be the easiest path, but it is the right one."

Dad straightened. "Now is the time to stand firm. Sarx needs the colonies. He needs the resources from your mines. Most of the wealth that drives his economy comes from the goods you produce. He knows this, and he's afraid. He'll move quickly, but just let him try to take our homes away from us."

"Sarx will destroy us all," Fred Morton said.

"He will certainly try." Dad turned toward him. "But his power isn't limitless. He's never needed a large army. He's ruled by threats and lies. He can't be everywhere at once."

Dad gazed down the line at the Delegates. "Each of you must continue to build your defenses. We have been designing weapons to help you retrofit your existing equipment to make it battle worthy. My son, Hamilton, will transmit these blueprints to you within the next couple of hours."

Dad motioned for General Roosevelt to come up onto the platform. "I've also been working closely with the general to develop a plan to keep Sarx busy. The general believes that several small, targeted attacks at key locations can at least slow the Poligarcy down, giving you time to prepare.

"General, could you talk with the Delegates and field any questions they may have?"

General Roosevelt nodded.

Dad looked at Ollie. "Oliver, I'd like to talk with you in private. I'll connect with you in a few minutes." He turned and left the platform, waving for the rest of us to follow. "Hamilton, please stay behind and give the general any support you can?"

"Of course." Hamilton walked up onto the platform.

We followed Dad to the magspheres and took a quiet ride to the bridge. We all wondered what was next, no doubt trying to come to grips with the idea that we were now at war with the Poligarchy.

As soon as we entered the bridge, Dad said, "Computer, connect me with Oliver Wolcott at Earthome."

Ollie appeared on the screen. He looked off to the side. "General, I must take my leave. We'll be in touch." He waved his hand over a console in front of him, and turned toward us.

"That was quite a show you put on in there." He looked at me. "You did an outstanding job, Noah."

I felt my cheeks burning and glanced at Adina to see if she noticed. She was looking right at me, grinning, so that would be a yes.

"It was nothing," I said. "I just read what Adina wrote."

"What I *modified*," she corrected.

Ollie looked back at Dad. "So the rat's out of the bag."

Dad smiled. "It's cat."

At least Ollie knew what a cat was. I saw a pair or two in Earthome when we dropped off the original settlers. Most everyone else alive in the thirty-first century had never seen one.

Dad's face grew serious. "Now that Sarx heard you declare Earth free, there's no way he'll let that stand."

Ollie nodded. "I saw the look on his face."

"The only thing we have going for us, is he doesn't know you're actually on Earth. I'm sure he's got all kinds of questions about who you are. Why some, excuse me for saying, *child* has declared independence for Earth. Where—"

"He knows who I am."

Dad stared at Ollie, and then the realization hit him. "He recognized you from Earth. Back before the Cataclysm."

"Correct. When Noah and I destroyed his lab." He grinned. "I imagine it'd be hard for him to forget some kindergartener jump-kicking him in the chest."

Dad smiled. "That doesn't mean he knows where you are. You could be anywhere declaring for Earth."

"But we need to be ready."

"Agreed. We're on our way, since you're the only colony without any real defense." Dad nodded my way, and I moved into the pilot's seat. "The first thing we'll need to do is neutralize the Poligarchy's base on the moon. We don't think Sarx has much of a force there, but it would be the ideal location to coordinate a search for Earthome, so we must take it over."

Ollie smiled. "That took some nerve to declare yourself for the moon."

"It was our home for years." Dad glanced at the rest of us. "Besides, Dr. Fletcher dreams of a day when he can return to the LCAS when this whole thing is over."

Dr. Randolph Fletcher was a teacher both Dad and Mom had studied under in college. He founded the Lunar Center for the Advancement of the Species, but then was forced to flee and even feign death to keep Prime Senator Sarx from meddling in his work.

"If anyone has a claim to the moon, it's Dr. Fletcher. He was feeling a bit under the weather, so I stood in for him."

I input the coordinates for Earth and gradually brought the *ARC*'s engines online.

"We should be there in...." Dad looked to me and raised his eyebrows.

I glanced at the screen. "Six days, twelve hours."

Ollie stood from his seat. "We'll do our best to still be here when you arrive."

***

I'd been itching to log some hours flying the J-3500s we'd captured from the Poligarchy in their failed attempt to take over the *ARC*. I was made for flying, and it wasn't a stretch to say I was better at it than nearly anyone else in the Solar System. I'd had a lifetime of practice controlling machines with my neuro-processor, starting with my magchair. Now I had the chance to try my hand at the state-of-the-art in fighting spaceships.

During the flight to Earth, Dad told me to practice as much as I could. It would be a bit tricky with the *ARC* traveling at nearly one-point-five million kilometers per hour, as any flight I took with the J-3500s had to match that speed. Fortunately, the ships were perfectly capable, especially with the momentum already gained by traveling in the *ARC*.

The first couple of days, I hadn't even taken them out of the hangar yet. I just sat in one of the pilot's chairs, located on the floor of the hangar, and familiarized myself with their systems. The ships were flown remotely, so I wouldn't be inside them. This made Mom and Dad very happy. Even so, Dad made it clear I had to do whatever it took to keep the ships safe. We didn't have many weapons of such advanced technology.

Hamilton wanted to retrofit the J-3500s with warp manifolds, but he'd been too busy working on creating weapons for the colonists.

On the third day, I got up early and went down to the hanger to practice. Comfy in the pilot's chair, my neuro-processor allowed me to interface directly with the ships, but the range was limited. The chair itself functioned as a transmitter. Hamilton had rigged it so I could fly any of the three J-3500s from one chair.

I had named the three ships *Destruction, Annihilation,* and *Big Boomer,* and programmed their computers accordingly.

I turned my back to the ships and brought *Annihilation* online, then raised her into a hover behind me. It helped to not look at the ships, but to use the sensors onboard instead; I wouldn't be able to see them when they were outside the ship.

I was just considering taking her outside the *ARC* when Sam, Hamilton, and Adina walked in. I was barely aware of them as most of my concentration was on the ship behind me.

"Looking good, runt," Sam hollered over.

Her voice broke my concentration a bit, and the ship dropped toward the floor. I caught it in time and raised it back to hover two meters up.

"Do you mind?" I wasn't in the mood this morning. I'd begun to get a little nervous I wouldn't be able to fly the J-3500s properly by the time we got to Earth.

Sam laughed. "If you're having trouble concentrating, maybe Adina should leave."

I glanced at Adina and saw her blush. *Annihilation* dropped to the floor with a crash.

"Careful with that," shouted Hamilton.

Sam continued laughing and strode into the workshop. Hamilton followed her. Adina stood for a moment in thought, then realized she'd been left alone with me and turned and ran after my siblings.

Why did I have to have a sister who made it her goal in life to torment me? Why not pick on Hamilton? Of course the answer to that was Hamilton wouldn't notice if she did. Why couldn't I be more like him?

I watched them through the windows of the workshop. Hamilton had asked for their help in replicating the final parts for his small army of mechs he'd built. They lined the walls of the Hangar.

Hamilton fired up the 3-D printer and was showing Adina how to load it with raw material. She figured it out immediately and started fabricating the first part.

Maybe it was time to quit guessing how she felt about me. There was something there, but every time I talked to her, she seemed just as flustered as I was.

A thrill ran through me, thinking about actually telling her how I felt. What was the worst that could happen?

She could laugh at me. It could ruin our friendship. She could say she felt the same way.

I wasn't sure which would be more terrifying.

CHAPTER TEN

The moon nearly filled the window of the bridge. Farther off, Earth floated like a blue eye, watching to see if mankind would take care of her this time around. We all sat, waiting for Dad to give the order.

This morning, as I lay in bed thinking about the battle to come, it had hit me: today was my birthday. I'd decided it'd be the perfect day to tell Adina how I felt. I had it all planned out: a nice picnic lunch next to an artificial waterfall in the black bear habitat, some actual time alone, without someone interrupting, or some excuse to avoid each other.

It hadn't dawned on me that we'd be in the middle of a battle.

I hadn't mentioned my birthday to anyone either, because it seemed insignificant against the backdrop of what we were about to do, but as the day progressed, and no one brought it up, I got a little more annoyed.

Now, as I watched everyone preparing for the invasion, I felt guilty for worrying about something as silly as a fourteenth birthday, or time alone with someone that probably just wants to be friends.

Dad studied his holo-pad. "There's a lot of chatter on the SolWeb. It's encoded." He looked around "Hamilton, can you and Adina see if you can decrypt it?"

"On it." Hamilton pulled Adina over to a terminal and the two of them went to work.

Dad shook his head. "I would've thought we'd see some resistance from the forces on the moon by now."

General Roosevelt stood looking over his shoulder. "Two possibilities come to mind. One, they're waiting until we get closer to launch their attack. Or, two, they're otherwise occupied."

"Looking for Ollie," I suggested.

The general nodded. "Either way, the faster we hit the moon base, the better chance we have. We should suit up."

Dad considered a moment then nodded. "Let's get going."

General Roosevelt and I moved toward the door. Mom came with us; she'd be overseeing the infirmary.

The three of us climbed into a magsphere and headed off. Once it came to it, my heart was beating out of my chest. Much of this mission depended on me providing air support to the ground troops.

Mom placed her hand on mine. "You'll be fine, Noah."

I smiled weakly. "Thanks."

General Roosevelt nodded toward me. "I have faith in you, son. I've seen what you can do with those ships." Somehow, his words helped. The general had a commanding presence, especially in the tight space of the magsphere. If he said I'd do fine, then I'd do fine.

We stopped at the infirmary and, with one last squeeze of my hand and no mention of my birthday, Mom got out.

I watched the general as we continued on. He actually had a pretty strong resemblance to the pictures I'd seen of President Roosevelt. He had the same big, round face and bushy mustache, but his was cut more sharply, and his hair was cropped in a standard military cut.

"I—I hope you and your men stay safe."

He looked at me with his eyebrows scrunched together. "Safety isn't something we strive for. We aren't reckless, but going into danger is what we do." He laughed. "At least that's what I like to believe." He leaned over like he wanted to tell me a secret. "To tell you the truth I'm scared, just like anyone else, but I can't let the men see it."

My eyes widened. He didn't look like someone who was ever scared. "Well, you do a good job of hiding it."

He grinned. "That's good. Maybe I'll make an okay general after all."

We both laughed.

"Today's my birthday."

He looked over, surprised at the sudden change in conversation.

"I'm fourteen. Everyone forgot."

His face softened. "I'm sorry."

"I know they have a lot on their minds."

"But a boy's fourteenth birthday only comes around once."

Somehow telling General Roosevelt made me feel better.

The magsphere stopped. He stepped out in front of me, then turned. "Happy birthday, Noah."

I smiled. "Thanks."

The general's men were lined up and came to attention when we entered the hangar.

"Suit up, men. We've got a *moon base* to take." He sounded like he still couldn't quite believe he'd gone from security detail on a Martian colony, to leading an invasion force on the moon, nine hundred years in the future.

His men marched down the row of mechs Hamilton had fabricated. Each stood with its windshield up, and a ladder dropped to the floor. The soldiers climbed into them, one per mech, the machines whirred as they came online.

The general reached has hand forward and shook mine. "Watch our backs, son."

"I will."

A couple of the soldiers were experienced pilots. Of course they had never flown anything like the ships we had, but Dad and I had taught them enough to be able to fly the *DUV IVs* — at least for simple landings and takeoffs. They boarded their ships and moments later their engines fired up, and the mechs split into two groups and marched into the holds of the ships.

General Roosevelt climbed into the last mech. He caught my gaze just before the windshield closed, and nodded.

I hovered over to my pilot's chair and pulled myself in. *Annihilation* came to life with a simple command through my neuro-processor.

"I'm ready, Dad."

"Landing Team One, ready."

"Landing Team Two, ready."

The sound in the hangar was almost deafening as the three ships readied for departure.

"Okay, Noah, you are go for liftoff. Landing Teams stand by."

It was my job to make sure the space around the *ARC* was clear before the other ships departed. I brought *Annihilation* into a hover and turned her toward the hangar doors. Dad had already started opening them, and the twinkle of stars shimmered through the energy shield. I gave the ship a little thrust and started moving her toward the exit.

When she was clear of the other ships, I gave Annihilation a little more thrust and she shot out into space. Cameras mounted on the ship became my eyes. It almost felt like flying in a thermsuit rather than a J-class ship. There was nothing between me and the vacuum of space.

I swung around and did a quick scan of the *ARC*: nothing unusual.

"Okay, Dad, all clear."

Moments later, the landing ships pierced the energy shield in succession. Inside, the sound of their engines dissipated as they left the hangar.

We turned toward the moon and within moments were close enough to make out some of the geography. I started naming some of the craters and places I remembered from the years we spent stationed here in the *ARC*, but was brought out of my memories by a couple of bright flashes from the surface.

"Incoming missiles," the computer said.

"I'm on it." I pushed the J-3500 into a dive and headed straight for the missiles. "Lock on targets one and two."

"Lock confirmed."

"Fire missile interceptors, now." Twin rockets shot off, one from each wing, and a heartbeat later, they destroyed the missiles.

"Computer, locate the coordinates of those missile launchers."

"Calculating trajectories."

"Bring it up." An image of the moon appeared, with a grid pattern overlaid on it. A red light flashed inside a crater, and I pushed the J-3500 toward it. "Lock on and destroy target when ready."

"Acknowledged."

I held my breath, hoping we'd get the missile battery destroyed before it fired again.

"Lock confirmed. Firing." A single missile shot from my left wing, and a silent flash of light was all I saw when the missile hit. I turned, looking for another target.

There were actually two main colonies on the moon, one on the side facing Earth. It was the most heavily populated, and consisted of several huge domes covering a metropolis, and even some large gardens for growing food — or at least the raw plant matter that the colonists' food is synthesized from. The people living there were mostly scientists and their families. Even though Dr. Fletcher's Lunar Center for the Advancement of the Species had closed down decades earlier, many of the scientists remained on the moon.

The second colony was much smaller and on the side of the moon facing away from Earth, situated inside a huge basin called the Sea of Moscow. The LCAS was originally built there, and more recently the Poligarchy had established it as a base dedicated to the defense and protection of the moon, and Earth.

I now circled the basin, the domes of the military base off to my right. The plan was pretty simple: take out the anti-spacecraft missile systems along the basin's perimeter, and then drop the mechs in to take control of the base itself. The biggest unknown was what Poligarchy ships they had stationed here. So far we hadn't picked up any on the sensors.

Another couple of missiles fired from the surface, and again I was able to destroy them and the launchers themselves. This continued all the way around the basin. In the end, I destroyed twelve missile installations, and still no sign of enemy spacecraft.

"Okay, we're ready to start deploying the mechs," I said.

"Roger that," General Roosevelt said. "Cover us."

I throttled back the power and lifted *Annihilation* a couple hundred meters higher. The first of the *DUV IVs* passed underneath and dropped toward the moon's surface. The ship slowed when it looked to be about one hundred meters off the ground, and the rear hold door opened. A soldier backed his mech down the ramp and then jumped. The mech fired its boosters, which slowed its descent, and it landed with a running hop. It then stopped and turned toward the center of the huge crater. The next mech did the same thing.

I was amazed at how well the soldiers were handling the machines. They'd hardly had more than a few hours of practice in the hangar. It helped that Hamilton had done an amazing job on the mech's artificial intelligence systems. The machines would not let them fall over or hit the ground too hard as long as they were in working order.

Around the basin we flew. When the first ship was empty, the second one flew into place and started dropping her mechs. Once I completed a whole circuit, thirty-three mechs stood ready.

"Okay, General, all your men are in place."

"Acknowledged. Watch our backs." The general gave several orders, and the mechs began marching forward.

I brought the J-3500 up to about a thousand meters, hovered over the center of the giant crater, and held my breath waiting for the defenses to come online. Meter by meter, the mechs tightened their ring around the military base.

Just when I thought maybe the missile batteries were all they had, the outer walls of the compound lit up. Hundreds of streaks of light arched toward the incoming mechs.

The seasoned soldiers piloting the mechs didn't panic, even as several took direct hits. The shields held up on most, even though they were knocked backward. At least two suffered more damage than they could recover from. One mech's left leg had been ripped off, and the other looked like it sprung a fuel leak in the main engine. I just hoped their life support systems weren't compromised.

The mechs fired back, and the missile defense systems didn't seem to have much in the way of shielding. Slowly the general's men pushed forward, and as the missile installations were destroyed, the confidence of the mech pilots grew. It looked as if they'd be within the walls of the compound in minutes.

A flash of light caught my eye, and I spun *Annihilation* to get a better look. On the horizon to the northwest, three ships glinted in the sunlight, which was now to my back. They were rocketing at full-speed in our direction. Seconds later, they came into full view — J-3500s, not good.

Two broke off, left and right, and the third headed straight for me. An alarm blared in my ear. "Missile lock confirmed. Perform evasive maneuvers." I punched it and rocketed straight for the central ship, which fired two missiles. I almost misjudged the speed of the missiles, combined with my flight right toward them, but just before impact I pulled *Annihilation* up. The missiles passed harmlessly underneath and I rocketed directly over the enemy ship. As I passed, the wide eyes of a pilot in the cockpit stared up.

Those ships are manned!

I brought up a view from the rear cameras. All three ships looped around and followed me. At least I could keep them busy while General Roosevelt did his job below. Much faster than expected, the ships were on me, and all three fired.

I spiraled and plunged off to my right. *These guys are good!*

Again two ships split and tried to box me in. I sped along the lunar surface looking for some advantage. Unfortunately, there were no canyons on the moon, only craters. I tapped into the cameras on the left and right wings, keeping the front and rear cameras up. It was a little disorienting at first, but my brain resolved the images into one large scene. I was now looking at a 360 degree view all around me.

The two ships had caught up, and were nearly even with me, and the ship behind was closing fast. I pulled up and tried to do a loop, but had to call it off when the computer projected a collision with the ship behind.

I spun left, and the ships followed; twisted right, and they matched my moves. I couldn't shake them. Three against one was just too much. If only we had more—

I stopped myself. We *did* have more ships. "Dad, I need the hangar doors opened."

I locked missiles on the two fighters on either side of me and fired.

"What? Why?"

The ships spun away to avoid the missiles, but they also fell back, giving me a little breathing room

"No time to explain."

"Okay. The doors are opening."

I pushed the image of the battle to a corner of my mind, still watching what was going on with *Annihilation*, but at the same time, I probed into my chair's computer and located *Destruction*. I sent a command to power up her mag-lifters. *Annihilation* pitched forward. *Oops.* I shut the mag-lifters down and *Annihilation* straightened out. It was trickier than I thought to keep the two ships separate.

The two J-3500s were catching back up. *Better make this quick.*

I modified the commands to the ships to include the ship's name and brought the mag-lifters to life on *Destruction*. I brought up an image from her cameras, and was looking at myself seated in the chair in the hangar. My head spun and a wave of nausea washed through me. For a heartbeat, I lost my grip on *Annihilation* and the image started to dissolve.

Maybe this wasn't such a good idea.

I thought of the general and his men; without me there to stop the J-3500s, the soldiers wouldn't stand a chance. I pushed the nausea away and brought the views from *Annihilation* back up. The two ships had caught back up and were coming in closer. I pushed the ship into another spiral and picked up a little distance, but I also held onto the image in the hangar.

James had told me one time he could do something he called "dual screen mode." He said he was able to see what I was seeing, while at the same time experiencing what was around him. This had to be what that was like. Of course his brain was an actual computer.

Pushing my doubts aside, I turned *Destruction* and pointed her toward the hangar doors.

The ships flanking *Annihilation* fired at me. I waited until the last possible moment, then dropped. The missiles hit each other and exploded above the ship.

The *Destruction* pierced the energy barrier over the hangar door and headed out into space. I immediately turned her toward the moon and fired her main thrusters. I briefly thought about trying to bring out the last ship, *Big Boomer*, but decided that was a bit too much for now. Two would have to be enough.

I swung *Annihilation* around and brought her back in the direction of *Destruction*. The three enemy ships followed, and I fired missiles at each of them. Again they all dodged the missiles and fell back for a moment.

Just a little bit farther.

I could just make out the four ships coming toward *Destruction*. I pushed the ship down and stopped within a crater.

Annihilation sped over the lunar landscape, surprise the only thing I had going for me. Seconds later I rocketed over *Destruction*, and for a moment, I saw both ships from the vantage point of the other. Then from *Destruction*, I saw the three J-3500s trailing behind *Annihilation*.

I gunned it and brought *Destruction* out of the crater. "Lock on all three enemy ships."

"Missile lock confirmed."

"Fire!"

Six missiles leapt from the wings of *Destruction*. The middle J-3500 didn't have a chance to react. First one missile hit, weakening the magnetic shields, followed immediately by the second. The missile sliced through the failing shield and hit the main thrusters. A bright flash momentarily blinded me. Debris flew out in every direction, flaming out in mere seconds in the vacuum of space.

I felt a stab of pain for the pilot, but at least he had died quickly.

The two remaining J-3500s had a few moments warning and were able to spin away from the incoming missiles. I rocketed after the one on the left with *Destruction* and slowed *Annihilation* enough to get behind the one on the right. Now we were even. Maybe I had a fighting chance.

In my limited practice runs with the J-3500s, I'd discovered that the biggest issue with space-based dogfighting was that the ships themselves were nearly as responsive as the missiles they fired. This meant a good pilot could almost always outmaneuver an incoming missile. I'd already witnessed this in the ease with which I could avoid the shots fired by the enemy ships, and vice versa. So surprise, or out-thinking my opponents, seemed more important than outflying them.

The two ships in front of me dodged and weaved, trying to break me off their tails, but we were evenly matched, ship for ship.

The question then was how to surprise, or out-think them? Yet how could I do that when it took all my brain power to fly two ships at the same time?

I desperately wanted to check on the general's progress, but couldn't risk it. Then it hit me. "General Roosevelt, can you hear me?"

He came on the comm, his voice almost drowned out by the shouting of the rest of his men. "I hear you. A bit busy at the moment, though. We just broke through the southeast wall."

"Sorry, but I need your help. Do you have any men still outside?"

"Yes. To the northeast. Five mechs."

"Good. Have them pull back and get ready."

"Ready for what?"

"To help me shake these pesky J-3500s."

General Roosevelt was quiet for a moment. "Sounds risky, but we'll give it a shot."

"Okay. Tell them I'll be the one in front, but we'll be moving so fast, they'll probably have to aim at me to have any chance of hitting the guy behind me."

"They'll be ready."

I took a quick look to see which ship was closest to the compound. It was *Destruction*. I pulled her into a dive, then immediately broke right.

The J-3500 I'd been tailing continued on for a few moments until the pilot realized I'd broken off. He immediately took advantage of the situation and swung around. Seconds later he was behind me.

I pretended to try to shake him, while working my way towards the base. I took the ship even lower, skimming the lunar surface. It wouldn't do if the pilot saw the trap I was leading him into.

"Ready, General?"

"They're standing by."

I gunned it and zigzagged around the rims of a few craters. A ridge of rock appeared that indicated the edge of the Sea of Moscow. Meters from the ridge, I pulled back and skimmed just over the top of the rough stone wall, then dove down into the giant crater.

The enemy J-3500 followed me.

Five mechs stood in a row just ahead, and I adjusted slightly and flew right at them. If I could just keep *Destruction* between my pursuer and those mechs....

Moments before I reached the mechs I yelled, "Fire!"

The mechs launched a hail of missiles right at me. My heart stopped for a second as I opened the throttle full-blast on *Destruction*. It wasn't enough; a handful of missiles clipped the rear of *Destruction*. I prayed the shield would hold, but it didn't. A bright flash lit the basin, just before my connection to *Destruction* was severed. Images from *Annihilation* flooded the void left by the destruction of, well, *Destruction*.

I shook my head. Maybe that wasn't the best name for a ship. "Did we get her?"

"Yup. Sorry about your ship though," the general replied.

"Not as sorry as I'll be when I tell Dad." Now wasn't the time to worry about it. I had one more ship to deal with.

The other J-3500 had been all over the place, trying to shake me, but now he flew in a wide arc. Obviously, he figured out there was no way to lose me. Maybe I could just chase him around until the base was taken. Then what choice would he have but to surrender?

This thought made me smile... until I realized where he was headed. The J-3500 was flying straight toward the base.

"General, we have a problem."

"Yes?"

"The last ship is headed your way. I'm not sure I can stop him."

"Roger that."

I pushed to close the distance between us. "Computer, how many more missiles do I have?"

"Seven."

Maybe I just needed to use a bigger hammer. "Target one missile at the ship, and the remaining six in a circle around it. Fire when ready."

The computer only took a split-second to comply. I could see the base just a few kilometers ahead. I'd only get one shot at it. Seven missiles launched off *Annihilation's* wings, and quickly formed a ring and headed straight for the target, the central missile aimed right at the J-3500's engines.

He dodged and weaved but the missiles followed. An instant before impact, the pilot did the unthinkable and fired his braking thrusters. He slowed and the central missile slammed into the rear of the ship. His shields held for a moment, and then flickered out.

I yanked *Annihilation* off to the right, barely missing a collision. The remaining six missiles flew off into space and the enemy J-3500 fell behind me. I'd never seen a move like that. He had used the shields to hold off the one missile, while allowing the others to pass him by. I didn't have time to marvel at the pilot's skill, because he immediately fired his thrusters and headed toward the compound.

"Incoming!" I yelled.

Without any missiles I wasn't sure what I could do, but I pushed after the J-3500 anyway. It crested the basin's outer ridge just as I caught sight of another ship screaming in from the west. My heart sank. No way I could take out two ships, especially without weapons.

The second ship fired a halo of missiles, and I pulled back before realizing they weren't aimed at me.

The enemy J-3500 exploded in a huge flash of light, and the new ship streamed through the falling debris. A retrofitted transport ship, it looked just like... *Lady's Revenge.*

Sastra's voice came over the comm. "It seemed like you needed a little help."

Draben's voice rose in the background. "He'll never admit that."

'He's right, you know.' James's voice in my head filled me with a sense of relief. They'd all made it off of Mars safely.

"Thanks," I said. "I'm sure I would've have figured something out."

'See, what did I tell you?'

"Oh, be quiet."

James and I laughed as I turned back to the battle below. "I guess if you want to stay and help, Sastra, I won't deny you that pleasure."

"Thanks." Her voice dripped with sarcasm.

CHAPTER ELEVEN

Dad brought the ARC in to land on the ancient volcanic sea next to the colony. I took Annihi*lation* into the hangar bay, and Sastra followed with *Lady's Revenge*. I powered down the J-3500 and pulled myself from her computers. For a moment, I sat in the chair trying to reorient myself, and looked around the hangar at *Lady's Revenge*. Steam poured from her engines as I climbed into my magchair.

Sastra had helped so many times before, running us all over the solar system, really. She liked to play the hardened, loner space pilot, but I knew she really cared what happened to us. Now she'd come through again, safely getting Draben and James off of Mars.

The door to *Lady's Revenge* opened and Draben walked out with a swagger. Of course he'd try to figure out a way to make it look like he was the hero today. Without him, the whole mission would have failed.

He spied me and came over. "Brilliant, eh?"

'Here it comes,' James said in my head.

"We got here just in time. Good thing I made Sastra push it." He grinned and looked over his shoulder as Sastra and James strode out of the ship.

"I wouldn't have had to push it if you didn't take so long to pack." She shook her head. "My word, how many suitcases did you bring?"

James and Sastra looked at each other and broke into laughter.

"Hey, you never know when you might have to impress the *ladies*." Draben winked at Sastra, who quickly socked him in the arm. He let out a yelp.

She laughed again. "You might be more inclined to *impress the ladies* if you could take a punch to the shoulder — from a *girl*."

"Hi, Draben."

He stopped at the sound of Adina's voice, looked over my shoulder as she walked up behind me, and stood up straighter.

She gave Draben a hug then stepped back. "Sastra, James, it's good to see you, too."

I could feel a wave of annoyance coming from James. I'm guessing he felt the same from me.

Sastra took us all in as we stood there staring at each other. "Looks like you've got some catching up to do." She hitched a thumb over her shoulder. "I'm gonna go get *Lady* fueled up."

We broke into nervous laughter.

"The gang's all back together," Adina said. She watched the three of us watching her, and then cleared her throat. "You must be famished."

Draben nodded his head. "I know I am. Not sure about robot-boy here."

James glared at him.

"I'm pretty hungry myself," I said. "Fighting off a squadron of J-3500's can do that to a man."

"Oh, *man* is it?" Draben snickered. "You'll be a man when you can sport one of these." He pointed to his mustache, which I had to admit was thicker than last time I'd seen him.

Adina rolled her eyes. "Then let's go get something to eat." She started toward the door.

Dad walked in and slowed a moment when he saw all of us. "Ah, I thought maybe that was you." He looked at Draben and James. "Good to see you boys."

"You too, Mr. Zarc," said Draben.

James just nodded. He still had trouble trying to sort out his feelings for our dad. It didn't help that Dad struggled with it, too.

Adina pushed her hair behind her ear. "We were headed up to get something to eat."

Dad turned to me with a frown. "Noah will catch up."

"Um, okay." Adina waved her hand at Draben and James to follow her... quickly. They dashed out of the hangar.

"What happened out there?" Dad stood with his hands on his hips. His nearly white beard spilled over his ample belly. It was hard to take him seriously when he stood in his 'Santa pose'.

I suppressed my smile. "I kept General Roosevelt's men safe."

His frown grew even deeper. "Don't get smart with me. I know *what* you did. I'm more interested in how you decided to do it. I expressly told you to be careful with those ships."

"I know, Dad, but I couldn't figure out any way around it. Those pilots were the best I'd ever seen." I had a sudden vision of the man I'd shot, being incinerated in a fireball. "There were real people inside those ships."

Dad's frown softened and realization dawned on his face. "I'm sorry, Noah. I think worrying about the ships was my way to avoid thinking about what was really going on. People died today." He put his hand on my shoulder. "Forgive me."

"Nah, I get it. This is war. In war you either kill, or be killed."

"But you're only thirteen."

Fourteen, Dad. I'm fourteen!

Then I shuddered as it hit me: I had killed a man. At least two other Poligarchy soldiers had died, people with families of their own, soldiers just following orders. Somehow, it hadn't mattered that much in the heat of the battle, but now....

Tears poured down my cheeks. "Dad — ?"

He bent down and wrapped his arms around me. "I know, son. It's going to be okay."

How could he say that? It would never be okay for those pilots.

He held me in his arms for a few minutes, and I started to feel uncomfortable. What if Adina saw me like this?

He stood up and gave me a smile. "So, how *did* you fly those two ships at the same time?"

I appreciated the change of subject. "I honestly don't know. It was amazing, like I had two holo-displays in my head, one for each ship. I just kept my eyes on both of them."

He just looked at me, kind of amazed. "Do you think your reflexes were slowed?"

I thought about it. "Maybe. The main thing I had going for me was the ships were basically equal with the enemy J-3500s. By the time I brought the second one out, they knew, that I knew, that they knew, we were at a standstill. I also think the ship-board computers helped a lot."

"Okay, well maybe you should practice it some more, see how much control you actually have."

"Good idea." I moved toward the pilot's chair.

He chuckled. "Not now. Go spend some time with your friends."

I managed a laugh and turned toward the exit.

"Noah?"

I swiveled back around.

"I'm proud of what you accomplished today. You protected our soldiers and we captured the base without any serious injuries."

"Thanks, Dad."

"Mom's got a special meal planned for you."

"My birthday?"

"Of course. You didn't think we'd forgotten, did you? I heard there's going to be cake." Dad grinned. He could never resist cake.

* * *

Draben's voice echoed down the hallway as I approached. "I told my Dad I was going anyway."

I entered the dining hall, but no one looked up.

"So, what'd he say?" Adina asked.

"He told me if I left the apartment, then I should never come back."

Adina put her hand on Draben's arm. "How awful."

"Yeah, well, who needs him?"

Adina looked horrified. "Don't say that. Family is the most important thing."

Mom came in and sat a cake in the middle of the table. Then she wagged her finger. "Don't touch it until Noah gets here." She turned and went back into the kitchen.

Draben looked at James and Adina. "You guys are all the family I need."

I was about to speak up when Adina gave Draben a hug. "You're definitely important to me."

It was just too much. I turned my chair and headed out the door.

Adina must have spotted me, and yelled, "Noah."

I didn't stop, and headed for my room. Today was my birthday. Today was supposed to be the day I'd tell her I....

What will I tell her? Okay, so I wasn't totally sure, but Draben and James appearing messed it all up.

The lights came on when I entered my room. I pushed over to my bed and pulled myself onto it, trying to relax my pounding heart. The adrenaline of the past couple of hours was making my head spin.

"Noah?"

I turned toward the door.

Adina peeked around the doorjamb.

Ugh, why didn't I shut my door? "I'm kind of tired right now," I said.

She stepped into my room anyway and glanced around at the mess. "What's going on, Noah?"

"I told you, I'm tired. It's been a pretty hectic week." I felt on the verge of tearing up. That would not be good.

"That's an understatement." She glanced at my desk chair, covered in clothes. "Do you mind?"

"Nah, just push that stuff on the floor."

She pulled the chair around, picked up my clothes and placed them next to my bed. Then she slid the chair up next to me and sat.

I pushed myself into a seated position against the wall.

"You know, you've been absolutely amazing." She looked up at me through her eyelashes.

"Not really. Did you see what I did to that ship? Dad wasn't real happy."

"But you kept the soldiers safe. You outfoxed three seasoned Poligarchy pilots. Not to mention your speech in front of the Senate."

"*Your* speech you mean."

She smiled. "Thomas Jefferson's, really. I just tweaked it a bit."

"Still, it was amazing." *You're amazing.*

She blushed slightly. "So, what's going on? Why have you been avoiding me?"

I laughed nervously. "Avoiding you? I thought you'd been avoiding me. Every time we've had a chance to talk you take off."

"Well, it *has* been hectic." She glanced around the room again.

We sat in silence for a moment. Now that it came to it, I was scared to death to tell her what I'd been thinking.

Finally, she broke the silence. "We're still friends, aren't we?"

"Of course." *How could she think otherwise?*

"It's just... you seem different somehow. Like—"

"I like you, Adina." I just blurted it out.

"I like you, too." She looked up at me with a smile, but then her smile changed as her mouth dropped open slightly. "Oh, you mean...?"

"Ever since we met, I've tried to figure out how to tell you."

"Noah, I...." She glanced around the room, almost like she was trying to think of something to change the conversation.

"It's Draben, isn't it?"

She looked back, confused.

"I mean, I understand. He's so much cooler than me. He's tall. He's got a mustache."

Her eyes grew wider. "I don't know what to say."

She didn't need to say anything. "Maybe you should go."

"Noah, I—"

I flipped my body toward the wall. "Just go!"

She was silent for a second, then the chair squeaked against the floor as she stood. A few moments later the door closed and I was alone.

Mom tried to get me to come back for cake, but I just stayed in my room until I fell asleep.

CHAPTER TWELVE

The next few days, Adina went out of her way to avoid me. If I walked into a room, she left. Of course I did the same thing, especially if Draben was around. Every little glance he gave her or smile she directed at him was like a stab to my heart.

I spent most of the time in flight, searching for any remaining Poligarchy ships, either in orbit around Earth or down in her atmosphere. Sastra and James both helped. Sometimes my ego wouldn't let me acknowledge that James was just as good a pilot as me—after all, he *was* me—but he flew the *Big Boomer* while I flew *Annihilation*.

It took us two days, but we ended up destroying six J-3500s and capturing eight more. General Roosevelt put the pilots in holding on the moon base along with the other soldiers they had captured during the invasion.

The third day after we took over the moon, I was pulling myself out of the pilot's seat into my magchair when Dad called me on the comm. "Can you meet me in my office?"

"Right now?"

"If possible."

I looked over at James, who had been patrolling with me. Even though he was a robot, he looked just as tired as I felt. The mental strain was every bit as difficult on him as it was on me.

"Okay, Dad, I'll be there in a few minutes."

"I nodded to James and headed to the magspheres.

Minutes later I pushed into Dad's office. General Roosevelt looked up from his chair, and so did Dad from behind his desk. A third man was sitting in another chair.

"Ah, Noah," Dad said. "You remember Dr. Fletcher?"

The old man smiled broadly and stuck out his hand. I took it and was greeted to an arm-wrenching shake. "Good to see you, Noah. I hear you've been up to no good."

"Good to see you too, sir."

"None of that. Just call me Dr." He looked deadly serious, then broke out into laughter. "I'd say call me Randolph, but not even your Dad here can bring himself to do that, even though he's significantly older than me now."

"You'll always be Dr. Fletcher to me." Dad smiled. He looked at me and frowned. "You look a mess, Noah."

"I've been busy the past couple of days."

"Maybe you should get some rest."

"I was planning on it."

Dad smiled. "Okay, we'll make this quick. We figure we've only got about four more days before the Poligarchy gets here with backup." He looked at the doctor. "Dr. Fletcher is now Governor of the Lunar Colony. He and General Roosevelt are working on a plan to protect the citizens from attack."

The general nodded. "I've already been working with your friend, Sastra—quite a little firecracker that one—to train my men on those captured J-3500s. She thinks they'll be competent enough when the Poligarchy gets here."

Dad tapped his fingers on his desk. "General Roosevelt needs you to take him and several of his men down to Earthome. Governor Wolcott is expecting you."

"Ollie?"

"Yes. Also the general has a shipment of arms he discovered at the lunar base, which he wants you to take down. Use one of the *DUV IVs.*"

The idea of giving guns to the citizens of Earthome bothered me. Not that the people were dangerous, but they were... innocent. They'd been living in isolation from the rest of the solar system for hundreds of years.

I sighed, but it was better than letting them get butchered by Sarx.

"Get some sleep," Dad said.

"We'll be ready at 0600 hours," General Roosevelt said.

I groaned. I was definitely not a morning person.

* * *

We landed just as the sun peeked over the horizon. Uluru, called by some Ayers Rock, glowed a fantastic deep red. I was surprised to see so much activity when I opened the hold doors.

Men ran here and there, carrying large boxes. Others rode horses, some in formation, as if they were practicing military drills.

General Roosevelt walked up behind me. "Always wanted to visit Australia. There's some beautiful country out here." He looked around at the rich vegetation and large trees. "I don't remember seeing anything like this in the brochures though."

A young man, dressed in what appeared to be a new green and white uniform, approached. He saluted awkwardly. "General Roosevelt." He looked at me and scrunched up his forehead. "Founder Noah—"

"Please, just Noah."

The young man shook his head as if he didn't like that idea. "Governor Wolcott asked me to escort you to his offices."

General Roosevelt stood aside and waved his arm. "After you, *Founder.*" He cracked a smile under his big, bushy mustache, then turned to our guide. "What's your name, son?"

"Hardin. Ben Hardin, sir." He reached his hand toward his forehead as if to salute again, but stopped midway.

We moved toward the center of town, which housed the main government buildings.

"Looks like you've been busy down here, Private Hardin," the General said.

"Yes sir. We're ready for any attack."

General Roosevelt watched the men and women we passed. Some practiced hand-to-hand combat, while others fought with long staves. He shook his head almost imperceptibly.

He must have been thinking exactly what I was: these men wouldn't last five minutes against even a small force armed with blasters.

"Well, we'll see that you are."

Private Hardin took us through the main gate I'd entered the last time we were here. The buildings were all the same, mostly low, one-story structures made out of red sandstone. I expected the private to lead us into the hall where we had eaten before, but he turned left as soon as we passed through the gate. He opened a door and entered a smaller building off to the side. We followed, and General Roosevelt closed the door behind us.

An older woman with graying hair at the temples sat behind a small desk. A couple of chairs lined the opposite wall. She smiled at the three of us. "He's expecting you."

Private Hardin nodded his head. "Thank you, ma'am." He strode to a door on the far wall and knocked once, then opened it.

Ollie was out of his chair and walking over when we came in. "So good to see you, Noah." He reached out and shook my hand. "It's been a while."

"I just saw you last week." I chuckled.

"That doesn't count. I don't care much for those holo-hootenannies." He turned and extended his hand toward the General. "Give me a real flesh and blood hand to shake and I'll know if I'm talking to a man I can trust."

I was struck by how strange it was to see Ollie like this. His actions, and inflections in his words, reminded me of Gramps, but his voice itself was that of a six-year-old. Even though his eyes displayed a true wisdom, the rest of him looked like a little kid.

He motioned toward a couple of chairs. "Please, have a seat."

The general sat, but Private Hardin remained standing at attention.

"Governor," General Roosevelt began.

"Please, call me Oliver." He climbed up on his desk chair.

I pictured his feet dangling above the floor behind the desk and smiled.

"Oliver, we have a shipment of weapons in the hold."

Ollie looked at the young man standing by the door. "Private Hardin, please see to the cargo onboard their ship. You are to lock it up in the storerooms in the rock. Set a guard until such a time we can train the men on their use."

The private saluted. "Yes sir." He turned and left, closing the door behind him.

"I trust the flight down was uneventful."

"Fine, just fine," General Roosevelt said.

Ollie studied us both for a few moments. "Give it to me straight. How bad is it going to be?"

The general shook his head. "About as bad as you can imagine. The Poligarchy has weapons so far beyond your comprehension—"

"Wait," Ollie said. "Aren't you from a thousand years ago? What makes you think you know more about their weapons than I do?"

General Roosevelt laughed. "Because I've been spending nearly every waking moment reading up on it. Oh, then there's the time I've actually been fighting against the Poligarchy."

Ollie smiled. "Point taken. So let me have it."

"Well, it really depends on what they throw at you. If it's just a drone attack you should be okay. With the weapons I brought along, and some training, your men can keep them at bay." He shook his head. "But if Sarx sends in a battleship, there's not much you can do. They could level this whole place from orbit."

"We won't let that happen," I said.

General Roosevelt looked at me and smiled. "Of course. We're training some pilots on the moon base, and they'll do what they can to protect you."

"Thank you for that." Ollie stared out an open window.

"I'd also like to prepare an evacuation procedure," the general said.

Ollie turned from the window. "Evacuation?"

Roosevelt nodded. "Yes. If it comes to it, we can get a ship in and load up the citizens of Earthome and get you out of here."

Ollie frowned. "And abandon our home?"

"Better than losing your lives."

Waves of emotion rolled over Ollie's face. He appeared torn by his love for his home and his duty to his people. "Of course. Let me know what you need."

"It's only a last resort." General Roosevelt tried to assure him. "And even if we do evacuate, it'll only be for a while. We're going to win this thing."

Ollie gazed back out his window. "I sure hope so."

CHAPTER THIRTEEN

General Roosevelt stood outside the hatch of the DUV IV. "I'll get these soldiers whipped into shape. You'll see."

In fact, I was having a very hard time seeing it, but what else could I do? "We'll be back in a few weeks." *If Earthome is still here.* "Thank you for being here for Ollie."

I pushed aboard the ship and closed the door feeling a certain dread that I would never see any of these people again.

After checking to make sure everyone was clear, I put the ship through her pre-launch sequence and lifted off. With one last look at the stone buildings of the village, I pushed upward and pierced the dome that had protected these people for two hundred fifty years. Nothing but lifeless, barren desert filled my sight now, as the energy shield made it appear Earthome didn't even exist. I hoped that wouldn't be reality next time I returned.

It seemed like I was losing everything. Ollie was directly in harm's way, and James and I had worked to separate ourselves as much as possible, the idea being we shouldn't be inside each other's heads unless we both allowed it. Draben and I had drifted apart, or more to the point, a wedge had been driven between us by....

I couldn't even bring myself to say her name. Of course, that didn't stop me from picturing her, imagining her. Always I'd see her with Draben — how she laughed at his jokes, how she comforted him over his dad.

James's voice in my head cut me off. *'Noah?'*

Ugh, why can't he leave me alone? Can't he see that – ?

'Because you're thoughts are practically screaming at me.'

I could tell James was feeling much the same way. *"You aren't supposed to be listening in – "*

'I'm not, but there are times I can't keep you out. Emotion is much harder to block.'

"Sorry." I wasn't at all happy to hear he'd been part of my pity-party.

'Don't be. But are you sure this is all necessary? Did you talk to her?'

"Yes. She likes Draben." I couldn't believe James was so blind to the facts.

'I don't know. It seems like she'd be in a better mood if that was the case. She's been moping around, just like you.'

"Well, I don't have time to deal with it right now."

'Okay.' I could tell James was hurt, but I didn't feel like worrying about his feelings at the moment. *'I'll see you when you get back to the ship.'*

He severed the connection and once again I was alone.

"Nice job, Noah." I pulled back on the yoke and punched it, and the *DUV IV* rocketed toward the blackness of space.

***

"But we can't leave them!" I glared at Dad, who stood in the door to my room. He'd just woken me with the news we were headed to Venus.

"I'm sorry, Noah. We picked up a lot of chatter on the SolWeb. It's pretty clear the Poligarchy is going after Venus."

"But I told Ollie we'd protect him."

"We can't be everywhere."

"But what if they send a battleship? Earthome would be helpless." I just couldn't believe Dad was going to make me go back on my word.

"Not helpless. They've got a few ships, and Sastra's staying to help train the pilots." He shook his head. "Besides, long-range scanners don't show any signs of Poligarchy ships headed toward Earth. We'd definitely see a battleship."

"The could send drones."

"You're right, but they're in good hands. General Roosevelt can hold off a drone attack."

I shook my head. "I don't like it."

"I don't like it either, Noah, but I'm doing the best I can. Our resources are so limited compared to the might of the Poligarchy. We need to out-think them, and be in the right place at the right time. Right now, I think that's on Venus."

He watched me for a moment. "Please meet me on the bridge in a half hour. I'd like help lifting off the moon."

"Yes sir," I mumbled.

* * *

The next few days were endless. I spent much of the time with Dad on the bridge of the *ARC*. We worked to see if we could intercept any transmissions from the Poligarchy over the SolWeb. I kept waiting for that message that said Earth was under attack.

On the fourth day it came, a short, encoded message from Ollie. "Attack began this morning. Enemy slipped past defenses on the moon. Drones."

I immediately contacted Sastra.

She popped up on my screen. "A little busy here, Noah." She was aboard *Lady's Revenge*. The room pitched and bounced around her, punctuated by the whine of her engines and an explosion in the distance.

"Okay, call us back when you get a chance." I waved my hand over the image, disconnecting.

Dad glanced over. "'Drones is a good thing."

"Yeah, I guess so."

I felt so helpless as the hours dragged onward, and had chewed my fingernails down to the skin by the time the computer chimed, indicating a call.

"Put it up on the big screen," Dad said.

General Roosevelt appeared in the middle of the bridge, covered from head to toe in red grime. He had a blaster slung over his shoulder. "It was a hard fought battle, but we were victorious."

I let my breath out in relief.

"We lost a lot of good men and women though. They fought valiantly. I've never seen people willing to give so much for each other." He allowed a smile to play across his lips. "It was an honor to fight alongside them."

I held my breath. "Is Ollie...?"

"The governor is fine. However...." General Roosevelt frowned and glanced at Dad, who nodded. "Your pilot friend, the spitfire—"

"Sastra?"

He shook his head. "Yeah. She—"

"No!"

"I'm sorry, Noah. She was absolutely amazing. Two pretty sophisti-cated fighters with nukes onboard accompanied the drones. Sastra took them both out—one , just moments before it hit Earthome. We wouldn't be here if it wasn't for her."

I pictured her as I had seen her just a few hours before. She was defi-nitely right where she liked to be, in the thick of things. Then I thought of Draben and Adina. They knew her the best, and would probably feel responsible for bringing her out here.

General Roosevelt cleared his throat. "I've got to see to my men. I'll contact you later for a full report."

"Thank you, General," Dad said.

The holo-display flickered out.

***

"No!" Adina shouted.

Dad pulled her into a hug. "I'm sorry, Adina."

Draben looked like he wanted to hit something. "How?"

"General Roosevelt said she single-handedly saved Earthome. A bomber-drone was about to drop a nuclear warhead on the dome. Sastra was out of missiles and the only way to stop the drone was to ram it."

"Maybe she ejected," James said.

Adina glanced up at Dad's face with a glimmer of hope.

He shook his head. "No, I'm sorry. They recovered her... remains."

She buried her face in Dad's chest again, her black hair standing out in stark contrast against his white beard.

I longed to go over and hold her myself, tell her it'd be okay, but I didn't know that any better than she did.

Draben looked around in frustration and finally just stormed out of the room.

"I'm so sorry, James."

Our eyes met and he nodded. *'She saved all our lives, you know. So many times.'*

I just nodded, too. Not much more I could say.

CHAPTER FOURTEEN

Getting onto Venus was going to be much more difficult than it had been on Earth. The planet was more tightly controlled by the Poligarchy, and by the time we got within long-range scanner distance, we discovered a battleship orbiting her.

Dad immediately jumped the *ARC* back a hundred years so we wouldn't be spotted, then called a meeting on the bridge. Mom, Sam, Hamilton, James, Draben, Adina, and I were all present.

"The way I see it we've got two main choices." Dad held up a finger. "One, we forget Venus for now and go straight for Sarx. If we can get to him, maybe we can stop this whole war before it goes any further."

"But—"

Dad cut me off with a look. "Or two, we secure Venus, gain more support, and hopefully go after Sarx with a stronger presence."

Mom glanced around at all of us. "I don't know how you can even consider going after Sarx now. This is it." She waved at the eight of us. "This is the extent of our *presence.*"

Dad nodded. "I know, but we aren't going to beat Sarx in an all-out war anyway. We'll have to go in quietly and take him out."

"You mean assassinate him?" Mom looked shocked. "You expect one of us, one of our kids, to kill the Prime Senator in cold blood?"

"Of course not. I would have to be the one to do it."

"No way, Dad." I didn't like the idea of assassinating Sarx, but there was no way I'd let Dad go in there by himself. "I hate to say it, but some mornings you can barely get out of bed."

There were several nods around the room.

Dad frowned but then seemed to agree. "Then our only alternative is Venus."

"I don't think we have a choice," Mom said.

"Well," Hamilton said, "to formulate any kind of plan, we're going to need more information."

Dad nodded. "We can't take the *ARC* in so it'll have to be something small."

"The J-3500s are small," Sam said.

"What about a thermsuit?" Everyone looked at me. "I could probably get down there without anyone seeing me."

Mom shook her head. "No way. You are not going in there alone."

"It's a moot point," Hamilton said. "The thermsuit would never hold up in the Venusian atmosphere. The sulfuric acid would eat through it in seconds."

Sam pointed to the holo-screen. "Can't we just call down there? Talk to someone and find out what's going on?"

"Again, not a good idea. The Poligarchy has to be monitoring all channels."

Dad shook his head. "This isn't getting us anywhere. We can't go down there. We can't call anyone down there. What does that leave us?"

"Haon." We all turned toward James. "I don't know why I didn't think of it sooner."

"You're going to have to give us a little help here," Dad said. "How can my brother help us?"

"Not your brother, exactly." James looked excited. "Noah, you remember what Haon said when you confronted him about being a robot? All those times we came across him in the past?"

I shook my head, not quite following.

"When you blew up that ship, back on Earth over Yellowstone, Haon said that was a robot. When he captured your Mom, and you tried to save her and broke Haon's arm, that was a robot." He was getting more animated. "And obviously the whole time he was with us, after he was thrown in prison, he was a robot."

"We know all this," I said.

"The question we never asked ourselves was, just how many Haon robots are there?" James slapped his hand against his thighs. "Isn't it possible there are still more, on Venus?"

"So you think Haon is still down there, walking around in another robot body?"

"No. Haon was very particular about his own robots. With me, he embedded your mind in my body. The same with Ollie. But Haon did not want two of *himself* around. Sure, he had multiple bodies, but he always maintained a level of control over those bodies, never allowing them to become a separate entity from himself."

I tried to put it together. "So, if there is a Haon body down there, it's just a robot, no mind?"

"Exactly."

"How does this help us?" Mom asked.

"I—" James pointed at him and me. " —or we, might be able to find it and connect to it remotely, just like Haon did from Deimos." He sat back in his chair, grinning.

Draben shook his finger at James. "Then one of you could be on Venus, without actually going to Venus."

"Bingo," James said.

It sounded almost too easy to me. "Don't you think his labs have been torn apart already?"

"Most likely, but what you saw was only a fraction of his operation. If I had to guess, he'd keep his robots close, probably in his apartment building."

"Okay," I said. "So how do we put your theory to the test?"

"That's the hard part, of course," James said. "He had a central server where he stored all his important information. My guess is there's a lookup database in there with the connection information, but I don't know how to get to his server, even if it's still running."

"I do," Adina said. We all turned to look at her. She hadn't said a word since we had all gathered.

In fact, I hadn't heard her say a word in days.

"When we were in his apartment, on Venus, Draben and I hacked into his network." She glanced over at him. "Do you remember?"

He nodded, as did James.

"I still have that information stored in my holo-pad."

"What are we waiting for then?" I swiveled around, trying to decide if we should do it here or —

"Hold on," Dad said. "Let's figure out our goals here before you go running off to Venus. Even if it is only virtually."

"Well, like you said...." *Why does Dad have to slow everything down?* "We need to get in and find out what's going on with the Poligarchy, and see if we can find some allies."

"Where are you going to start, Mr. Smarty Pants?"

"Well, umm...."

"As I thought." He considered for a moment. "I think we should start with that scientist who worked for Haon. What was her name?"

"April," I said.

"That's right." Dad nodded. "She certainly didn't have a high opinion of Sarx."

"So I go down there, contact April, and see if she has an army hidden somewhere we can borrow." I think I about summed it up.

"Hey," James said. "Now it's *you* going down there?"

"Of course. You need to practice your flying."

"Noah's probably right," Dad said. "He's got quite a few more hours than you do on the J-3500s."

James didn't look too happy about the idea.

"But I'm sure he and Adina could use your help finding out if this robot of Haon's even exists."

I shook my head, but then Adina nodded. Apparently, she still wasn't ready to be alone with me, and right now, I also wanted to avoid that at all costs.

"It's settled then," Dad said. "We'll take the *ARC* back into the present so we can get into the SolWeb. Please let me know before you actually go to Venus." He turned toward his console and began preparing for the time-jump.

I turned toward James. "Where do you think we should do this?"

"Probably somewhere you can lie down. Might as well go to your room."

I glanced at Adina and swallowed. "Okay. Let's go."

***

I pulled myself into bed and lay back, thankful to have James in the room with Adina and me.

Adina, for her part, sat down in the desk chair and pulled out her holo-pad. "The first thing I have to do is figure out if Haon's servers are even online anymore." She pushed her fingers across the screen and pulled them out toward her face. Cubes of data slid out of the screen and floated in front of her.

Just like always, I had no idea what she was looking at. It might as well have been in a different language, which I guess technically it was.

"Ugh, I can't even connect to the SolWeb."

"Are you sure we've finished jumping?" I asked.

She turned and glared at me, then shook her head. "I guess not."

I glanced at James, who just raised his eyebrows. It was highly unusual for Adina to not think of something so simple.

A tiny shift in the vibration of the ship told me we had come out of warp. "Try it now."

Adina pinched and twisted some data-cubes. "Ok, I'm in." For the next couple of minutes she sat in complete concentration, flipping bits of information here and there, and opening and closing data-cubes.

Finally she smiled slightly. "I've found it."

"Haon's servers?" James asked.

"Well, his network at least. That's a good sign." She pinched and opened and closed a few more cubes. "Yup, there it is." Her fingers flew through the holographic images floating in front of her. "He didn't change any of the security protocols since I was in here last."

"So...." James leaned forward to look at the projection. "Is there anything that shows if there are any remaining robots?"

"I'm not exactly sure what I'm looking for." She sat back and cracked her neck, then leaned back in. "Let me check the connected devices." She flicked through a list of number strings, and pointed at several that flashed red. "These are inactive." Then she cocked her head sideways. "I don't recognize this structure." She clicked a number, and tt enlarged and swirled around her finger. Then she flicked her thumb and forefinger open and the numbers flew outward, forming spiraling patterns, lit with blue and green strings of numbers and letters.

"I've never seen anything like it." She leaned back again, puzzled.

"I have." James pointed to his own head. "In here."

"Is it...?" I said.

"It's a robotic neuro-processor," James said.

We looked at each other, and even Adina smiled.

James walked around so he was standing between the projection and my bed. "Can you back out?"

"Sure." Adina reached out and squeezed the data together until we were looking at the original list of IDs.

"So it was this one here?" James pointed to a number.

"Yes."

He glanced over at me. "Okay, I'm going to try to connect."

I opened my mouth to complain.

"Do you know how to connect to anyone, other than me?" James looked at me with his eyebrows raised.

"No."

"Okay then. Let me get in and see if I can connect, see if it's indeed an inactive robot. Then I'll show you how to sync up with it."

I nodded.

He turned back to the holo-display. His body went stiff and he just stared straight ahead, unblinking.

I glanced at Adina, who sat watching James intently. Almost too intently.

'Noah?'

"You're in?"

'Yes. Close your eyes.'

I did.

'Okay, I'm going to open a tunnel.'

A flash hit me right between the eyes, and I blinked a few times until the image resolved. I was looking at *a thin sliver of light."I think we're in a closet."* I tried to reach up and touch the dark wall in front of me. It felt like I was fighting against a hidden force.

'Let me drive for a minute.'

"*Oh. Okay.*" I relaxed.

A huge hand reached forward and pushed against a panel. *Click!* A door swung open, and we stepped into a dimly lit room, which I immediately recognized as Haon's bedroom in his apartment. James looked around beside me. It was the same room, but many of the furnishings were different than I remembered.

A voice rose, and James moved toward the bedroom door.

"I don't really think that's necessary." It was a woman's voice.

James quietly opened the door a crack and peeked through.

A woman paced back and forth, and a small image of a man floated above her wrist. "But I told you, I don't need them anymore."

"Bookshelves are highly prized in most apartments," the man she was talking with said.

"But I don't have any books!" She was getting irritated.

'*Obviously, someone else has moved into Haon's apartment,*' James said.

"*Yeah, and she didn't know she had a huge robot hiding in her walls.*" I smiled, thinking what she would have done had she discovered Haon's robot. He was a pretty intimidating figure. "*Let's get out of here.*"

'*Agreed.*' James pushed the door open all the way when she had her back to us. Then, he took a deep breath and dashed for the front door. Unfortunately, there was a small table in the front hall that wasn't there last time. He smashed into it, knocking little knickknacks all over the floor with a crash.

The woman whipped around. "What! Who are you?"

"Nobody." Haon's deep voice boomed in my ears. "Um... wrong apartment. Sorry."

James scrambled for the door and dashed out into the hall. Looking left and right, he headed for the elevator. Thankfully, it came almost immediately after pressing the button. We stumbled inside and the door shut. James leaned against the wall, and we both let out a deep sigh.

'*That was close.*'

"Yeah."

'*Okay, I guess it's time for you to take over.*' He wasn't happy about it. '*Go ahead and drive.*'

I pushed further into the robot, trying to get a feel for the size, and looked down at my huge feet. A scratchy beard tickled my neck as I took a few steps around the elevator. *"It's going to take a little getting used to walking, especially in a body of this size, but I think I've got it."*

'*All right, I'll tell your father we ran into a little trouble and you had to start right away.*'

"*Sounds good. Thanks, James.*"

'*Sure. As soon as you know anything, let me know.*'

"*Will do, and James?*"

'*Yeah?*'

"*Tell Adina thanks.*"

He withdrew from my mind — well, from Haon's robot's mind.

I reached down and pressed the button for the ground floor. *Time to go find April.*

CHAPTER FIFTEEN

I walked out into the streets of Onissya. The heat hit me immediately, but I knew from experience it wasn't near as hot as it would be once I got outside the city-center. I stumbled over Haon's big feet while stepping off the curb, and a few curious onlookers stopped to stare. One woman, who was sitting on a bench across the street, watched me much longer than I was comfortable with.

I turned in the direction I remembered as being the exit to the outer parts of the city. The combination of being inside a body that weighed a good three times my own weight, and the excitement of actually walking, made me hyper-conscious of each step. I looked up from watching my feet, just in time to avoid a woman pushing a stroller. A young boy walked next to her and the mother pulled him out of my way.

"Sorry about that." I smiled at the boy.

He smiled back, but then his eyes grew wide. "Mamma, isn't he the man from the SolWeb?"

She turned and looked up at me, and her eyes about doubled in size as well. She grabbed the boy and hurried off in the opposite direction.

I glanced around, and several people were watching me, some scanning through images on their wrist displays. I hadn't thought about Haon being recognized, and quickened my pace. I could get lost much easier outside the main dome.

After walking about a kilometer, I spied my target: the street entered a tunnel, which pierced the walls of the dome. I lowered my head and hurried toward it.

A shadow flitted out from a side alley. "You don't want to be going out there."

I turned to see a scruffy teen, probably sixteen or so.

He smiled, showing his front teeth had been knocked out. "There's nothing but trouble out there. The Poligarchy is rounding everyone up."

"Thanks for the advice." I continued on, but the boy dashed in front of me and walked backwards with his palms toward me.

"I don't think you get my meaning. I can't let you go out there." He looked me up and down. "I know who you are, and if you don't give me something to forget, I may have to talk to the Poligarchy m'self."

"Look, kid, I—"

A scuff of a shoe behind me caused me to spin around.

A tall, lanky fellow with a scar across his forehead was swinging a metal pipe where my head was a moment before. Faster than I thought possible, my hand flew up and caught the pipe. He made the mistake of holding onto the pipe with both hands as I twisted my body and threw him across the street. He hit a street sign and fell to the ground.

I felt a stab of pain in my side and whipped back around to see that it was indeed an actual stab. Scruffy boy held onto a long knife that stuck out of my new robot body, just below the ribs. I pushed the pain away, and like turning off a switch, it was gone.

I reached over and grabbed him by the front of his shirt, and drew him closer. "You picked the wrong guy to mess with today."

His eyes went wide. Obviously he expected me to be lying on the pavement, bleeding to death. I shoved him backwards, and he smashed against the wall of the building behind him. His eyes rolled up into his head and he slumped to the ground.

I pulled the knife from my side and turned back toward the tunnel. A couple steps later, I heard a commotion behind me and glanced over my shoulder to see two Poligarchy policemen running down the street toward me. I started running myself.

"Stop!"

No way. Who knows what they'll do to me.

I plowed into the tunnel. The small booth next to the road was there, just like I remembered, but the shield was down. A mag-truck was coming into the tunnel, loaded with crates. The guard stood outside his booth with his hands on his hips watching the truck as it drove by.

One of the policemen shouted from behind me, "Stop that man!"

The guard looked over, startled, then moved toward me.

Again a shout from behind me. "Raise the shield."

The guard hesitated, then seemed to take in my size. He spun around and dashed into his booth. Just as he dove for a big red button on the wall, I ran past.

An electrical hum echoed down the tunnel, and a blue shield shimmered into view just a few meters ahead. The cops raised their weapons, and the guard came out of the booth and reached for his own sidearm.

There's nothing for it. I ducked my head down and barreled forward.

Electrical energy lanced through my robot body. Every pain receptor erupted as if on fire. I couldn't shut them down fast enough. My legs quit working and I stumbled forward. I couldn't even get my arms up to keep me from landing face first on the ground. Yellow and green light arced across my vision, and a loud buzzing filled my ears as I slid a meter or two on my face. The robot system was shutting down.

Darkness enveloped my sight just as several shadows flitted across the road.

* * *

I opened my eyes. Cool air enveloped me. I was back in my room on the *ARC*.

"What happened?"

I turned over to see James standing in the doorway.

"Were you watching me the whole time?" I asked.

"What do you mean the whole time? You were only gone a few minutes. I was just leaving."

I nodded. "I guess you're right. I... um...."

"What did you do?" James walked back into my room, stepping over some piles of clothes on the floor.

"I think I fried the robot."

"What? That didn't take long." He just looked at me, waiting to hear the story.

So I told him.

He shook his head when I finished. "Believe me, I've got a pretty good handle on how much one of these bodies can take, and it's considerable." He placed his palm on his own chest. "But I'm not sure going through a barrier shield was such a good idea."

"I didn't have a choice."

He stared at me a few moments longer.

"So, do you think I destroyed it?"

"I don't know, but there's only one way to find out." He sat down in a chair and swung around toward me. "Let's go back in."

I wasn't so sure I liked that idea, but I didn't say anything.

He closed his eyes, and so did I.

'Okay. Just like before. I'll go in and then open a tunnel for you.'

"I could do it on my own this time."

I felt his annoyance.

"Or you could go in and open a tunnel for me."

'Okay. One sec.'

I held my breath, hoping for the best.

'It looks like he's rebooting.'

"That's good, right?"

'Well, it depends on what happens after the reboot.'

A few tense moments later. 'He's back online. Let's see what's going on. You can drive since it's your mess.'

"Thanks." Just like before, I could feel James pulling me into the robot.

Long lights flashed overhead. I could feel a rough floor sliding under my back. My head banged against the ground as my body was pulled along in jerks. I looked down along my legs, and saw a couple of men straining against the weight of the huge robot body.

"Hey," I said.

They stopped and looked at me, startled.

"No way," the one holding my right foot said. "You should be dead." He and his partner dropped my feet.

I sat up and rubbed the backside of my head. "Obviously, I'm not."

"But you went right through that shield." The other one spoke up. He was a huge kid, probably not much older than me, but I got the impression that if I stood up, I'd be looking him in the eye. "No one can go through the shield and live."

The other kid, smaller but still a good size, looked over my shoulder. "We need to get out of here. They've got to be looking for you."

I pushed to my feet. "Show me the way."

'Do you think that's such a good idea?'

"I'm not sure I have much of a choice."

'Okay. Well, I guess you've got everything under control.' James didn't really believe that, but I didn't say anything. *'Try not to take any electrical baths again.'*

"You can be sure of that. I did not like it one bit."

'Talk to you in a little while, Noah.' James withdrew.

"You coming, mister?" The giant kid waved me on.

"Right behind you. Just had to catch my breath."

We wound through cramped tunnels that seemed almost carved between the buildings that piled up against the sides of the long tube we were in. Whereas all the buildings inside the main dome appeared orderly and planned, those outside, in tubes and smaller domes, were just smashed together, built out of material most likely left over from construction projects inside the city center.

I had to squeeze the massive frame of Haon's robot through several areas, and had the distinct impression that if I pushed hard enough the whole area would come toppling down upon us. The smaller of the two guides kept turning around to make sure I was still following. I was surprised at how nimble the larger one was.

"I didn't catch your names," I said.

"I'm Jerry," said the smaller boy. "And that's Ander."

"Thanks for pulling me out back there."

Jerry just nodded. "Not too much farther."

We got to a particularly tight spot, and Ander squeezed through; followed quickly by Jerry. I turned sideways and stuck my foot in the small hole, and then pushed the rest of my robot body through. The pocket on the khaki-colored pants Haon had dressed the robot in caught on a protruding piece of metal. There wasn't much I could do but push on, and the pocket tore and I nearly stumbled.

I looked up and discovered I was in a small area, surrounded by buildings on every side. There was no sign of Jerry or Ander.

I couldn't see any way out, other than the hole I had just come through, and as I spun around, something blocked it, too.

I was trapped.

CHAPTER SIXTEEN

"Hey, what's going on?" I looked up at a small patch of Venusian sky between the ramshackle walls and the protective tube.

"Just calm down, Mr. Zarc." A muffled voice came from somewhere behind me.

I swung around but didn't see anyone.

"Trouble seems to follow you everywhere you go."

I scanned a little higher on the wall, looking for a window or peep hole in the mishmash of material. "You've made a mistake. I'm not who you think I am."

"Oh? You've got a face that's a little hard to mistake." The voice definitely came from a dark square in the wall, about three meters up.

"Looks can be deceiving."

"Then why don't you tell me who you are?"

"I'm afraid you wouldn't believe me. Besides, how can I trust someone who isn't even willing to show his face?"

Some whispering came from the hole, and I strained to hear it. A crackle and hum filled my head, and suddenly I understood every word. I must have unconsciously tapped into the robot's sensors and increased the reach of its ears.

"....but we know he's Haon."

"That doesn't mean he can be trusted, although he definitely doesn't work for the Poly."

"We need to get the lady down here. She'd know."

"I'll get her. Keep him busy."

After some rustling, the soft patter of footsteps receded into the distance.

"So, mister, how'd you get through that shield?"

I didn't know who "the lady" was, but I had no choice but to play along. "There's more to me than meets the eye."

"You some kind of superhero?" A little bit of awe colored his voice. He was obviously just a kid, but not Jerry or Ander.

"I guess you could say that."

"So why were you running?"

"I didn't want the *Poly* to find out my identity."

"How come you don't have a mask on?"

I smiled up at the dark hole in the wall. "Maybe I do."

Some commotion came from behind the boy — echoes of several foot-steps, followed by a woman's voice. "I'm not climbing up there."

"It's the only way to see him."

"Jerry got a good look at him," the woman said. "I trust him. It's got to be Haon."

"If you say so."

"Open the gate."

Some more shuffling, then a grinding noise, and dust fell from a crack in the wall, just below and to the left of the hole where the boy sat. The poorly mortared brick split along a hidden seam and slid back, revealing a door.

Two figures stood within the shadows of the door: one small, and the other tall and slender.

"Dr. Zarc!" A woman dashed forward with a grin on her face.

I recognized her at once, although her black hair was cut short, and her clothes where worn and dirty — not the white lab coat she had worn last time I'd seen her.

"April."

She seemed like she was about to give me a hug, and then stopped short, thrusting her hand out. "It's so good to see you... alive." There was a bit of a question in her voice.

"It's good to see you, too." I looked her over. "Your arm is healed?"

She grabbed her left arm with her right. "Yeah. Still hurts some days, but the doctors did a good job with what they had."

"That's great. It looked like it hurt something awful last time I saw you."

April studied me for a moment. "I think we need to talk." She glanced at the boy standing behind her. "Somewhere private."

I nodded, and she turned and passed back through the door.

I followed her through another warren of alleys and tunnels, none quite so packed together as before. We passed several people who, while dirty and dressed in ratty clothes, seemed somewhat happy. Many smiles were given to April, but almost unanimously they disappeared when gazes shifted toward me. Two boys followed behind, trying to look official. Even Jerry and Ander peeked out through a grimy window.

She led me to a crooked building, with what looked like a piece of a ship's wing for a door, and shooed the boys off. "That'll be all. Thanks for your help."

The boys puffed up their chests with pride, but couldn't hide the disappointment in their eyes; they wouldn't be able to find out more about the "super-hero" in their midst.

April and I ducked inside the building. It was a small, one room apartment with a tiny kitchen area built into the wall on one side. Next to that sat a rickety old table and a couple of chairs, and on the opposite wall was a shabby looking bed.

April gazed around in embarrassment. "I know it's not much."

"Oh, it's fine. You should see the room I share with my brother—" I clamped my hand over my mouth.

"I knew it wasn't you." She edged toward the door. "Do I need to call the guard?"

"No!" I took a step toward her. "I'm not here to cause you any trouble." Well, that wasn't entirely true. "I came here to find you."

"So who are you?" She had the door to her back, with her hand on the makeshift handle.

"Noah. I was with Haon when your lab was destroyed, when those people...."

Sadness washed over her face. She shook the memory away. "So you're a robot?"

"No. Well, sort of. I'm on a ship out in space, but I'm connected to this robot body, remotely."

She smiled. "Amazing."

"I know, right?"

"I had my suspicions when I found Haon's body before. After I left the lab, I discovered him just lying there. At first I thought he was dead, but then I found the hole in the back of his head and saw the circuitry inside. I've actually done quite a bit of...."

"It's okay," I said.

"Once I was up to it, I did an extensive study of the robot, trying to figure out how it worked. Whoever made it was a genius."

"Haon did it."

"No big surprise there. He had an incredible mind. Is he...?"

"He's still locked up on Deimos." *Along with Gramps.*

"I assumed he was, but when I heard you were on Venus...." She frowned and looked away.

"I'm sorry to have gotten your hopes up."

She swallowed and shook her head. "It's silly to hope for the impossible." She took a deep breath. "You said you were here to find me?"

"Yes." Where to begin. "I'm sure you've heard by now that the colonies have declared their independence from the Poligarchy."

She nodded. "Many of us were disappointed not to be included."

"We couldn't get into Venus safely, and we didn't know who to contact."

"Fair enough. The only thing keeping us alive is our secrecy."

"So there *is* someone in charge? You've got some kind of leadership here?"

She watched me as if trying to gauge just how much to tell me. "There are those we follow, but they wouldn't call themselves leaders."

"Can I meet them?"

"That's up to them, of course. I'll ask." She glanced around her apartment. "If you want to make yourself comfortable, I'll go talk to the one we follow in Avalon."

"Avalon?"

"That's the name we give this area of the city."

I scrunched up my forehead.

She smiled. "It's supposed to be ironic."

April opened the door. "Help yourself to anything in the kitchen." Then she was gone.

I looked around and decided something to drink would be nice. Not that I was thirsty in Haon's robot body, but it would feel good in this heat. I'd suspected before that James could regulate his own heat, but I hadn't figured out how to do that yet in this body. I found a plastic cup in April's lone cupboard, went to her sink, and turned the knob. All that came out at first was the sound of banging pipes, but then the spigot spurted and hissed and, finally, water flowed out in a steady stream. A brown color at first, the water quickly cleared up, and I filled my glass. Had I been in my real body, I might not have been too keen on drinking the water here.

Neither of the chairs beside her table looked like they'd support the weight of my robot body, so I walked over and sat on the edge of the bed. It creaked under my weight as well, but it held. I took a sip and, as I suspected, the water tasted terrible. Worst of all, it was warm, almost to the point of being hot.

I went back and poured the water down the sink. "So much for that."

I sat back down. An old plastic crate next to the bed functioned as a night stand, and a small holo-frame sat on top of it. I waved my hand over it, and an image of a group of people, all dressed in white smocks, sprang up about a half meter off the table. April was one of them. I slid my finger through the image and flicked sideways. Haon appeared, the image taken from the side, as if he didn't know someone was shooting it.

"It seems like April may have had a thing for him."

Voices outside caused me to wave my hand across the holo-frame. The image of Haon disappeared just as the door opened.

April walked in, followed by an old man that couldn't have been more than a meter tall, slightly bent over with age.

"Noah, this is *Memory Keeper*." She guided the old man by the shoulders to one of the chairs. He took a few moments to position the chair to his liking, and with some effort pulled himself into his seat.

April swung the other seat around so the three of us faced each other in a triangle. "You'll need to speak up. Memory Keeper is a bit hard of hearing."

"Good to meet you, sir," I said, trying to match April's volume.

The old man waved his hand in sort of a salute/bow gesture.

I sat watching him expectantly, and for a moment I thought he'd fallen asleep.

Finally, he said, "You are not what you appear."

"That's right. How did you know?" Already, I attributed magical powers to the old man. He did look kind of like a wizard.

"Because, this beautiful woman told me." He bared a toothless grin at April, then turned back toward me with a serious expression. "You have come to us with a purpose."

I wasn't sure if that was a question or statement so I kept quiet. He seemed like the kind of person you didn't push. When he was ready to talk, he would.

Unfortunately, it took him longer to speak than I had patience for. "Why did April call you Memory Keeper?"

He jerked up as if I had awakened him. Was he sleeping with his eyes open?

"Because that's my name."

"Your name? It's not a title?"

"No, of course not." He looked at me with his milky grey eyes as though I'd said the dumbest thing in the solar system. "My father was Memory Keeper. His father was Memory Keeper. And so on. Back until the first."

"It just seems like a strange name."

April frowned at me.

"Umm... I mean I've never met anyone with a name quite like that."

He let out a raspy chuckle. "I imagine the first time anyone heard the name Noah, they thought it strange too."

"I guess, but that was a very long time ago."

"Every name has a beginning." He pointed a bent, gnarled finger at me. "Yours began with a man who lived through the first destruction of Earth. Mine began after the second."

"You're from Earth?"

He shook his head so hard I thought he'd fall out of his chair. "No, no. The Red Planet."

"You're from Mars?"

Memory Keeper dropped his eyes. "No, not for me. Maybe for others but never for me."

Clearly an amazing story lay locked in this man's head, but I was growing more and more impatient. "April said that you're a leader. Er, I guess she said you have followers. Do you have an army?"

"An army? Where do you think I'd be keeping an army?" He patted his chest and his pant legs. "In my pocket? Do you think I have an army in my pocket?"

I glanced over at April.

She just shrugged then said, "Maybe you should tell him why you are named Memory Keeper."

The old man calmed down and settled back in his chair. "Ah, yes, yes, that is a good tale. It starts with the first colonists on Mars. The year was 2062. There had been a small colony on the moon for fifteen years, but now had come the time to try something on a much grander scale. It was thought that Mars could one day actually support life, much like Earth, without the need of domes and habitats to protect its inhabitants."

None of this was new to me. Draben and I had done a report on this very subject last year in school.

"The Colony on Mars thrived. Nearly every industrialized country sent ships with people looking for a new life. In the year 2076, it was agreed upon by all the nations with a stake in Mars, that a coalition government should be created. This would give Mars a certain level of autonomy from Earth. Not wholly separate, but enough that they could make basic laws and direct their lives for their well-being. This new government, of course, was called the Poligarchy. From the Greek words, *poly* meaning *many*, and *archo* meaning *to rule*. The many nations would rule together. A central capitol was built, and a vision of a peaceful future began to take shape. At last it seemed mankind could put away her warring past, and enter a new world. It lasted exactly twenty-five years."

"Until Sarx invaded."

April and Memory Keeper both looked at me, stunned.

"You know of this?" the old man asked.

"Yeah... I was there."

He looked at April, who nodded slightly.

"You are a time-traveler?"

"Yes. Well, my family is."

"A Zarc?"

I nodded.

"What more do you know?" The old man sat forward with excitement. "I would love to fill in gaps in my own memory."

I shook my head. "Not much more than that. I saw the invasion being launched from Earth, and I saw the final battle at the Capitol building on Mars. After that I'm pretty much like every other living being, except Sarx. I know nothing of what happened during the Forbidden Years."

A smile stole across Memory Keeper's face. "Oh, there are a few of us that know the truth."

He leaned back and continued his story. "Shortly after the invasion you witnessed, Sarx declared himself Prime Senator. Up until that point, all the Poligarchy members were equal, none standing above another."

"Why did they let him? I mean didn't Earth send help?"

"No. They tried, of course. I think they sent one ship with some men tasked with assassinating Sarx, but any kind of full-scale retaliation would take time. Unfortunately, they had problems of their own. Shortly after Sarx launched his invasion of Mars, the Emperor of China launched one of his own. He released a weapon, unlike anything the Earth had ever seen, on the continent of Australia. Within a matter of days, the entire population was killed."

I cringed, as did April. We both knew our role in the destruction of Earth, and apparently it all started in Australia.

"The Chinese held the rest of the world hostage for another five years, then nothing. All communication with Earth ceased, and Sarx declared that no ship from Earth was allowed to land on Mars. Several tried, of course, and each time Sarx destroyed them before they even reached orbit. That's when the Prime Senator began his systematic efforts to clear up his own name. Everyone knew, of course, that Sarx invaded Mars, and most everyone figured out he had something to do with the destruction of Earth. After all, he showed up with a mostly Chinese army, and mere months later the Chinese destroyed Australia. Yet there was nothing they could do about it. He had the army."

The old man rubbed his temples, as if all this remembering was giving him a headache. "Sarx announced a plan to colonize Venus. This was crazy. Venus was inhospitable, and always would be, but he said we should never put all our eggs in one basket. 'Look at what happened to Earth,' he would say. So it started off innocent enough. Protective domes were built on Venus, and settlers went to begin a life outside the immediate control of Sarx. But then the forced transplant of civilians began. It became quickly known that if anyone mentioned anything about the invasion of Mars, they found themselves on Venus. If anyone made any statements about who or what caused the destruction of Earth, they were forcefully relocated to Venus."

He shook his head and frowned. "Sadly, it didn't stop there. Sarx built a police force on Venus whose primary goal was to wipe out any memory of his atrocities. So even on Venus, if someone was suspected of talking about the invasion or Cataclysm, they simply disappeared. Sarx was relentless in his determination. Within only a couple of years, no one ever spoke anything against him. Within one generation, he succeeded. No one remembered."

Patting himself on the chest and grinning, the old man said, "Except Memory Keeper."

"You were there?" *Is he a robot too?*

"No, no. Like I said, I am descended from the first Memory Keeper. He saw what was happening and decided someone had to know the truth, even if it was only a handful of people. He swore to pass down through the generations the memory of what Prime Senator Sarx did, hoping that someday all mankind could learn again of his horrific crimes against humanity. We have protected that secret, even to the point of not letting our families know the truth. Sarx would wipe us out if a whisper of the truth got out. Only me, my granddaughter—" He glanced at April. "—and the handful of Memory Keepers across Venus know the truth. Most think I'm just an old man who tells stories of Earth and the way it used to be."

"Maybe it's time the real truth got out." I wasn't sure even Memory Keeper could convince the Poligarchy of the truth. Stories handed down from generation to generation weren't the best evidence.

He shook his head. "I don't know. There are changes, but will they be enough?"

"I can tell you that right now —" I sat up straighter in my chair. "—we are doing everything we can to make sure Sarx doesn't remain in control."

"Sarx controls everything." He sighed and shook his head.

"Not anymore. Not Earth. Not the Moon."

He perked up. "So it's true? The rumors we've heard?"

"Yes, we are fighting back. We are going to win."

April seemed excited. "So if you have taken over the Moon and Earth —"

"It's time to take Venus." That would be easier said than done, but no sense beating around the asteroid.

Memory Keeper shook his head. "But Venus isn't like Earth or the Moon. Sarx has a formidable army here."

"How many soldiers?"

The old man thought for a moment. "Three thousand. Maybe more. Maybe less."

"And how many men and women live out here?"

"It's hard to say, but probably around fifty thousand."

I sat there and blinked.

"But the soldiers are armed." There was genuine fear in the old man's face.

"How many people live inside the city?"

April said, "The official count is twenty thousand."

"Would they put up a fight?"

She shook her head. "No way. They like their way of life, but not enough to risk their lives over it."

"So fifty thousand people, subtract out the children and those too old to fight...."

"We'd probably have twenty to thirty thousand able-bodied people." April's eyes gleamed. "We could overwhelm them."

"People would die," I said.

Her face grew serious. "People have already died. Maybe it's time we put an end to any future bloodshed."

Memory Keeper sat with his eyes closed as April and I talked. "The people will not follow you without my blessing."

I turned and he was staring right at me.

"How can I ask them to?" His eyes filled with tears.

"You can give us the choice." April reached out and held his hands in her own. "For too long, we've had no choice. Give us that opportunity."

The old man squeezed his lips together and closed his eyes. I could almost see him running the scenarios over in his mind and comparing them to what he knew about Sarx. Finally, he nodded slightly and opened his eyes. "We will give them the choice."

April smiled and stood. "I will call a meeting of the Elders."

CHAPTER SEVENTEEN

April said it would take until the next morning to get everyone together, and I said I'd check in with my father and return in twelve hours. She offered to keep Haon's robot body in her apartment.

After she left with Memory Keeper, I looked around. At first I considered lying down in her bed, but thought she'd need that. I sat in the corner against the wall, closed my eyes, and withdrew from the robot's mind.

I opened my eyes, smiled at the sight of Obadiah asleep at my feet, and glanced over at the clock. It was getting late, but I needed to fill Dad in on everything that had happened. I moved to sit up, almost forgetting that my legs didn't work. How quickly I got used to it. I pushed my hands under me and shoved myself into a seated position, then pulled myself into my magchair.

Obadiah jumped up and wagged his tail.

"Computer, locate Dad."

"Your father is on deck thirty-seven, pod ninety-four."

"Thanks." At least he wasn't sleeping.

I pushed out of my room and headed for the magsphere. Obadiah padded along beside me. "Come on, boy, let's find out what Dad's up to."

A few minutes later I was looking at the door with 3794 on the door — the Irish Deer habitat. I sighed. This is where it had all started a couple of years ago. News came that Mom and Dad were missing on their trip back in time to get the Irish Deer. Dad got stuck in the Ice Age, and Haon had taken Mom captive.

The thought of the Ice Age brought Adina to mind, and I smiled, remembering all that hair she had.

I glanced at Obadiah. "Wonder what Dad's doing down here?" The habitat was still empty, as far as I knew.

When I opened the door, Obadiah dashed past me and bounded into the underbrush. I hovered inside and took a deep breath. It smelled just like the woods back on Earth, a deep loamy smell of decaying leaves and wood.

"Dad!" I yelled out. My words seemed to die almost as soon as they left my mouth in the dense growth. The habitat had definitely grown since I was here last. I heard a muffled grunt, then the clang of metal on metal. I pushed down a path to a small clearing, where Dad's old Jeep sat, a pair of legs sticking out from under it.

I pushed over beside the Jeep. "Dad?"

The legs jerked, followed by the distinctive sound of head meeting metal. Dad slid out from under the car and rubbed his forehead. "You shouldn't sneak up on me like that."

I laughed at the sight: Dad with black smudges on his face and a big, goofy grin. It had been a while since I'd seen him smile like that.

He reached out a hand. "Here, help me up."

Grabbing his hand with both of mine, I lifted my magchair into the air, pulling him with me.

He groaned as he stood. "I'm definitely getting too old for this."

"What are you doing out here?"

He looked around. "Ah, well, this is where I like to go to think. You're mother calls it my 'man-cave'. More like a man-forest, but I like it. It's so quiet. It reminds me of...."

"The Pacific Northwest," I finished.

"Yup." He grinned. "That's the best place on Earth."

I smiled. "Remember when we got lost?"

"I wasn't lost." He ruffled my head. "Just didn't want to go home just yet."

"Sure, sure." I waved at the red Jeep. "And this?"

"Last time I took her for a ride, the CV ioints were making a racket. They're shot, all right. I was thinking about replacing them."

"Maybe we should get Sam to help."

"Yeah, you're probably right." He studied me for a moment. "So, how'd it go on Venus? Did you find out anything?"

I nodded. "Yup. I got in touch with April, and she introduced me to this old man."

Dad raised his eyebrows.

"Well, not as old as you, of course."

"Of course."

"Anyway, his name is Memory Keeper."

"His name?"

"That's what I said, but that's his name. He remembers everything, from way back when Mars was first colonized."

"Everything?"

I told Dad all about my time on Venus, about everything April had said—I left out my suspicions about her feelings for Haon—and all that Memory Keeper had told me.

When I finished, Dad said, "Amazing. To think that all these hundreds of years there have been those who knew the truth about Prime Senator Sarx."

"I know."

"I'm still not sure I understand what they hope to accomplish against the military. They have no weapons to speak of."

"I know, Dad, but they want to fight. It's their right, isn't it?

He nodded. "We'll do what we can to help. At least we can try to keep Sarx's ships busy, but people—"

"Are going to die," I finished. "I know."

My face must have shown the turmoil I was feeling because Dad placed both his hands on my shoulders. "I want to tell you something, son."

I looked up into his clouded, brown eyes.

"There will come a time in your life when you reach a crossroads. Hundreds of times, really. One direction seems to go down a path of comfort, the other into danger, or pain, or just plain hard work. Everything within you screams to take the path of ease. You ask yourself what good could possibly come from taking the hard road. You may offend someone. You may make yourself look stupid. You might even put yourself in physical danger. But you know what? Life wasn't meant to be lived in safety. We weren't put in this universe just to be happy people who drift along looking for what feels good. Deep, rich, full life comes from taking the hard road. Do you understand?"

I nodded.

"Of course you don't, really. Not yet. Not until you've come to the end of living life and look back and realize that the hard road was always the best one." He gazed off into the forest. What hard roads was he remembering?

"Dad, I do get it, at least a little bit. Look at you. There have been so many times you could have taken the easy way, but you didn't. Do I wish you hadn't gone back in time and lived nearly a hundred years without us? You bet. But does that make me love you less? No way. I can't imagine it any other way now. You are who you are because of the hard things you've done. And I'm the person I am because of those hard things you've done too."

He smiled broadly and patted my shoulder. "When did you become so wise?"

I laughed. "Probably about the same time you got so old."

He looked at me a bit longer, then turned and gathered up his tools. "You should probably get some sleep. Sounds like you have a big day ahead of you."

"Okay." I turned my chair toward the exit. "Thanks, Dad, for everything."

"You are most welcome, son."

* * *

I woke up the next morning feeling as if I'd forgotten something. It wasn't until I was dressed and in my magchair that I realized Obadiah wasn't around.

"Ugh. I left him in the habitat." I glanced at the time. There was still an hour before I had to be back on Venus. "Let's go see what kind of trouble you've gotten yourself into."

During the ride in the magsphere Sam called me over the comm. "Noah, I think you're going to want to see this."

"What's that?"

"Just come on up to the bridge."

"But I've got to get Obadiah."

"He can wait." Sam was really agitated. Of course, when wasn't she?

"Okay, I'll be there in a few minutes."

On the ride up, I thought through what I'd say to the Elders on Venus. My first instinct was to come up with all kinds of arguments as to why they needed to fight the Poligarchy. Then I thought of people dying, and I'd go through all the reasons why they shouldn't fight. By the time I reached the bridge, what I'd known all along was confirmed: it was their choice. I just needed to make sure they knew what they were getting into.

When I pushed onto the bridge, I was surprised to see everyone there.

Dad sat in the captain's chair. Mom and Adina stood by the front window talking. Hamilton sat in a chair, with Draben and James standing behind him. They watched a projection above a holo-pad in Hamilton's lap. Sam paced back and forth nervously.

"What's going on?"

Sam whipped around at my voice. "The Poligarchy's going to make some big announcement."

"Announcement? About what?" I pushed over beside Dad.

"We don't know," he said. "They just came on to say a discovery has been made which will rewrite the history books."

I didn't like the sound of that. From what I'd learned yesterday, Sarx had been rewriting history for a thousand years.

"It's starting," Hamilton said. He grabbed the image above his holo-pad and flung it to the main monitors.

A podium shimmered into the middle of the room, with the official seal for the Poligarchy on the front. A voice filled the bridge. "Please welcome the honorable Prime Senator Sarx."

Sarx strode into view, stood behind the podium, and cleared his throat. "Ladies and gentlemen of the united Solar System. I come to you today with disturbing news. What began as a glorious example of human ingenuity, and humanitarianism, has turned to horror. We have learned that our National Heroes, the Zarc family, have turned into the perpetrators of history's vilest crime. With the unimaginable power of time-travel, they have transported themselves back one thousand years and unleashed the biological weapon that destroyed the inhabitants of Earth."

He paused to let that sink in. "We believe their overwhelming desire to have a pristine home for their beloved animals has driven them to this horrendous act. We have irrefutable evidence of this crime, and our highest courts have issued a warrant for their arrest. Anyone with information as to their whereabouts, that leads to their capture, will be the recipient of a generous reward of one billion credits."

The Prime Senator stood tall, his face resolute. "It is a dark day for humanity, but at last we can put to rest the speculation and uncertainty that has haunted us for nearly a millennia. Thank you, and may peace remain our deepest yearning."

A hidden crowd erupted into a chorus of questions, but then the image vanished and the bridge was silent.

"How can he do that?" I yelled.

The vein in Dad's temple throbbed. "He can do that because he has absolute control over the Senate and media."

"But what he said about us — people will believe it." I wanted to punch something.

Mom sighed. "All we can do is speak the truth. Eventually the lies of the enemy will be brought into the light."

"This changes nothing," Dad said. "We'll continue on as we are, but —" He looked at each of us. " — be careful."

Everyone nodded, and I turned for the door. *Time to show the Solar System who the real villain is.*

CHAPTER EIGHTEEN

I rushed back to my room, Obadiah jogging along behind me. "You've made me late, you dumb dog."

It had taken several minutes to find Obadiah in the Irish Deer habitat. Even though no living creatures occupied the forest, he just couldn't stop sniffing every bush and tree. He didn't seem to believe no squirrels were hiding in there somewhere.

I tore into my room, gave Obadiah some food and water, then pulled myself into bed. It took me a few minutes, lying there, listening to the dog crunching his food, before I could settle my mind enough to connect to the robot on Venus.

Finally, I felt the oppressive heat and opened my eyes. I was leaning against the wall in a room about twice the size of my bedroom, while at least twenty men and women stood about having heated discussions. I pushed myself to my feet and spied April the same time she saw me stand.

She walked over to me. "I wasn't sure what to do with you. The meeting was about to start, and I couldn't wake you, so I brought your, umm, body here."

"That's fine. I got held up."

"Watching the announcement?"

"Yeah." I looked sidelong at the rest of the people in the room. "How did they take it?"

"There was some belief at first, but then Memory Keeper spoke up on your family's behalf. He has much respect in our community. I think he allayed their fears."

"That's good."

At first, I didn't see Memory Keeper, but then the crowd parted slightly, revealing him sitting in a chair on the far side of the room.

He looked at me and smiled, then stood slowly to his feet. "Gentlemen, ladies, our guest has arrived."

The noise in the room died down immediately as everyone looked around. When each saw me standing next to April, they backed away slightly and stood waiting for me to speak.

"Umm, thanks everyone for getting together." I nodded toward April. "I've been told you saw the broadcast from Prime Senator Sarx. I want to make it very clear that the Zarc family, first and foremost, wants nothing more than the equal treatment of all people."

The Elders mumbled among themselves.

"Memory Keeper and I spoke yesterday, and I told him about the alliance that has been created by the colonies. We would like to welcome Venus into that alliance. It's our goal to unseat the Prime Senator and build a solar system where we can all be free. If it's okay with you, I'd like to show you a recording that we made of the Declaration of Independence that I, as a representative of the colonist delegates, presented to the Poligarchy."

Some of the Elders nodded, while others looked toward Memory Keeper. He bowed his head.

I turned to April. "Do you have a holo-projector?"

"Yes." She moved to a small console on a desk in the corner as people began talking among themselves again. "Here you go." She flipped up the holo-screen.

I tapped in and opened a channel to the *ARC*. "Computer, please play back recording, *Declaration 07043027*."

A small projection of Prime Senator Sarx seated on his dais with the Senate around him appeared on my chest.

"...you, we all know. The boy who saved Earth." The speakers emitted some static as I adjusted the sound, then stepped aside so the senator's projection would display in the center of the room.

"What have you to say to us today?" Sarx asked.

The Elders moved toward the outside of the small space as an image of me, in my magchair, appeared. I looked like I might puke. Most of the

Elders seemed surprised that I — the me who was talking — was just a kid. The robot me that stood before them was far from it.

They quieted when I began to speak. "When in the course of human events, it becomes necessary for one people — our people — to dissolve the political bands which have connected us with another...."

These men and women recognized the words immediately. They had studied history just like I had. They took it all in as the recording continued.

It was amazing to watch these men and women as I spoke. I knew it wasn't the fact that some thirteen-year-old kid was addressing the Senate; it was the historical significance of the words.

The Elders stood taller. Their faces began to shine with a light that hadn't been present only moments before. These men and women had only known suffering and pain under the rule of the Poligarchy.

The recording got to the list of Prime Senator Sarx's offenses, and the Elders cheered. Especially the section about his mistreatment of Venus. When I finished up by accusing Sarx as the perpetrator of the destruction of Earth, the Elders were yelling, down to the last person.

Memory Keeper walked to the middle of the room, part of his body piercing my projection. He held up his hands, and eventually the Elders grew silent.

April paused the playback.

"Please, let the boy finish," the old man said.

Murmurs of agreement rippled through the crowd, and Memory Keeper looked at April and nodded. She resumed the recording.

"A leader whose character is shown by such terrible acts is, by definition, a Tyrant and unfit to be the ruler of a free people...."

The recording continued on until I read the names of the signers. When it finished up, one of the Elders yelled out, "And Venus." Several others joined in. "Venus agrees to the Declaration."

My image disappeared from the center of the room.

Memory Keeper raised his hands once more, and the room grew silent. "I will put my name on this document only if we have a unanimous agreement."

Everyone around him nodded.

"You understand that this means we are joining in a war against a merciless enemy. It could very well mean the death of many of our sons and daughters."

The Elders looked at each other.

One woman, dressed in near rags, lifted her chin. "I will not stand by as the rest of the Solar System fights against this tyrant. I vote yes."

A small man with graying hair stepped forward. "I vote yes."

One after the other, the Elders stood forward or lifted their hands, and a chorus of yeses filled the room.

"Opposed?" Memory Keeper asked.

No one spoke.

"Then it is so. Venus declares itself free from the Poligarchy."

CHAPTER NINETEEN

Over the next several days, we worked with the free people of Venus to prepare for the revolt. The Elders decided it wouldn't be enough to just declare their independence from the Poligarchy. The Free Venusians must gain control of Onissya, which served as the Government City Center. Not only was it symbolic, but the bulk of the Poligarchy's forces were in a garrison in the city. Also, they controlled access to the main port there.

I would be leading the defenses of the city from space and the skies above. The biggest issue for the spaceborne defenses was the battleship in orbit around the planet. Dad had agreed the only hope we had was to draw it off, and the only prize big enough would be the *ARC*, with the Zarc family on board.

Dad, James and I stood around a projection of Venus. The battleship held an orbit directly above Onissya. "We'll draw the ship off before the attack begins."

"But the *ARC* doesn't have any defense against a ship like that," I said.

"Except for our ability to time-travel."

"It won't do you any good to jump as soon as they start after you, though. They'll just come right back to Venus."

Dad nodded. "We'll have to take our chances."

I didn't like that idea at all. My whole family would be aboard the *ARC*, not to mention all the animals, and—

'*Adina,*' James said in my head.

"*Cut that out.*" I smiled. He knew me far too well. "Maybe one of us should stay behind to protect you."

"I appreciate that," Dad said. "But what's one J-3500 against a battle-ship? No, you'll both be needed down there." Then he frowned. "That leads us to the biggest problem, though."

I looked at James and smiled grimly. "We know, Dad. With you jump-ing through time in the *ARC*, we won't be able to use the remote pilot chairs. We'll actually have to be in the J-3500s."

"Your mother and I talked about it. At this point we're not sure where you'd be the *safest*, but we know where you would be the most *effective*."

"We'll be careful, Dad."

He pursed his lips together as if trying to talk himself into it. "I know you will." He studied us for a few moments longer, then reached over and turned off the holo-projector. "You boys better get some sleep then. Tomorrow's the big day.

* * *

Hamilton helped me climb into the cockpit of the J-3500 I'd named *Annihilation*, while James climbed into the other ship, *Big Boomer*. Hamilton buckled me in, and then mussed up my hair. "Keep safe, little brother."

I looked at him in surprise. It had to be the first time he'd ever called me that.

He climbed down the ladder and I started my preflight checklist. When finished I said, "*Big Boomer*, this is *Annihilation*. Are you ready?"

James came over the comm. "Ready, *Annihilation*. This is *Lady's Revenge II*."

I glanced over at James in the cockpit. "That's a good name."

He saluted. "Much better than *Big Boomer*."

"Okay, Dad, we're ready to go." I lifted off the floor and turned *Annihilation* toward the bay door.

"Opening bay doors now. And boys, stay focused. Stay safe."

"Yes sir," we both said.

Once the doors opened, I punched it and launched out into space. James followed right behind.

The plan was to head toward Venus, but we would be circling around as the *ARC* went directly for the planet—the goal being for the battleship to see her first and head off after her. Then we'd come in with Venus between us and the ships. If it worked, we should be able to get in and provide what support we could. If we were extremely lucky, we wouldn't have to do anything but wait for the revolt to play out on the surface.

I didn't have high hopes for that happening.

It was an eerie feeling leaving the relative safety of the *ARC* behind. I watched her recede into the blackness of space to be lost among the stars.

James was thinking the same thing, and I said to him in my thoughts, *"We'll see them again. Don't worry."*

'I know. It's just, I lost them once when Haon created me. I don't want to lose them again. I know that's selfish.'

I laughed. *"Well, if worrying about the people you love is selfish, then I'm the worst offender."*

'No more than me.'

We both laughed. It was hard to remember sometimes that James and I were so similar. At the same time, it was pretty cool to hear him say things that I wouldn't have, or talk about doing things I'd never done. Even though at one point he was an exact copy of me, he was becoming his own person. In another ten years we'd have similar personalities, but we would be completely independent people—and he'd still look twelve and I'd be twenty-four. Already we were starting to look quite a bit different.

I could barely make out James sitting in the cockpit of *Lady's Revenge II* as we rocketed toward Venus, his ship a speck against the vast darkness beyond. It was good to have a brother so similar.

The thought took me off guard. That's what he was: in every way, a brother. *"I'm glad Haon made you."*

He laughed. "Me too," he said aloud.

"No, seriously."

"I know, Noah. Thanks."

* * *

It was kind of painful flying for such a long time in the cramped cockpit of the J-3500, and it would take us nearly twenty-four hours to make it to Venus. At least I was used to being confined to a chair all day long, except when in a robot body.

"Hey, I'm going to check on the progress on Venus."

'Okay. I'll watch your back out here, make sure no one sneaks up on us.'

We both laughed. Catching us by surprise out here in the middle of nowhere would be impossible.

I reached out to Haon's robot on Venus. The smell of something cooking immediately caused my stomach to rumble. The complexity of these robots astounded me at times. When I opened my eyes, I rested on the floor in April's small apartment.

She stood over her stove, cooking something in a small pan.

"Hi there," I said.

She jumped about a half-meter off the ground, nearly toppling her pan as she whipped around toward me.

"Sorry."

She pointed her spatula at me with a mock stern expression. "You about scared the heebie-jeebies out of me."

"What exactly are heebie-jeebies?"

She just looked at me and grinned. "So, are you hungry?"

"Actually, I am. I'm not sure how this robot body can feel hunger, but I can definitely eat."

"Then pull up a chair." She waved the spatula at the table.

I was about to protest when I saw a new chair, much stronger than the previous ones. I pulled it out and took a seat. "So, is everything ready?"

"As ready as it's going to be. I'm still not sure about this, but the Elders think we have a chance." She pulled a couple plates off a shelf and grabbed some mugs with her pinkies.

I helped her put them down on the table without dropping them.

"Elder Brooks—he's the only one with any kind of military experience—says he's got a secret weapon. I have no idea what that could be, but it'd have to be pretty advanced to take down the Poligarchy. I guess he would know. He used to be one of them until he got kicked out." She tilted her head sideways. "Never did hear why."

She picked up her frying pan and brought it over to the table. It smelled absolutely amazing.

"What is this?"

"Oh, not much, sorry. Just a mixture of potatoes, onions, a little bit of red peppers."

"Let me stop you right there." I shoved a forkful into my mouth. "Oh man! I've never had anything like this, except maybe that fresh wooly mammoth back in the Ice Age."

April sat with a bemused expression on her face, waiting for the punch line.

I snickered. "I'm not kidding. Wooly mammoth."

We both cracked up. It was nice to laugh at something so simple as some fried vegetables, and breakfast with someone who wasn't related to me somehow. I emptied my plate in a matter of minutes and eyed the pan in the middle of the table.

April nibbled at hers and just sat watching me. "Go ahead, you can have the rest. I'm not that hungry."

I felt bad eating all her food, especially since I was a robot and really didn't need it, but it sure looked like she wasn't even going to finish what was on her plate.

"You know, it is so strange." She rested her fork on her plate.

"What's that?" I said between mouthfuls.

"You look *exactly* like him, but it's so easy to see the kid you really are inside."

For a moment I was offended. Then I saw her gaze drift away. "You really cared for him, didn't you?"

She was startled back to the present. "What? No. I mean we worked together for quite a long time, spent a lot of time together, but I—"

"I was raised to hate him."

She scrunched her eyebrows together. "He wasn't an easy man to understand."

"Don't I know it. It wasn't until I found out he was my father—"

Her mouth dropped open. "Your father?"

"Umm, yeah. He's my dad's brother."

She nodded. That was pretty common knowledge.

"But he's my real dad, umm, my blood-dad I guess. My mom died giving birth to me, and he just couldn't handle the idea of taking care of a baby, so he gave me up."

She reached over and placed her hand on mine. "I'm so sorry."

"No, it's okay. I'm not mad at him. Not anymore. In fact, I can understand why you might have liked him. He may have been a bit mixed up, but he was certainly —"

"Passionate," she said.

"I was going to say driven, but that works too."

"It was really hard, you know?" She glanced out her only window. "Loving a man whose actions you sometimes hated." Tears pooled in her eyes.

"Do you know why he's in Deimos right now?" I asked.

"Because of what he did on Earth."

"I don't mean that. He escaped in a robot body, just like this one."

She nodded. "I told you I studied the robot, but it was missing a key component."

"Exactly. That was the neuro-processor, basically the brain that drives the robot. He gave a friend of mine that processor. He sacrificed his life, or at least his freedom, to save someone else."

April looked at me, a hopeful smile on her face.

"That's the Haon I think of now, the man who finally gave up his own desires for someone else. He wasn't the man who gave me away as a baby. I believe he would most definitely do things differently now."

"Thank you." She sucked in a sob. "You don't know how much that means to me."

"I think maybe I do."

We sat in silence for the rest of breakfast, both lost in our own thoughts about a man we'd probably never see again.

Finally, April stood. "I've got something to show you." She gathered up the dishes and placed them in the sink, then went over to a trunk at the foot of her bed. She lifted a key on a chain from around her neck, bent and opened it, then after pulling a few blankets and old photos out, she dug to the bottom of the chest and lifted a long bundle wrapped in cloth.

"This is completely illegal, and if the Poligarchy Police discovered I owned it, they'd probably kill me on the spot." She laid the bundle on the table and unwrapped it.

Inside was an old rifle. Well, that might be giving it more credit than it deserved. It was actually a length of iron pipe and various other pieces of junk metal, welded together into the shape of an old rifle.

She held it up with a look of awe on her face. "This was handed down in my family, from generation to generation, for nearly one thousand years."

"It looks it."

"Hey!" She slapped me on the shoulder. "You don't understand the significance of this old thing. Back when Sarx first invaded, many of the people of Mars just rolled over and let him do what he wanted. There *was* a resistance, but they had no weapons, of course, so they had to fashion their own. Eventually, when it was apparent Sarx would exterminate everyone who stood against him, even the resistance faded away. But their spirit did not. All over Venus there are people just like me, pulling out guns similar to this one. It's time to put these secret weapons to the use for which they were originally created: remove Sarx from power."

"Wait, is this your *secret weapon?" They think they can overthrow Sarx with a bunch of old hand-built guns?* "Does it even work?"

"I'm not sure if this is what Elder Brooks means when he said secret weapon, but they should at least give us some advantage. And as to the question of whether it works or not... I think so. My grandfather said he tried it once."

"Do you have ammunition?"

She nodded and walked over and pulled an old box from the chest. It rattled as she sat it down on the table.

I opened the lid, exposing dozens of long bullets. They looked to be made from smaller pieces of pipe and some softer metal melted for the points. "I have to be honest with you. I don't know anything about guns, but these sure look dangerous."

April snickered. "They're supposed to be dangerous."

"So what makes you think you can fight the Poligarchy with these things?"

"That's the thing. The Poligarchy uses energy blasters."

I nodded. "I've seen the damage they can do."

"They fire a concentrated projectile of super-charged plasma, held together in a electro-magnetic casing. This is the kind of weapon the Poligarchy soldiers are trained to fire, and the kind of weapon they know how to defend against. Standard issue for all military and police is body armor designed to disperse the plasma charge. You shoot them with a modern blaster, and it doesn't even slow them down, but—" She patted her gun. "—hit them with one of these, and the bullet will go right through their armor."

I winced at the picture of the hunk of metal tearing through another human being.

"I know. It's not a pretty thought, but I can't see any other way."

Neither could I. "Well, I should probably get back to my ship. You're gathering at twelve hundred hours?"

She nodded. "I'll be leaving here twenty minutes prior. The Free Venusian Army is gathering. I'll be leading one of the teams."

"Okay, I'll be back then. We should have our ships in place and, hopefully, the battleships drawn off." I pointed to the chair I was sitting on. "Do you mind if I—?"

"Sure. No problem."

I closed my eyes and pushed back to my body.

CHAPTER TWENTY

James and I did what we could to pass the time. We played I Spy with star clusters, until I finally gave up trying to find the two-headed bunny dragon. We also sang several variations of one hundred bottles of synth-root beer on the wall.

I took a nap, thought about Adina, took another nap.

At last we were getting close.

My long range sensors showed the battleship still in orbit around Venus. *"Keep alert. If we can see them, they can see us."*

'Except we're a lot smaller.'

"Hey, James, I've been thinking."

'Yeah?'

"It'd be good to know what's going on down on the surface, with the attack on Onissya."

'Right.'

"You remember that time you talked about running in 'dual-screen mode'?"

'Yeah, but —'

"I've done it before."

He snickered. *'But we both know how that turned out. Only this time if you blow up a ship, you'll be in it.'*

"I know, but how will we know where they need cover? What if the Poligarchy takes ships in and starts attacking the outer domes?"

'There's always the comm. We could keep in touch that way.'

That idea concerned me. I was pretty sure they could track any signal coming from our ships. We'd be sitting ducks. *"We'll see. Maybe I could try, and if it doesn't work, just pull out."*

I felt his skepticism. He knew me well enough to know I'd hang on as long as I could, probably longer than I should.

'Well, let's just – '

Long-range scanners lit up at some movement. The battleship had begun lifting out of orbit.

'Uh oh.'

It looked like they were headed toward us. Sensors picked up another ship quite a ways off in the opposite direction. It was huge, and could only be one ship.

"I think they've just seen the ARC," I said.

The battleship broke free from orbit, and turned. It was headed around the planet.

'They've taken the bait.'

I sensed James's relief, then his guilt. Just like me.

Bringing up the nav-com, I punched in a trajectory that would take us into orbit. *"I'll go give them the news, and be back before we reach orbit."*

'You better. I don't want to have to win this battle all on my own out here.'

***

April fidgeted with her collar as she stood in front of a mirror. She had donned an old patched-together uniform. She turned to see me smiling at her.

"You look so official."

She laughed. "You think so?" She glanced one more time in the mirror, then grabbed a small backpack off a chair, slung it over her shoulder, and picked up her rifle. "Are you ready to go?"

I stood and followed her to the door.

Her hand shook when she reached for the door handle, and she laughed nervously.

"It's okay," I said. "You'd have to be stupid not to be nervous right now." It felt strange being the veteran, but even at fourteen, I'd seen my fair share of fighting. "It just means you're alive, and that means there's something worth fighting for."

She nodded and pulled the door open.

Crowds of people all moved in the same direction. Each wore their own version of a uniform, and most carried some kind of old weapon slung over their shoulder. We stepped into the flow and several curious stares were directed my way. Word must have spread pretty quickly about the giant robot that was really a fourteen-year-old kid inside.

We made our way to a familiar door—the entrance to Haon's old labs. The crowds continued on, but April stepped up to the door and rapped three times. The door opened a crack and she whispered to someone inside, then stepped in and motioned for me to follow.

A man stood back at attention, an old rifle held across his chest. The hangar had been turned into the Free Venusians' war room. One wall displayed a huge projection of Onissya. A couple of the Elders I'd seen the other night stood before it, moving flashing blue lights around to various spots around the city. Onissya was laid out like a giant wheel, with twelve roads fanning out like spokes. Each of these main roads pierced the dome that surrounded the City Center. Outside the dome, things were much more chaotic. A series of smaller domes and tubes made up the habitable space, with little rhyme or reason to their layout.

One of the Elders in front of the map spied us and walked over with his hand thrust out. "Welcome, Noah. I'm glad to have you with us."

I shook his hand.

"This is Elder Brooks," April said.

"Good to meet you, sir."

"Please, call me John. What's going on out there?" He waved toward the ceiling.

"It looks like they took the bait. The battleship left orbit and is headed after the *ARC*."

"Excellent."

"And even if they come back, my brother James and I will keep you all safe."

"James? Isn't he a kid?"

"Yeah, same age as me." I smiled.

He looked a little worried.

Then it hit me. "You understand this isn't me, right?" I waved my arms down my body. "This is just a robot. I'm back on a ship, about to enter orbit around Venus."

"Yes, I understand that, but—"

"And you know I'm fourteen, just like James?"

"I guess it's hard to understand, exactly."

I nodded in agreement. "You've got that right."

He was still skeptical, but what more could I say? If my being in a grown-up's body gave him more confidence, I'd have to go with that.

An alarm buzzed.

"Can you give me a second? I need to check in with my brother."

Elder Brooks nodded.

I pushed out but kept the connection open. Looking around, I saw that we had settled into orbit around Venus.

'You said you'd be back before *we got to orbit.'* James frowned through the cockpit window of his J-3500.

"Sorry, I was meeting with the leaders of the Venusian army."

Whispers filled my head as Elder Brooks and April talked. I pushed them over to the side of my consciousness.

'So they have an army?' asked James.

"Well, I'm not sure yet."

'Okay. So the plan is to just sit tight up here until we're needed?'

"Yup. Let me know if you see anything. I'm going back down."

'Roger.' James saluted me through the windshield.

I opened my eyes back in the war room.

"...we've got men positioned around the police stations here, and here." Elder Brooks pointed to a couple of flashing lights near outside tunnels into the City Center. He glanced over his shoulder and saw me watching. "Ah, you're back."

"We're in orbit," I said. "Still no sign of the Poligarchy up there."

"Good." He turned back to his map. "We're just about ready down here. The plan is to overrun the police on the outside, then launch the invasion from all points at the same time. The coordination will be a bit tricky, but we should be able to pull it off."

"They have no idea you're coming?" I just couldn't believe Sarx wouldn't think we were going to try to take Venus.

"We're having to plan as we go, but right now it doesn't appear they're on to us."

Men and women around me cinched up their uniforms and hoisted weapons onto their shoulders.

"I'd like to be in one of the groups that goes in," I said.

Elder Brooks' brow shot up. "I thought you'd stay here."

April moved over to join a line forming at the exit.

"I think I can react more quickly if I'm actually inside the city."

"Whatever you think best." He looked around and spotted a young man running across the room. "Akbar, get this man a gun."

The boy nodded and dashed off.

"Here." Elder Brooks held out his hands. "So you we can keep in touch." He dropped a comm into my hand.

I fitted it into my ear. "Thanks."

He nodded and turned back to the screen. "Okay, people, we are twenty minutes from launch."

CHAPTER TWENTY-ONE

After a quick lesson from Akbar on how to load and fire the rifle he gave me, I followed April and the other soldiers out of the war room. We climbed down a few flights of stairs, then out into a large, domed room. I gasped; it was the hall where Sarx had all those people killed — the event that finally made me realize what a monster he was, and that maybe I had misjudged Haon.

I looked around expecting to see the bodies of the slain, but saw only rows of men and women, close to a thousand of them.

April waved me on. "You'll go in with my team."

She jogged over and stopped in front of a group of about twenty men and women who stood at attention when she approached. They were an odd mixture of people. All were hard and lean, used to very hard work, but none looked like soldiers, as much as they tried. There were a few kids my age, including Ander, who towered over those around him. He caught my look and smiled. A few of the men and women appeared too old to be fighting — maybe in their eighties or nineties.

April turned to me. "Zeta Team, this is Noah. He'll be joining us for today's adventure."

A nervous laugh rolled through the group as they gave me an appraising look.

"The Advanced Strike Forces should be positioned outside each entrance to the city. We're on the Bandow Street tunnel. Are we ready?"

A few half-hearted nods, but Ander pumped his fist in the air and yelled, "Ready!" His voice echoed off the dome as he looked around, his face turning red.

"Thanks for your enthusiasm," April said. "Let's move out."

Several teams around us were already marching out.

April turned and headed toward one of the many exits, and we all fell in line behind her.

We were running through a small tunnel when a hail of gunfire erupted, followed by several muffled explosions.

"That's the ASF. They've blown the barrier!" April yelled.

The Advance Strike Force had been sent in to blast a way into the main dome.

"We need to move faster!" She picked up the pace.

Moments later, we broke onto the main road. A billow of smoke poured from the tunnel to our left. Gunfire sounded from inside the dense fog and blue energy blasts shot out, hitting the buildings around us.

April motioned with her hands to follow her. She ran along the edge of the street to the wall just outside the tunnel. We all packed in beside her, avoiding the blasts coming from inside.

She checked her gun and then yelled, "Pick your targets, and fire as soon as we're in."

Everyone nodded.

"Now!" She lunged into the smoke, firing.

I ran after her.

A blue flash indicated a blaster being fired. I pointed my rifle in the general direction and pulled the trigger. I was thankful for the size of Haon's robot, because the gun had quite a kick. Several people around me fired at the same target, and no more shots came from that direction.

Another light flared up and we fired again. A blast shot past my shoulder, and someone screamed. I kept moving forward.

"Stay close," April shouted.

It was a good idea, as I couldn't see more than a few meters ahead. Several more flashes indicated a Poligarchy soldier. I took a second longer and actually aimed the rifle and fired. A scream accompanied a blast toward the ceiling; I'd hit my target. The idea that I most likely had just killed another person made my stomach lurch, but I couldn't afford to dwell on it.

The smoke started to clear, revealing the end of the tunnel. Silhouettes of another Free Venusians team scattered to either side of the exit.

The team leader yelled back, "We'll cover you."

April waved her arm and started running forward, and a burst of gunfire sounded from outside the tunnel. We all ran forward and broke out of the tunnel into the greenish light of the main dome, following April into a small alleyway to the left of the tunnel.

I peeked out into the main street as the rest of the team stopped for a short breather. ASF soldiers worked their way up the street, from alcove to recessed doorway. Meter by meter, they were gaining a foothold.

Elder Brooks' voice crackled in my ear, "We've taken all but one tunnel. Teams Delta and Epsilon met fierce resistance on the Howard Street tunnel."

"Roger that." April's voice sounded in my ear and behind me. "Okay, let's move." She pushed past me and headed up the street.

The ASF did a good job of taking out soldiers ahead of us, so we didn't need to be as cautious. Zeta Team fanned out, and we jogged up the street.

'Noah!'

I pulled back slightly, into the cockpit of *Annihilation*. "Yeah?"

'There's a ship headed our way. A big one.'

"Dang! They must have gotten wind of the attack."

I could still see an image of the street my robot version walked down. Everyone was diving to either side as a series of blasts erupted around us. I rolled right, firing at a blue pulse from a second-story window ahead, and a figure slumped back inside.

The scanner in the cockpit showed the ship James was talking about. "*It looks like a battleship,*" I said.

'Yup. They must have decided Venus was more important than getting the ARC.'

"Okay. I don't think they'll risk damaging the main dome, but we'll have to watch out for attacks on the outer city."

Zeta Team continued their push down the street.

"Elder Brooks, we have an incoming battleship," I said over the comm.

"How soon?"

I looked at the scanner. "About thirty-five minutes."

"Okay, keep me apprised."

I was impressed by the Elder's calm. I'd just told him a ship capable of leveling the whole city was headed his way, and he took it all in stride. Clearly he had plenty to worry about immediately.

When James had told me about the dual-screen mode, I had pictured it more like two different holo-monitors that I would look back and forth between. That's how I had approached trying to fly the J-3500s back on the moon. But it was more like two images appearing at the same time. I could see the street around me, dodge out of the way of incoming fire and shoot at enemy soldiers, while at the same time sitting in the cockpit of *Annihilation*. It really was like being in both places at the same time, and as such, I didn't really need to concentrate on one or the other. I could do both at once.

"James, we'll have to wait to see what the battleship does before we can do much. Keep your eyes peeled to see if they launch any smaller craft."

A handful of Poligarchy soldiers ran in a full-on retreat up the street toward the government center. They stopped every few meters and fired back, but their shots were wild and ineffective.

'Maybe we should drop into the atmosphere a bit,' James said. *'That way we'll be harder to spot.'*

"Good idea." I fired the reverse thrusters on *Annihilation*, and immediately she started to fall.

The men and woman of Zeta Team surged forward after the retreating enemy, and I looked at April and grinned. She smiled back, but kept running with her rifle ready.

It went on like this for the next half-hour. April's team and I worked our way forward, with the enemy in retreat, while James and I waited in the broiling upper atmosphere watching the approach of the battleship.

It was an immense ship, but still only about a third the size of the *ARC*. Where the *ARC* was all graceful curves and deck after deck of blue lights, the battleship was nothing but angles and guns—big honking guns. Its shape reminded me almost of a lighting bolt. Each major angle toward the ground held a large array of weapons. I had read that all of them firing at once produced so much energy that giant engines had been built on the opposite side of the ship to counteract their thrust.

I hoped never to see it in action.

At about the moment the battleship came close enough to know we were there, we ran into heavy resistance on the ground, the street in front of us blocked by a row of soldiers two deep. One row kneeled in front, firing their blasters, while the second row fired over their shoulders.

Four smaller ships dropped from the underside of the battleship and headed our way. *"Split up, James."*

We both fired our thrusters and rocketed away from each other. Two fighters pursued him and two came after me.

"We've got to break through," April said in my ear-comm. "Do we have any more of those charges?"

"I'm on it," said an ASF soldier. They'd lost a lot of men and women, but apparently some were still fighting.

Acid sizzled on my windshield as I pulled *Annihilation* out of a dive. This is where the J-3500 really shone. It was made for both space and atmospheric flight.

An explosion rocked the streets around me. Rubble flew through the air, and chunks of steel and concrete smashed into the street.

"Into the breach," April yelled.

We charged forward before the last of the debris hit the ground, and I searched for targets.

The two ships on my tail were older J-2500s — still agile, still deadly, but they couldn't quite keep up. Battleships were developed mainly for orbit-to-land attacks. Any fighters they carried onboard were for unexpected attacks like ours.

I put *Annihilation* into a climb and twisted around to tail the two ships.

A Poligarchy soldier charged through the smoke toward me, guns blazing, and I fired twice. One shot hit him squarely in the chest. I turned away; he had family, just like me — hopes, dreams for the future.

The J-2500 on the right peeled away. I let it go to pursue the other, locked on a missile, and fired. It rocketed through the acidic air and hit the ship's right engine, and a huge ball of fire filled my vision. Pieces of the ship bounced off my windshield, then we were through. The J-2500s couldn't outrun the missiles.

"How're you doing, James?"

'Fine. Lining up for a shot.'

I got a glimpse of the Capitol building when I scrambled down and out of the crater made by the blast. We were only a couple blocks away. The city had been unprepared for an assault of this scale. They had no large weapons, and the numbers of troops seemed far below what was projected.

'Got them!'

"Both?" I asked.

'Yup. What, you only got one of yours?'

"Hold on, smarty-pants." The second J-2500 had pulled around behind me again. "Watch this."

I pulled back and headed straight up. The fighter followed, and I nudged the ailerons left and right, getting a feel for the amount of atmosphere. When they quit responding, I knew I was free. I fired the left nav-thrusters and spun *Annihilation* around completely, then fired one missile straight at the J-2500. It never had a chance and exploded in a ball of fire and debris.

'Ok, I have to admit that was pretty fancy flying.' James pulled up beside me and gave me a thumbs-up.

"Why, thank you."

Elder Brooks' voice sounded in my ear. "Converge on the Capitol."

We all started running forward. Periodic blasts came from within the building itself, but we met no real resistance and quickly reached the bottom of the steps. They were made to look like white marble, but they must have been synthetic, unless Venus had a marble quarry I didn't know about.

Light flared along the back of the battleship. "*She's firing up her dampening thrusters!*" I pushed *Annihilation* in the direction of the massive ship. "*They're going to fire.*"

'What do we do?' James asked.

"I don't know."

"Elder Brooks, the battleship is preparing to fire."

"Target?"

"We have no way of knowing." I glanced at the navigation array. "We're definitely above Onissya, but that doesn't tell me exactly where they're going to strike."

"Acknowledged. The moment you know anything, let me know."

"Yes sir."

I reloaded and ran up the steps of the Capitol two at a time. It had been a struggle to not run ahead of the rest of the team, but this time I couldn't help myself. Maybe if we took the building quickly enough, we could get everyone inside the main dome where they'd be safe from an orbital attack.

A soldier stepped out from behind a huge column and fired at me.

I spun right and squeezed off a shot. It ricocheted off the column as the soldier ducked back behind. He didn't expect me to move so fast, though, and I whipped around the marble pillar and swung my arm, catching him in the throat.

He crumpled to the ground.

A blast hit the stone above my head. I spun around and fired, knocking another enemy soldier back. The main doors were only a few meters away, now free of defenders.

"April, we're clear up here."

"Copy that."

I wanted to charge through the door on my own, but thought better of it. Turning, I looked back down the steps at Zeta Team bounding toward me.

James and I rocketed toward the battleship. A greenish glow appeared along the bottom of the ship as well.

I glanced over at James. *"We're just going to have to hit her with everything we've got."*

Small navigation thrusters fired on the side of the battleship as it lined up to take a shot. The glow intensified along the bottom, and the thrusters on the top spouted yellow flame.

I scanned along the ship. *"Let's both hit the same place. Target the first gun at the front of the ship."*

'Okay.'

James and I pushed toward the sharp front of the lightning-bolt shape.

I lowered my shoulder and smashed against the door to the Capitol. Several Zeta fighters joined in, and after three tries the door splintered and burst inward. Immediately, blue bolts of energy shot out, and a man to my left screamed as he was spun around by a shot to his arm. We dropped and fired into the gloom.

Fire erupted along the battleship's back as the dampening thrusters sprang to life. At the same moment, the guns along the bottom launched a massive beam of green energy.

"*Fire!*" I yelled, and launched everything I had at the front gun on the battleship. Twelve missiles tore free of *Annihilation*, and a similar number rocketed away from James's ship.

"The battleship is firing!" I screamed as Zeta Team pushed inside the Capitol building.

"Still no idea where?" Brooks said.

"We'll know soon enough."

A sound like thunder rose and I dashed back outside the Capitol building. An intense beam of green light emanated from the top of the dome directly above us and burned a hole straight up through the swirling atmosphere. It pulsed in bursts of energy, each wave causing great cracks to appear in the dome. Chunks of steel and concrete fell and smashed into the top of the Capitol.

"They're hitting the main dome!"

"Get out of there!" Elder Brooks screamed.

I spun around. Several soldiers on Zeta Team looked around in confusion.

April ran toward the door. "You heard him. Let's get out of here!"

That's all it took. The soldiers ran through the door and jumped down the stairs several at a time.

The missiles hit the battleship at almost the exact same time, and the explosion momentarily blinded me. The beam emanating from the front gun winked out.

As we ran along the street in front of the steps, everyone kept glancing at the top of the dome. A huge concussion threw us to the ground as a massive hole tore through the dome. The pulsing beam of energy hit the Capitol building, and it exploded. Huge pieces of the structure flew outward.

"Run!" April yelled, even as several soldiers around us were smashed by chunks of marble and concrete. Something tore by my head, ripping into my cheek. Automatically, I stopped the flow of artificial blood to that area of my face.

I risked a glance over my shoulder. Where the Capitol once stood, nothing remained but an ever-growing crater. The edge expanded as the beam's super-heated energy melted everything around it, and the pavement below my feet grew hotter by the moment.

The explosion along the front edge of the battleship had done the trick. Slowly, the ship listed to the side, and the beam of energy changed angle, then winked out. We'd stopped the attack, but it was too late.

The energy beam had slid along the crater toward us, before exiting the hole in the dome above, then shutting down altogether.

I breathed a sigh of relief as I looked at April and the remaining Zeta Team members, but then the rushing sound of wind hit us. It struck me as odd at first; there shouldn't be any wind inside a protected dome. Then I looked up.

Green and yellow smoke poured through the opening in the ceiling as the air inside the great dome was sucked outside. Already a fine mist of acid fell onto my robot skin.

"We have to get out of here. Now!" I started running down the street toward the exit tunnel. "Elder Brooks, the dome has been compromised. You need to get the tunnels sealed off."

"How are we going to do that? We destroyed the shields."

"I don't know, but if you don't, everyone's going to die."

Panic filled the citizens of the capital when they realized what was going on. Throngs of people poured into the streets and everyone surged toward the exit tunnels.

April helped one of her wounded, his arm around her neck as she practically dragged him. People jostled and knocked the two around as they rushed past.

I waded through the crowd and grabbed hold of the wounded soldier. "I'll carry him. Follow closely behind me." I hoisted the man into my arms and pushed forward, April's hand on my shoulder.

Members of the Poligarchy police and military, as well as soldiers fighting for the Free Venusians, commingled with government elite. All were equal here. All feared for their lives. We now had a common enemy, as only Sarx had control over the battleships. He had exposed himself as a man who didn't care who died, a man who had no greater respect for those who followed him than for those who opposed him. Sarx.

The crowd slowed as we drew close to the exit. Like a funnel, everyone pushed to enter the tunnel. The air thinned, and the man in my arms labored over each breath. I took in a huge gulp of air, then sealed off my throat. It was so strange having this almost instinctual idea of how to operate the robot body.

The battleship turned and fired its main thrusters. Apparently having completed Prime Senator Sarx's mission, it was leaving orbit.

James and I stayed where we were.

"James, we've got to do something about those people below. They're losing air too quickly."

'What can we do? There are thousands of them.'

I looked around the street as people began to topple over from lack of oxygen.

"We've got to save as many as we can. Come on." I pushed *Annihilation* forward and dove down into the boiling atmosphere.

The man in my arms shuddered and then lay still. April slumped against my back. I turned and caught her as she fell toward the pavement. There were thuds all around me as people collapsed.

"No!" I yelled.

I searched for someone to help, but those who were still standing were already moving into the tunnel. I laid the soldier and April on the ground. Sores peppered their skin where the acid touched them. I checked the man for a pulse and found a faint one, so I bent over him and pinched his nose closed, then breathed into his mouth. His chest rose. I turned and did the same for April. With very few breaths left in me, I grabbed the man around the middle and lifted him onto my shoulder, then grabbed April and pressed her against my chest.

Even for a robot, it was a large burden, but I pushed to my feet and turned to the tunnel. They didn't have much time. I started running, had some difficulty dodging the bodies that lay everywhere, but didn't stop.

Visibility was near zero as we plunged toward the surface in our J-3500s. I worried we might run right into the dome before we saw it, but then the mist parted.

A huge hole topped the dome, plenty big enough for us to fly through. I went in first, then James, and we got a view of the city beneath us. A massive crater filled the center where the Capitol building had been. I didn't see a single living person.

We dodged in and out of the tall towers that surrounded the City Center, looking for people in the streets. There were many, but they all lay still on the ground.

'Look in the buildings,' James said. I slowed and turned toward a skyscraper to my left. There, peering out of the windows in terror, were hundreds of faces.

"Of course. They'd have some limited oxygen supplies in the buildings." I brought *Annihilation* into a hover. Then it hit me: there was no room in these ships for any more people; they'd been made for combat, nothing more.

"What are we going to do, James?"

I staggered into the tunnel with April in my arms and the soldier over my shoulder. It was empty except for a few bodies of people that hadn't made it. The light at the end was much smaller than I remembered. I stumbled forward as a couple of men pushed a massive piece of steel in place over the last bit of opening.

"Wait!" I yelled.

They glanced up, startled to see anyone still alive.

I pushed the robot to its limits and squeezed through the opening. "Help them!" I said as I collapsed to my knees, laying April and the soldier to the ground.

Their faces were white as death.

"Noah?"

At first I couldn't place the voice, then I realized.... "Dad! Where are you?"

"Look up." His voice came through the comm.

I looked through the cockpit window of *Annihilation* toward the ceiling of the dome. A *DUV IV* flew through the hole.

"Where do you need us?" Dad asked.

I'd never been so happy to hear Dad's voice. Except maybe when we found him alive in the Ice Age.

"There are people in these buildings. We need to shuttle them to safety."

"Okay. Why don't you and James head back to the *ARC* and get some ships better suited for transport?"

I pushed toward the opening in the ceiling as two more ships came through. We let them pass by, and then James and I headed out.

CHAPTER **TWENTY-TWO**

We worked for several hours, shuttling people from buildings inside the
Onissya dome to the port outside the city. People were universally
overjoyed at our help, and horrified that the Poligarchy would order a
strike against its own people. Venus now lay firmly in the hands of those
seeking independence from the Poligarchy.

Sarx might have committed his first major blunder.

Finally, after a long day, I pulled myself into my bed on the *ARC*. The
day's activities all blurred together as I struggled to keep my eyes open,
but before falling asleep, I turned all my focus to my robot self on Venus.

I sat in the cavernous hall where the original massacre had occurred.
It had been converted to a hospital, and hundreds lay on white sheets
around me. April's breaths came rhythmically as she slept. The doctors
had revived her after they pulled her from my arms. The soldier I had
carried out hadn't been so lucky. They'd worked on him for fifteen minutes before giving up.

My robot body wasn't really tired, but my emotions were drained.
Running in dual-screen mode took more out of me than I would have
thought. I glanced at April and smiled, but then I thought of the thousands who weren't so lucky.

It was just as I'd feared. After promising Elder Brooks I'd protect the
people of Venus, I'd failed. The Free Venusians had lost almost three
thousand soldiers. Untold more citizens and Poligarchy troops were lost
inside the city. I tried to add up all the people who died either directly or

indirectly because of actions I'd taken—the thousands who died in the massacre, the thousands in Onissya, and the billions on Earth.

I could hear Dad telling me it wasn't my fault, that Sarx was at the root of it all, but I just couldn't shake the feeling I was at least partly to blame. These people only volunteered after they heard me reading the Declaration of Independence. I had talked them into fighting, convinced them to die for the cause of freedom.

Was it worth it? Not for those who died.

Everything I touched—everywhere I turned—people died. I sat in a room of hundreds and felt totally alone.

Adina sprang to my thoughts. I hadn't seen her when I returned to the *ARC*. She was probably avoiding me. Maybe it was good she didn't want to have anything to do with me. I'd probably end up causing her nothing but pain, or worse.

I laid my robot body down next to April, her face pitted with marks where the acid had burned her. The doctors had already healed them as best they could, but she would always have some visible sign of what happened today. She'd remember every time she looked in the mirror.

There just doesn't seem to be anything I can do right. The connection faltered. I must have been falling asleep back on the *ARC*. Watching April breathe evenly, I realized even she was worse off because of me. The man she loved was in prison on Deimos, all because of....

***

I awoke the next morning, totally disoriented. I lay with my eyes closed, trying to remember where I was. In my bed on Mars? On the *ARC*? Down on Venus? In *Annihilation*? I almost didn't want to know, fearing that once I opened my eyes it would all begin again. The reality of everything that had happened would come crashing back down on me. Maybe if I just lay here, the Solar System would go on without me. Everything would right itself. I'd just be a footnote in an unfortunate time for humanity.

'Noah?'

No such luck. "*Yeah, James?*"

'We got a call from the Elders on Venus. Dad wants to go down and meet with them.'

"And?"

'He wants you to go with him.'

I groaned. That fantasy had shattered quickly enough. *"Okay, I'll meet him in the hangar shortly."*

James pulled back, and I was alone again. I thought about pushing down to Haon's robot to check on April, but I just didn't have the strength. I opened my eyes and rolled myself to the edge of my bed, and climbed into my magchair.

I was still rubbing sleep out of my eyes when I hovered into the hangar.

Dad was coming down the ramp of one of the *DUV IVs*. He spied me and smiled. "You did good yesterday."

"I'd hate to see things if I did poorly," I grumbled at him.

"Well, there's a whole bunch of people who owe their lives to your quick thinking. If you hadn't taken out that battleship, they —"

"I don't really want to talk about it right now, Dad!"

He seemed a little taken back by my anger. "Oh. Okay." He glanced over his shoulder into the hold of the *DUV IV*. "Hamilton and Sam are about done loading up. They think they can help the Venusians fix the breach in the main dome. We have a bunch of material left over from when we built the whale habitat."

I just nodded and headed for the cockpit. "I'll get her ready to fly."

"Okay, Noah."

* * *

As soon as we landed at the port outside of Onissya a crowd of men and women moved in to help unload the hold. Hamilton had said the goal was to get the patch in place as soon as possible. Most of the air had escaped the dome, but many of the buildings still retained some usable oxygen, and the less corrosive atmosphere they had to pump out, the faster it would go. Not to mention what the acid clouds buffeting the city were doing to the structures.

Dad and I exited the ship as a black hovercar pulled up. He held a long tube in his hand. Inside was the Declaration of Independence.

April got out of the car. She looked at my surprised face, took a hesitant step, and then ran over.

She bent and squeezed me in a huge hug. "Noah, thank you so much for what you've done!"

She held onto me far longer than was comfortable.

Then another voice said, "So, here you are in the flesh?"

April stepped back and smiled at Elder Brooks, who extended his hand toward me. "We can't thank you enough."

I didn't really feel like shaking his hand. I wanted to be anywhere but here today, but Dad glared at me, so I took it.

Elder Brooks saw the look on my face, and glanced at April and Dad, then cleared his throat. "Um... are we ready? The Elders would like to meet with you both."

April and Elder Brooks turned back toward the car.

Dad scowled at me and mouthed the word, *behave.*

Dad helped me into the car, then stowed my magchair in the back. I sat opposite April, and she didn't stop grinning at me the whole drive.

Fortunately, that wasn't long. We reached the part of the outer city I was most familiar with: the car pulled up outside Haon's lab.

The room was much as it had been yesterday, still with a big map of the city on the wall. Several areas outside the main tunnels were marked with a red X.

Elder Brooks saw me looking at the map. "We've sealed off all the tunnels, but some took longer, and the corrosive atmosphere from within the main dome did serious damage. We're keeping people away from there as much as possible."

I didn't really want to know, but asked anyway. "How many people died?"

Elder Brooks glanced at Dad. "We put the estimate around ten to fifteen thousand in total."

I frowned, my mood growing darker.

"But understand, many times that number were saved yesterday. And now we can truly call ourselves Free Venusians."

I glanced around the room, not wanting to make eye contact with him. He had no idea how keenly I felt responsible for the death of those thousands.

"Let... let's go this way."

Dad and I followed as April and Elder Brooks left the war room and entered a smaller room off to the side—April's old lab. Upon first entering, my gaze was captured by the old man himself, Memory Keeper, who sat in a chair near the center of the room. His gaze bore into me until I had to look away.

The other men and women milling about were, of course, the Elders. They all turned when we entered, and Elder Brooks held up his hands.

"Friends, I give you the heroes of the day: Noah Zarc, Sr."

The Elders cheered, and Dad nodded.

"And of course, his son, Noah."

There were whoops and yells of thanks. Everyone clapped their hands and grinned at me.

I couldn't stand it anymore. "That's enough!"

A few people laughed, thinking I was making a joke, but then they saw the look on my face and quieted.

"How can you cheer for me?" I could feel my face burning. "Didn't you see all those people die?" I spun my chair around. Tears filled my eyes. "I should have stopped it," I mumbled. "It was my job to stop it!"

Everyone stared at me in silence. Mouths hung open as they looked at each other.

"The child speaks truth."

I swung around to see Memory Keeper climbing to his feet.

"We have much to celebrate, but we also must not forget the cost."

A few nodded their heads.

"There won't be a living soul on Venus who hasn't lost someone in the horrific attack yesterday. So yes, the boy speaks truth." He walked slowly toward me, his cane tapping on the floor. "But to say this is your fault—I *cannot* allow it!" He pointed a gnarled finger at my chest. "You have done something that we should have done a long time ago. For centuries, we have huddled in our holes, afraid to stand up to a tyrant. I, my father, his father, on back for a thousand years—we have all been weak."

He shook his head. "No, you have nothing to be ashamed of. It is I who should weep." He turned and pointed his fingers at the Elders. "But, even as I weep for the foolishness of our actions, we *must not forget* who is at the root of our anguish."

Memory Keeper pointed at me again. "This brave boy is not the cause of our pain. *We* are not the cause of our people's misery. There is one man, and one man alone who must stand for his crimes."

"Sarx!" the Elders yelled. "Sarx!"

"Yes. He must not be allowed to go unchallenged. And we can say today that we, Free Venusians, are no longer under his fist. This planet is ours."

Again the Elders erupted in cheers.

"And for that," Memory Keeper yelled over the noise and turned back toward me. "And for that, we have nothing but thanks to give to you, lad. Don't be troubled. Mourn for the dead, yes, but don't carry the burden that belongs on someone else's shoulders."

I nodded and wiped the tears from my cheeks. "Thank you."

CHAPTER TWENTY-THREE

April and I turned to leave while the Elders and Dad prepared to talk about next steps. Before I exited the room, Dad pulled out the Declaration, and Memory Keeper looked my way and winked just before putting a shaky pen to the document.

Out in the street, April and I moved along in silence. People bustled about us. It was so different from the first time I came down this street. Then, everyone seemed so desperate. Now, although they all wore the same rags, there was a new spring in their step, and hope on their faces.

A tall boy lumbered by and almost ran into us.

"Ander, good to see you," April called after him.

The boy spun around and waved. "Sorry, can't stop now. On a mission."

I was happy to see he was still alive. He'd been separated from Zeta Team shortly after we entered the City Center.

We made our way toward April's apartment. "Can you stop in for one last breakfast before you go?"

I grinned. "I don't know. Do you have any of those potatoes and onions?"

"I'm sure I can rustle some up." She giggled as we reached her door. Once inside, she turned and frowned: Haon's robot sat in the chair.

"Oh, April. I'm so sorry."

She started out of her thoughts. "What do you have to be sorry for?"

"For Haon. For his imprisonment."

"How is that your fault?" She cocked her head in puzzlement. "Is this another burden you shouldn't be carrying?"

I thought about it a moment. "You know, last night it seemed so clear that it was all my fault. Now, I can't figure out how I came to that conclusion, especially with him."

"He did some horrendous things."

"That's true, but he also did some pretty amazing things."

She looked at the robot and just nodded.

"His name's Benjamin."

Her eyes grew wide. "Haon's?"

"Yeah. You didn't really think his parents were mean enough to name him that, did you?"

"Well, no, I guess not." A tear rolled down her cheek as she mouthed the name, Benjamin.

Finally, she smiled and pressed out a wrinkle in her shirt with her hands. "Thank you, Noah. You don't know how much that means to me."

"You're most definitely welcome."

CHAPTER TWENTY-FOUR

It took until the end of the day to get the hole patched up in the top of the dome. Hamilton and Sam were covered in grime when they walked off their ship into the hangar on the *ARC*.

Dad and I had landed just minutes before. Memory Keeper came with us. I hadn't asked Dad why, not wanting to offend Memory Keeper with such a question. Maybe Dad thought he'd be able to help somehow.

As we disembarked, I brought the robot Haon out of the ship, too.

Sam walked over and stood between me and the robot. "I'm beat. If it's okay, I'm gonna go take a shower and get some sleep."

It was an odd sensation seeing things from two different perspectives—almost like there were two Sams. I shuddered at the thought.

"That's fine, Sam," Dad said. "We've got a few days ahead of us to rest."

"Thanks." She turned and left the hangar.

"What do you think I should do with the robot?" I asked Dad.

He thought a moment. "Why don't you take him to the infirmary?"

"Okay." While I walked the robot out, I realized that even though we had accomplished a great deal, the war was far from won.

"So?" I asked Dad.

"So, what?"

"What's next? Are we headed for Mars?"

"Don't you want to rest for at least a few hours before worrying about that?"

"That's just it: I won't be able to rest until I know what we're doing next."

"Okay. We're headed to Earth first. I've been in touch with General Roosevelt, and he has some ideas on how to hit Mars and overthrow Sarx."

"And...." I nodded toward Memory Keeper, who seemed distracted by the sight of Venus through the bay doors.

"Our good friend has volunteered to take his case before the Poligarchy."

I frowned. "We've tried that."

"I know, but maybe they'd be willing to talk now, especially if word gets back to Mars about what Sarx did to his own people on Venus."

I shook my head. I just couldn't see Sarx losing his grip so easily. He ruled the Poligarchy with an iron fist.

"All right. I'm going to take Sam's lead and get some sleep myself."

* * *

I opened the door to my room and stopped at the sight of Adina sitting in the chair next to my desk. Hamilton stood behind her, the two of them immersed in some code cubes floating above her holo-pad, and they didn't hear me enter.

I thought about just sneaking back out, but was just too tired. "Hi there."

They spun around.

Adina almost dropped her holo-pad. "Noah! I thought you were still on Venus."

"Nah, we got back a little bit ago." I glanced at Hamilton.

He looked around the room then fumbled toward the door. "I—I have to go speak with Mother about something."

Just like that, we were alone.

"Noah, I—"

"Stop." I held my hand toward her. "It's okay. I understand."

Her eyebrows pinched together. "You understand what?"

"You and Draben."

She stared at me, her mouth hanging open. "Me and Draben? Draben is my—" Then her eyebrows went up. "Oh! You thought Draben and I were—"

"Well, yeah, it's pretty obvious." I was beginning to feel a little stupid. "I mean, after I told you how I felt, and the way you've been hanging out with Draben..."

She stood and took a step toward me, and laughed. "Draben's like a brother to me. Nothing more."

"And am I like a brother?" The lump in my throat grew even more painful.

"Well, you kind of *are* my brother, but...." She stared down at her hands. "Everyone I've ever really loved has been taken from me. I never knew my mother. The memories of my father are fading. Your family is all I've got. And you...."

I waited for her to continue.

"I guess I've been afraid to get too close, because if I get too close, you'll be taken away from me, just like everyone else." Tears filled her eyes.

"So, you — ?"

"Of course, Noah. It's always been you." She bent forward and kissed me, just one soft kiss on the lips.

I didn't want it to end, but she pulled away.

"We're still just kids."

I wanted to protest, but she was right.

"Let's just give it some time, okay?"

I nodded.

She smiled and walked past, brushing my shoulder with her hand. Then she was gone.

Just like that, the stress of the day melted away. Even after Hamilton returned, I couldn't stop myself from grinning. He had the good grace not to press me with any questions.

***

Dad jumped the *ARC* back and forth through time, just a few years each jump, but it shaved days off our trip to Earth.

I arrived in the hangar to find Mom, Dad, Sam and James all waiting for me.

Dad turned when he heard my chair coming. "Ah, here at last."

His jab at my tardiness couldn't bring my mood down. Everyone kind of stared at me when I came in with a big grin on my face. Sam opened her mouth, but Hamilton elbowed her into silence.

Dad cleared his throat. "General Roosevelt has a surprise for us. He wouldn't tell me what it was, but said we should bring every transport ship we had. So, let's get going."

It wasn't often that we all got to fly together. Most of the time, Dad or I flew. Mom and Sam were both competent pilots, but they didn't get much joy out of it. I just couldn't imagine.

I grinned at James.

He, of course, knew something was up, and probably knew it had something to do with Adina, but he didn't ask.

Dad was beginning to treat James more and more like one of the family. Flying one of the J-3500s was one thing, but letting James take out a ship that Dad built, one of the *DUV* classes, was something else entirely. That said, James got the *DUV III*, while the rest of us each flew one of the four *DUV IVs*.

When we were all aboard our respective ships, mine being the one I'd named *Firestorm*, Dad gave the signal to lift off.

I went out first. As always, the breathtaking view of Earth struck me. The sun was just rising, and the deep blue of the ocean seemed almost surreal after the dull red of Mars, and muddy yellows and greens of Venus.

"I'll race you down," I said as I fired the reverse thrusters. *Firestorm* slowed and began to fall toward the planet below.

"Nothing crazy, Noah," Dad said.

I nearly fell out of my seat when his ship went screaming by me. "Hey!"

He laughed over the comm until Mom chimed in. "Boys!"

Dad made a crackling noise with his mouth. "What's that? You're breaking up."

"Ugh, once a boy, always a boy," Mom said, but joined in the giggles.

Minutes later we were all burning through the atmosphere. Once through, Dad and I played cat-and-mouse all the way down to Australia. It was a great release after all the seriousness of the past few weeks, the five of us out on a beautiful day, flying through the blue sky.

We hurtled over the undulating lands of Australia until the great red rock, Uluru, rose in the distance. I eased up on the throttle, and Dad pulled ahead, piercing the energy barrier and disappearing. I immediately gunned it and swooped up over the dome that protected Earthome from prying eyes. *Firestorm* rattled and shook as I rose, then I pushed the nose down and dove straight for the Rock.

I pierced the shield and saw Dad about a kilometer out. I was coming in hot, but nothing I couldn't handle. Yanking back on the yoke, I brought the ship into a flat fall and used her underside to slow down.

After dropping to the ground in a large field, scattering a flock of sheep, I powered down and scurried into my magchair to depart the ship. I hovered above the green grass of the field, waving, as Dad landed beside me.

By the time he powered down and came outside, the others were landing around us.

"You didn't really think I thought I'd won, did you?" He came over and slapped me on the back. "Not when my son is the greatest pilot in the Solar System."

"That's debatable," a voice said behind us.

We turned to see James leaning against a fence post. His ship was parked behind him, hidden by a tall stand of trees.

"How'd you—?" I couldn't believe it. My own brother.

"While you two were trying to outsmart each other, I just took the shortest course. I've been here for ten minutes." He just stood there with a huge grin on his face.

"Oh no," Dad said. "I've got *two* hot-shot sons."

James looked at me and wiggled his eyebrows.

"I want a rematch," I said.

"I'm sure you'll get your chance," Dad said, then looked over to see Mom and Sam walking over. "But for now, let's go see what General Roosevelt's got cooked up for us."

We all started moving toward the red rock, when we heard hoofbeats. A horse came galloping around the stand of trees James's ship was parked behind. It reached a wooden fence and leaped over. The rider slowed the horse as it neared, and cantered over. It was the general, dressed in baggy, brown trousers and a matching button-up jacket. He wore leather gloves that extended almost to his elbows, and atop his head was a broad-brimmed hat.

"You look just like a holo of President Roosevelt I've seen," Sam said.

The general swung his leg over the pommel and dropped to the ground. "Why thank you, little lady, but I'm sure I'll never live up to his stature."

He reached out and shook Dad's hand. "It's good to see you all alive and well." He turned toward me. "I was glad to hear your adventures on Venus were a success."

"Not without a cost," I said, frowning slightly.

"Aye, there's always a cost."

"So, what's this surprise you want to show us?" Dad asked, not allowing me to darken the mood.

"Follow me." He turned and started walking back the way he'd come. His horse followed along behind him.

We moved along a dirt road with Uluru peeking out above trees just ahead. The road rose in front of us, momentarily blocking the view of the great rock. When we got to the summit, General Roosevelt stopped, and we looked out over a large field. Rows of horses stood facing us, each holding a rider dressed in the same type of uniform as the general.

Dad's mouth dropped open.

The general waved his arm at the mounted soldiers. "I give you Roosevelt's Rough Riders."

"A cavalry?" Dad said. "That's your big surprise?"

"Yes sir. One thousand strong." You could see the pride in General Roosevelt's face.

Dad laughed. "You do realize this is the thirty-first century, don't you?"

"Not what you were expecting, is it?"

"That's an understatement."

"Well then, Prime Senator Sarx won't be expecting it either."

"What?" I interrupted. "You're going to take these to Mars?"

General Roosevelt grinned. "You brought the ships, didn't you?"

CHAPTER TWENTY-FIVE

It was a sight to see: one thousand horses all grazing in a field in one of the
large habitats on the *ARC*—the American Bison habitat, to be exact. We'd
built a fence to keep the herd of buffalo separate from the horses, but it
wasn't really necessary. They didn't pay each other much mind anyway.

The men and women from Earthome were camped out near the edge
of the field, up against the wall of the habitat. They had tents set up, and
even some cook-fires here and there. It looked like a scene from twelve
hundred years ago in the Wild West, which seemed perfect, because most
of them were scared to death being on a spaceship. They were used to
dirt beneath their feet and blue sky over their heads, even if it was just a
ceiling of girders and metal painted blue.

Once we were headed for Mars, General Roosevelt laid out his plan,
a pretty simple one. We would land the cavalry outside the capital on
Mars, along with a handful of mechs and whatever ships we could put
together.

We all surrounded a projection of Capital City.

He pointed to the dome and the surrounding basin it sat in. "Basically,
the idea is to create as much noise as possible, drawing Sarx's army out."
He drew his finger out to the landing spot. "This will hopefully buy a
small group the chance to get in and try to bring the Poligarchy to its
senses." He indicated the Senate building.

"If that fails, then someone will be tasked with trying to assassinate
the Prime Senator."

We all looked at him in disbelief.

"I know it's not ideal," he said. "But it may be our only hope of victory."

Memory Keeper stood from the stool where he sat in the corner. "I will do it."

We all turned to look at him.

"What? No," I said. "If anyone's going to do it, it should be me."

Mom shot me a glare that said, 'No way.'

"I can't allow that, son." Memory Keeper hobbled over and looked straight into my eyes. "I know you still feel responsible, but this has been my failing since long before you were born. I must be the one to set it to rights."

I just looked at the old man. Even if he should be the one to do it, how would he—

"Begging your pardon, sir," General Roosevelt said, "but you're—"

"Old?" Memory Keeper spun around and held a small pistol against the general's stomach.

General Roosevelt looked down, his eyes wide.

The old man smiled, pulled the gun back and stuck it in his breast pocket.

The general laughed. "I guess there's always more than meets the eye."

Memory Keeper scanned everyone in the room and then rested his eyes on me. "Then it's settled." He turned and shuffled back to his stool and sat down.

* * *

"But I'm the best pilot we've got!" I just couldn't believe how unreasonable Dad was being.

"I wan't you to focus one hundred percent on the task at hand." The set of his jaw made clear he wasn't budging on this.

Still, I had to try. "And you know I've had the most time in the mechs."

"General Roosevelt's soldiers have been putting in several hours a day training on them."

"Haon's robot can help with the ground assault."

"Most everyone will be on horses. Have you ever ridden a horse?"

Ugh. I hated it when Dad used logic against me. "But—"

"Enough, Noah. You are amazing at everything you put your mind to. There's no doubt about that. I'm very proud of you, but you just can't do everything. This is one of those times I need you to focus." He shook his head. "Believe me, I don't even want you going into the city, but you have to. I believe you, Draben, and Adina have the best shot of getting in there unseen, and allowing Memory Keeper an audience with the Senate."

He was right, but I hated missing any of the action. After mastering dual-screen mode, I could at least operate a fighter at the same time I went after Sarx. Maybe I could even run Haon's robot—

"Besides...." Dad cut off my train of thought. "You'll be able to communicate with James. I know how you two work. You'll get to see everything that's going on."

I smiled slightly.

"But don't let it distract you." He jabbed a finger at my chest.

"I won't, Dad."

He watched me for a moment, probably trying to decide if I was truly in agreement. "And not to put too much pressure on you, but this whole thing is riding on your shoulders." He grinned and ruffled my hair.

"Thanks for that, *Dad*." I laughed.

"Be careful."

I looked into his lined face. All he'd done for me; now it was my turn. "You too."

CHAPTER TWENTY-SIX

The timing would have to be just right. Our part of the job relied wholly on stealth.

Draben, Adina and I escorted Memory Keeper to the bridge of the *Morning Star*. She was the smallest ship we had that would carry more than one person, and I knew her like I knew my own face—and after seeing James nearly every day for the past year, that was better than just about anyone else.

The only downside to the *Morning Star* was that she wasn't a jumper, meaning we lost our biggest advantage. But that could also help, because they might not recognize her.

We all buckled into our chairs on the bridge, Draben to my left, Adina to my right, and Memory Keeper seated on the other side of her. I glanced at Adina, but she kept her eyes on her monitor. We'd shared a few awkward smiles since the night before, but hadn't really had a chance to talk. Things had changed between us, but I still wasn't quite sure what that meant.

When Dad said that Draben and Adina were going with me, I was hit with a sudden fear something would happen to her, now that we were... whatever we were. Dad pointed out that Draben had spent most of his life avoiding the authorities, and Adina was excellent at moving quietly and remaining hidden due to her hunting experience during the Ice Age. I didn't like it, but once again his logic overruled my feelings on the matter.

Dad popped into the present time out near the asteroid belt. The plan was to find some ships heading in from deeper space and ride into port with them.

"Okay, son, you're go for departure." He used his captain's voice, but couldn't hide the nervousness behind it.

I powered up the *Morning Star* and lifted off the hangar floor.

"Remember, we'll be out of contact until just before the assault. James will connect with you when we begin our descent."

"I've got it, Dad." We'd been over the plan a hundred times. "We'll be all right. See you when Mars is ours."

"Roger that."

I pushed toward the bay doors, then punched it.

***

We didn't run into any trouble on our flight to Mars. Dad had been right in his hunch that the Poligarchy wouldn't be looking for us in a ship like the *Morning Star*.

Capital City sat right on the equator of Mars. We skimmed along the surface coming in from the south. The port lay just ahead, and pockets of green plants grew in depressions along the ground. I'd heard rumors that small plant life had started taking hold, but I hadn't seen it with my own eyes.

Memory Keeper watched the terrain fly by. "I never thought I'd see the day."

"We've got a long way to go, but it's definitely a start." I turned to Memory Keeper. "Are you ready?"

He swallowed hard and nodded.

On the way to Mars, I had thought about the last time Draben, Adina and I had flown together on a "mission." We'd gone back to see the asteroids pummel Mars during the initial terraforming of the planet. That little trip had resulted in Draben getting hauled off by the police because he wasn't in the registry of those allowed to time-travel. Sensors at every port on Mars checked the DNA of those debarking ships. Trace markers in our system showed right away if we'd been anywhere in time but the present.

The problem was that everyone aboard had traveled in time, even Memory Keeper, when Dad jumped the *ARC* to get us from Venus to Earth, then Earth to Mars more quickly. Those had been short jumps, however, just a few years back, so they shouldn't show up in the scans.

We could have landed outside the port, but Memory Keeper wouldn't be able to handle a long walk across the desert. Also, the Poligarchy would probably send someone out to check on why a ship had landed outside the city. It was a pretty uncommon scenario.

So, Memory Keeper would drop us off just outside the city, and then take the *Morning Star* into port. Autopilot would do the flying for him, but he was still pretty nervous about the idea.

"When the ship lands, I press this button." He pointed to his monitor.

I'd told the computer to allow Memory Keeper to pilot the ship. Since the *Morning Star* wasn't a jumper, she didn't require DNA authentication. *I hope that wasn't a bad idea.* "Yes, or just give the command written below it."

"You mean, 'Computer, power—'"

"Don't say it now!"

Memory Keeper jumped, his face going white.

"Sorry, I shouldn't have yelled," I said. "Yes, just press that button after the ship lands in the port."

He nodded. "And I don't have to do anything else?"

"Right."

He didn't look too sure of himself, but he didn't say anything more.

I wanted to be close enough to the city that we didn't have a long walk, but far enough away that the police didn't come looking.

I spied some tracks in the sand leading back toward the main dome. "This looks like as good a spot as any. We ready?"

Draben and Adina both nodded.

"Okay, I'm taking her in."

I settled the *Morning Star* to the ground, but kept her engines online. "Let's go." Climbing out of my seat, I pushed myself into my magchair.

Draben and Adina stood, each hoisting a small backpack onto their shoulders.

"We'll meet you just outside the main entrance to the port in an hour." Memory Keeper nodded.

I checked to make sure my pack was on the back of my chair, then headed for the exit. Once outside, I gave the *Morning Star* the command, through my neuro-processor, to initiate takeoff and set the autopilot to take her into the port.

Moments later, we were alone in a desert of Mars.

I took a deep breath. The air was thinner than I was used to, but quite breathable. "We'll have to take it slow while we get used to the air."

Adina smiled, and then saw Draben watching us. Her face turned red, and she spun around and started walking down the trail.

Draben watched her go, then looked at me.

I just shrugged my shoulders. It was going to be a *long* walk.

We passed a small patch of greenery, and I couldn't help my curiosity. I pushed my chair off the track and took a look. Tiny plants grew in a blanket on the dusty ground, their leaves no more than a few millimeters across, but they were dense. A few white flowers even peeked from within the plant.

"So this is how it begins?" I tried to imagine what the desert might be like in another hundred years — maybe some bushes, even some trees.

The scientists in charge of terraforming would have a better idea. It probably all depended on how much moisture was in the air before they could plant the seeds. We'd probably need actual rain before anything like a tree could grow.

I lowered my chair to the ground and plucked a handful of the green plant along with a few flowers, picturing Adina with the flowers in her hair. I shook my head shoved the plant into my backpack.

Get your mind back on the mission.

I turned back to see Draben and Adina disappearing over a small rise. Seeing the two of them together still brought up a twinge of jealousy. *No sense in giving her a chance to change her mind.* I pushed my chair to catch up.

* * *

Draben and Adina were breathing heavily as we neared the main dome of Capital City. I had been worried about how we were going to get inside, but several people actually milled about outside the dome. Many little kids ran around playing, with their moms or dads looking on. A young couple enjoyed a picnic lunch. The citizens of Capital City were learning the joys of being out in the open.

A doorway led into the city, and a policeman stood outside looking mostly bored, but still watching the people enjoying the sunshine.

I pushed toward him with Adina and Draben behind. "Beautiful day, isn't it?"

He nodded. "Yup. Supposed to get a dust-storm later, but doesn't look like it now."

I turned to go through the door.

"Hold on," he said. "What're you kids doing out here? Shouldn't you be in school?"

"Uh, yeah." I glanced at Draben and Adina. "We were working on our botany project." I reached over my shoulder to my backpack. "We're studying the new growth the terraformers have been planting." I pulled the plant out and showed it to him. "Pretty cool, huh?"

He looked at the little bit of green in my hand skeptically. "You know you're not supposed to remove any of the plantings."

I shook my head. "No, sir, I didn't know." I tried to put it in his hand. "Here, you take it."

He pulled back. "I don't want it. Just... just don't do it again."

All three of us nodded.

"Very well. Off with you." He motioned toward the door.

"Thank you, sir."

We turned and pushed through the door, and I breathed a sigh of relief when we closed the second door of an airlock behind us. "Phew, that was close."

"If that's all we run into, I'll be happy," Draben said.

The dome for Capital City was at least twice as big as New Cairo, where Gramps lived. *Or used to live.* The three of us stood with our mouths open, looking at the curve of the dome as it disappeared in a haze.

"Better get moving. Wouldn't be good to look like tourists." I moved onto the sidewalk for a main street that looked like it circled the outer edge of the dome. "The port is this way."

Even out here at the edge of the city, the traffic was amazing. Huge trucks barreled by and hovercabs honked their horns in a cacophony of sound. Adina, who was definitely more at home out in the deserts than in a big city, flinched and moved to the left of me, staying as far away from the street as possible.

A sign for the port pointed straight ahead. "Come on." I pushed through the crowds of people, searching for Memory Keeper.

A throng of people poured out of a tunnel with a large sign over it that read *Capital City Port: Gateway to the Stars*. It was going to be hard to find the old man in this crowd. He was, after all, half as tall as everyone else.

We worked our way against the flow until we reached the scanners.

"We can't go through there," I said. "Do you see him?"

Draben and Adina stood on tiptoes, and I raised my chair until I hovered near eye level with them.

"There," Adina pointed.

I could just make out a wisp of white hair as we pushed through the crowd. When we came upon the old man, he had his back to us.

"You made it," I yelled.

Memory Keeper turned around, and worry on his face turned into a big smile. "Yes, I did."

"How was your flight?" If anyone was watching, it should appear we were greeting our grandfather who'd just arrived.

"Oh, it was fine, very uneventful." He winked at me. "Let's head home. I'm famished."

"Sounds great."

We went back down to the street. This time we crossed over the traffic and headed toward the center of the city, where the Senate building was located. A knot formed in my stomach; it was becoming all too real.

'Noah, we're here. Are you guys in?'

"*Yes, we just left the port. No problems.*"

I sensed James's relief. *'Good. Your Dad is preparing the ARC for landing. We've already been spotted, so I need to scramble the J-3500s.'*

Dad had jumped near present-day Mars only long enough for us to leave in the *Morning Star*, then jumped back in time to wait while we landed on the surface. The plan was to jump back to the present and bring the *ARC* in as quickly as possible, so the Poligarchy wouldn't have time to scramble any of their defenses once they recognized it was in fact the *ARC*. Such efforts were important because time-travel was only possible to points in time that had already occurred. Strictly speaking, we couldn't jump into the future — at least, the future based on when our present was. Confusing stuff, and it always made my head hurt a little to think of it.

The good news was that there were no battleships in local Martian space. Apparently, the idea that we'd attack Mars itself had never entered Prime Senator Sarx's mind.

"Keep me updated, James."

'Actually, it might just be easier if we stay looped in.'

He opened up the connection, and an image of a hallway on the *ARC* flew by in a blur as James ran.

"Good idea. You can monitor our situation too."

'Sounds good.'

"The *ARC* is here," I said to the others. "They're beginning their descent."

Everyone nodded and we picked up our pace to as fast as Memory Keeper could go.

"What do you think about going for a ride?" I asked him.

"Oh, bless you. I was thinking the same thing."

We stopped and Memory Keeper turned and sat on my lap. With just about anybody else I wouldn't have been able to handle it, but he was all of thirty kilograms, if that.

"Hold on." I looked over his shoulder and pushed the magchair down the sidewalk, weaving around the crowds of people.

Adina and Draben kept up. The red sky began to darken.

"It's going to be night soon." *I just hope it helps the invasion.* The men on the ground would be harder to see, at least.

The image of James climbing into the pilot's seat flitted in the back of my mind. His heart was racing.

"You'll be fine," I told him. *"Even though you aren't quite the pilot I am."*

'I beat you.'

"Yeah, yeah. Wait until our rematch."

'For now, if you don't mind keeping quiet, I'd appreciate it. I'm taking both J-3500's out.'

My vision blurred slightly as James pushed into the other fighter. For a moment I saw three images at once: the city around me; the view from

James's ship, *Lady's Revenge II;* and the view from *Annihilation's* camera. I pushed the last one away as James launched out into space.

Once out, James turned back toward the *ARC.* The underside had already begun to glow. We'd never taken her into an atmosphere before, but she was designed for it.

At first we'd planned on taking the ground troops down to the planet just like we brought them up from Earth, aboard multiple shuttles, but General Roosevelt had said it would be too slow. He said we needed to hit them fast and in full force, so Dad suggested just taking the *ARC* down. He and Hamilton had argued for a while about the safety of it, but eventually Hamilton relented.

James peeled off after a couple small fighters that followed the *ARC* down. They were nothing more than patrol ships, and it only took a shot from each J-3500 to take them out.

Like most cities on Mars, and Venus for that matter, the capital was laid out like a wheel. The central government district was the hub, with roads like spokes radiating out. Only this city was immense.

Deep shadows were forming between the tall buildings, and lights began to wink on.

"I don't think we're going to make it to the Capitol building before dark." I slowed my chair, and Draben and Adina came to a walk beside me, both breathing heavily. "I was hoping we'd find a good place to scout the building, so we could plan how to get in. I also want to make sure the senators are inside."

"So let's keep going," Draben said between deep breaths.

Adina just nodded in agreement.

The crowds around us had thinned as the evening progressed, and while walking down the street at night might not be such a good idea, I couldn't think of any better ideas. "I guess there's no reason—"

A siren rent the air.

People stopped in their tracks and looked around. I nearly lost Memory Keeper from my lap when I swerved to avoid a man in a dark grey suit and hat standing in front of me.

The siren continued to blare.

"What is that?" I asked the man I'd nearly run over.

"The Emergency Signal." He put his hand on his hat and started running the opposite direction. "It means 'get off the street,' " he yelled over his shoulder.

Sure enough, the streets began to empty. First the people disappeared into buildings, then the hovercabs and trucks that clogged the roadway vanished down side streets.

Within minutes, we were alone. Still the siren filled the air.

"Obviously they know about the invasion," Draben said.

"What do we do?" I felt exposed sitting there in a pool of light from a streetlamp just above us.

Draben looked around. "I don't know, I—"

The siren cut off, but the ringing in my ears was quickly replaced by a rhythmic drumming. It sounded like hundreds of boots marching in step. I looked up the street.

It was exactly that.

From the direction of the Capitol, a mass of uniformed men and women marched toward us. They filled the street and were coming fast. Like a crashing wall of white water, the soldiers bore down on us.

"This way," Adina yelled, pulling Draben by the arm. We followed her into an alleyway just before the first rows of soldiers ran by.

"Are you seeing this, James?"

'Yeah. Apparently, they know we're here.'

James was trying to be funny, but I could sense his nervousness.

"Hey, you!"

I spun around.

A soldier peeled off from the marching column, lowered his weapon, and stalked toward us.

Draben grabbed my arm. "Let's get out of here."

We took off down the alley. The soldier yelled for us to stop, but we paid him no mind. Adina dashed through a maze of small side streets and alleys, some barely wide enough to squeeze my chair through. She pulled up when we turned into an alley that dead-ended into a wall.

She spun around, but Draben held up his hand. "Give me a minute."

Memory Keeper climbed out of my lap and stood stiffly, cracking his back. "I wasn't made for this."

Adina looked down to the end of the alley, her eyes wide. "I don't like this. We're trapped if someone finds us here."

The words were no sooner out her mouth than two soldiers stopped at the alley entrance. One held a flashlight, and he passed its beam along the street and walls.

We pushed back into the shadows as I looked around for a way out. "Can we make it back the way we came in?" I whispered.

Adina shook her head. "They'll see us."

Draben tried the handle to a door that was recessed into the wall.

He shook his head. "Well, they're gonna see us anyway," Draben whispered. "Let's just rush 'em. Their weapons are on their shoulders."

We all looked at each other, then back at the two soldiers who were working their way down the alley, searching behind crates and piles of trash. It was dangerous, but what else could we do?

Memory Keeper pulled out his gun.

"On three," Draben whispered. He held up three fingers, and counted. One, two—

"Psst."

Draben stopped with two fingers up, and we all spun around. A pale face peeked from a door that had opened in the wall to our right.

"Over here."

We took one last look at the soldiers, then dashed for the door.

A small girl opened it wide and we plowed through. She shut the door behind us, careful not to make any noise, then turned and leaned her back against it. We all held our breath waiting for the shouts outside. None came.

CHAPTER TWENTY-SEVEN

After several tense minutes, we all breathed a sigh of relief.

The little girl peeked out of the door, shut it, and twirled around. "They're gone." She flashed a big grin, her front teeth missing.

"Thank you," I said.

She eyed me and my chair. "My name's Clara."

"Noah." I stuck out my hand.

She reached forward and shook it quickly.

"This is Draben, Adina, and Memory Keeper."

She giggled. "That's a funny name."

The old man smiled. "Well, you have a very beautiful name, and it's lucky for us you are so brave too."

Clara stared at Adina. "You're hair is so pretty."

Adina glanced at me, then smiled at the girl. "You are very pretty yourself."

She grinned again. "You think so? Emalyne is always saying I'm ugly. She says pretty girls don't have freckles."

"Well, Emalyne doesn't know what she's talking about," Memory Keeper said.

"I don't, huh?"

We turned to see an older version of Clara walk into the small room. She was probably fifteen or sixteen with reddish-blond hair, and a splash of freckles across her nose. I suddenly thought freckles made a girl very pretty.

"Who do we have here?" she asked. "You know better than to let strangers into the house, especially from the alley." She tried to make her words sound stern, but she seemed more curious than angry. Her eyes passed over me and rested a moment on Draben. She smiled, then looked away.

Of course she'd smile at *him*.

"What were you four doing out on the street?" The tone in Emalyne's voice was clear: *only an idiot would be out after the siren's sounded.*

"We're not from around here," Draben said.

Sure, we had an emergency alarm system back in New Cairo, but it never went off; at least, not in my short time living with Gramps.

Emalyne looked between the four of us, then nodded. "Well, you can't go back out there tonight. They'll pick you up for sure." She smiled at Draben. "Looks like you have to spend the night."

He grinned back at her.

Adina pretended to study her fingernails, but she kept glancing at Emalyne. I also caught her watching me. Was she jealous of the older girl?

"Follow me." Emalyne spun around and headed through the doorway she'd entered.

We moved into a long, narrow apartment with a kitchen area to our right, then a living area with large cushions on the floor for chairs, and finally an area set aside with some curtains, for sleeping. Two small mattresses occupied the floor.

"Is it only the two of you?" Memory Keeper asked.

"Mamma died when I was born," Clara said.

Adina flinched.

"And my daddy—"

"That's enough, Clara," Emalyne said. "I'm sure they're tired from a long day and don't want to hear our sob story." She gestured toward the sleeping area. "It's not much, but it's warm and out of the eye of the Poligarchy."

Draben and Adina pulled their packs from their shoulders and set them against the wall.

Memory Keeper eyed the floor, and the big cushion chairs, warily. It wouldn't be easy to get back up once he got down.

"I'll see if I can find something to eat," Emalyne said as she bustled toward the kitchen area.

"I'll help." Draben went off with her.

Adina sat down on a cushion with a sigh.

Clara plopped onto the floor in front of her. "You have really pretty hair."

I couldn't help but smile. Adina's hair was the blackest I'd ever seen. Today she wore it in a long, glossy braid down to the middle of her back, but a few strands had come loose and hung along her left cheek. I had the urge to reach up and push it behind her ear—

"Tell me about your daddy," Adina said.

A loud blast from a rocket engine filled my head. I'd pushed James to a corner of my mind while we dealt with the soldiers outside. I pulled up his presence. It still felt like watching everything on a holoscreen in my head.

James banked sharply, then looked out of the cockpit. The ARC was just below him, and I was stunned to see just how huge she looked. Even next to the giant dome over Capital City, the ARC looked massive.

There had been quite a discussion about bringing the ARC down to the surface, putting her right in the middle of a battle.

Mom didn't like the idea at all. She thought it was too great a risk to all the animals. "We've been working for years to collect them, and it could all be lost," she'd said.

"But if we don't do something," Dad had replied, "Sarx will hunt us down no matter where we go. Then we'll never get these animals to Earth where they belong, anyway."

In the end, Mom had relented, but she wasn't happy about it.

Dad brought the ARC in toward the city, then spun her around so the tail was pointed at the dome, and James followed her down. At first it looked as though Dad was taking her in too hot, but he kicked on the mag thrusters and slowed her. A huge plume of red dust rose into the air from under the ARC's wings, and with a bump, she settled to the ground.

The ARC was sitting on a planet's surface for the first time in her history. The rear of the ship was about ten kilometers from the edge of Capital City's dome.

James swung around the back of the ARC and hovered just in front of the secondary hangar. It was designed specifically for ground deployment, and as such, we'd never used it. The massive bay door opened and dropped to the Martian soil. It was a few hundred meters across, and men and women on horses galloped down the ramp. In just a few minutes, all one thousand Rough Riders were off, followed by twenty mechs.

It was a sight to see.

The horses seemed uneasy in the strange environment, but the riders knew their mounts and controlled them with gentle pats to their necks. There had been some concern about the thinner oxygen levels on Mars, and what it would do to the animals, but Hamilton had come up with an ingenious plan. Each rider strapped an O^2 canister on his saddle, with a hose leading to the horse's bit. The tube fed a continuous supply to their mounts, and could also be used by the riders, via another tube, if need be. The horses were also loaded with weights to keep them firmly on the ground, since the gravity on Mars was only about a third of Earth's. We didn't want the horses to be leaping into the air and losing control.

Great lights from the *ARC* lit up the ground behind it, where General Roosevelt sat astride his own horse. He had decided a night assault would be best, providing some cover for their assault. The general rode down the line as his men formed up.

I wondered if he was giving some kind of speech, one that inspired men before battle, and felt a twinge of jealousy. Why couldn't I be down there?

The cavalry fell into ten groups of one hundred riders each. Each had one mech to help defend them. Once they formed up, the general moved his horse to the front of his army, and the remaining ten mechs marched up behind him. Being the point of the spear, with the ten battlegroups behind, General Roosevelt raised his fist in the air and held it for a moment, then dropped it down, and the army began to march toward Capital City.

The lights on the *ARC* went out, and the Martian surface went dark.

An alarm blared, and James glanced at his controls. Sensors showed a series of red dots flying toward him in formation. "Here we go," he yelled as he spun *Lady's Revenge II* around.

In the back of my mind I was aware of *Annihilation*. I hoped he was able to handle the two ships by himself.

Five J-3500s screamed toward James. He brought his two ships to-gether and rocketed straight for them. It wasn't exactly the move I would have done, but probably effective. He fired an array of missiles toward the enemy ships, then peeled off left and right. There weren't enough directions for the Poligarchy fighters to go, and two missiles connected. Explosions lit the night sky.

I sucked in my breath when I saw the fireball. I'd rarely seen explo-sions anywhere but in space, and those were short-lived and small. This was massive. The area for kilometers around was bathed in a red glow as debris fell to the ground.

James looked around and spied one of the remaining J-3500s rocket-ing toward the ground forces. He pushed his ship forward and tore off after it.

I opened myself up a little and saw him pursuing another ship with *Annihilation*. I wished there were a way I could help. Maybe I could work through my connection to James—

'Don't even think about it,' James said.

"Why not?"

'You'd be connecting to me, and then connecting to the ship. The lag would be too great. Any advantage we would have with you piloting the other ship would be lost because your response time would be too long.'

I shook my head. I wasn't sure that was right, but James had much more experience with linking.

It turned out he didn't need my help this time. He took down the two enemy ships he was chasing. The third and final one made the mistake of going straight for General Roosevelt's position. Twenty mechs behind the general fired, and the ship exploded before it got off a shot.

"We've got to stop those ships at the source," General Roosevelt yelled in James's ear.

"On it," James said.

He kept *Annihilation* with the army and tore off in *Lady's Revenge II* toward Capital City.

"Do you want cheese?" Clara asked.

I blinked. "Cheese?"

"Yeah, for your salad." She held a bag of synth-cheddar toward me.

"Uh, sure." I was so caught up in the battle I'd almost completely zoned out back in my body. I had somehow made my way to their small kitchen table.

Adina and Memory Keeper sat across from me. Memory Keeper was intent on his food, and Adina picked at hers while watching me from the corner of her eye.

I glanced around the room. "Where's Draben and Emalyne?"

"They went out," Adina snapped.

"Out?" I spun toward the door.

Clara got a frightened look on her face. "I told them not to go."

Memory Keeper mumbled through a mouthful of lettuce, "They were going to check on things, see if it's safe. We need to get moving the moment it's clear."

"Safe?" How could they just leave? The streets were filled with soldiers.

Adina looked toward the door. "Emalyne said she knew places to hide." She looked a little skeptical.

The way those two were looking at each other earlier, I wouldn't have been surprised if checking to "see if it's safe" wasn't the only thing Emalyne wanted to do with Draben in the dark.

"There's not much we can do now," Memory Keeper said. "Wait until they come back. Then we'll have a better idea of what to do next."

'I could use a little help here, if you're able.'

I pushed toward James. He was flying over the barren red surface of Mars. Capital City's dome was just ahead.

"What do you need?"

'I need to find the hangar for their ships.' James's gaze searched the dome.

"How can I help? I only see what you see."

'You could push into the camera system of the J-3500. Through me.'

"But —"

'This is different,' he said. *'The lag issue doesn't matter much. You're not flying the ship.'*

"Okay, I'll try." I imagined the ship's system, and felt my way through her complex circuitry. I could sense James there, right along with me, though in actuality he was seated in a pilot's chair back on the *ARC*, connecting to the J-3500's computers.

It wasn't really that hard to take control of a few of the cameras.

"I'll look through the port cameras," I said.

'Okay, I'll take starboard. We're searching for anything that looks like a shield covering the entrance, or signs of small ships leaving the dome.'

I scanned the edge of the dome. It shouldn't have been that hard, but the dome was massive. A flash of light caught my attention higher up, and I focused the camera and zoomed in.

Three J-3500s flew down along the curve of the dome.

"There."

'I see them. It looks like they're coming from the far side.'

"Should we go after them?" The thought of those ships firing missiles on General Roosevelt's men made me want to seize control of the J-3500 and shoot them down.

'No, I'll stop them with Annihilation. We have to find that hangar.'

James pushed the ship to maximum throttle. He hugged the terrain and circled the city. We were nearly on the opposite side of the dome from the general's forces when the shimmer of a shield caught my eye.

"There it is."

'Most likely. Let's see what we can do.'

As James rocketed forward, a larger ship pierced the shield and turned to fly over the dome.

'A bomber!' I could hear the fear in James's thoughts.

"Go after it!" I yelled.

Memory Keeper jumped at my outburst, and was about to say something, but Adina held her finger to her lips.

James was frustrated. *'I can't. I have to shut down that port.'* He pushed *Lady's Revenge II* down toward the energy shield. A green beacon on top of a tower flashed to the right of the port entrance. A tower on the left held a red one.

"Maybe those towers — "

'On it.' James locked onto the right tower and fired a missile.

Another ship was leaving the port when the bottom of the tower exploded. An instant later, James hit the left tower too. The ship, another bomber, had just cleared the shield when the two towers began to fall. James had hit them perfectly, and they collapsed toward the entrance to the port.

The right tower clipped the rear of the bomber and the ship lurched to the side, smashing into the dome. The towers crumpled into a heap in front of the port entrance, leaving only a small area clear of debris. The bomber was caught by girders from one of the towers, but the pilot pushed the engines to full throttle and it began to break free.

James fired another missile, and seconds later the main thrusters on the bomber exploded. It lost all lift and plummeted into the open space in the port entrance. A plume of dust and smoke billowed outward, but when it cleared, we could see that the entrance was completely blocked.

'It's going to take them a while to clear that out.' James turned the J-3500 and rocketed up over the dome.

"What's happening?"

I turned to see Adina staring at me, worry on her face.

"The invasion is under way. James was able to stop the Poligarchy from launching any more ships — at least for now."

She breathed a sigh of relief.

Memory Keeper was helping Clara put the dishes away. It was funny to watch them. Memory Keeper was almost exactly the same height as the little girl, and they had to use a step-stool to reach the top cupboards.

"Have you heard anything from Draben?"

Adina just shook her head, worry returning to her face. "No. Nothing."

At least she was talking to me again.

"I'm going to see if James needs any more help."

She nodded and stood up.

James shot over the top of the dome and headed down the other side. My breath caught in my throat.

Columns of Poligarchy soldiers spewed out of the city, forming up into regiments. Already, thousands marched in formation toward General Roosevelt's cavalry. We were already outnumbered four to one.

The bomber we'd failed to stop earlier flew over the Poligarchy army, and was only a few kilometers from our troops. The mechs in the front began firing at it, but even when they connected, the ship hardly seemed to slow. Its shields kept the missiles from causing any real damage. On the other hand, it had no difficulty destroying the mechs. Three of the machines crumpled to the ground before James was able to engage with *Annihilation*.

He fired several missiles at the ship with little effect, except that the bomber quit firing on the general's men and turned its attention to the J-3500. James dodged and weaved as rockets came at us.

He was frantic, trying to keep *Annihilation* from getting hit. *'We need to find a way past their shield.'*

The massive ship swung around toward us. *"What about the engines? I don't think they're as heavily shielded."*

'Just like the other bomber!'

"Yeah, something to do with losing efficiency in the atmosphere."

'It's worth a shot.'

James pushed back into *Lady's Revenge II*, which screamed over the enemy soldiers. Barely within range, he fired two missiles—one at each engine—and we both held our breath.

The missiles hit their mark and the engines exploded. The ship dropped toward the ground in what seemed like slow motion, but it wasn't slow enough for the soldiers directly beneath it to get out of the way. Hundreds of Poligarchy troops were crushed under the ship as it plowed into the red soil.

General Roosevelt's voice came over the comm. "Nice job!" His army cheered in the background. "Now it's time for us to do ours."

CHAPTER TWENTY-EIGHT

The front door of the apartment banged open, and we all spun around as Draben and Emalyne burst through.

"We've got to get moving!" Draben yelled.

Adina leapt to her feet. "Why? Did they find us?"

Draben shook his head. "No, but we found them."

Memory Keeper reached for his backpack. "Who?"

"The senators." Draben began gathering up his supplies and shoving them into his own pack. "Emalyne knew where some of them lived. We went to see if *they* were locked up in their houses, too."

"And?" I draped my pack over the back of my chair and glanced around. We were all ready.

"And we saw Senator Billingsworth," Draben said. "He looked like he was getting ready to leave his apartment."

I moved toward the door. "Let's go."

Clara grabbed a small bag and started toward the door as well.

Emalyne raised a hand, palm out. "Where do you think you're going?"

"I'm coming with you."

"Oh no you aren't. You're staying here." Emalyne pressed her hand against Clara's chest.

"You're not Daddy! You can't tell me what to do." Clara put her hands on her hips in defiance.

"I may not be Dad, but he made it clear—"

"You're both staying." Adina stepped between the sisters.

The girls were startled into silence. Their faces grew red.

"No way," Emalyne said. "I know the city much better—"

"We'll be fine. Once we find the senator, we'll just be following him." Adina wore that familiar look of hers, the one that said she wouldn't budge. "But you—" She put a finger on Emalyne's chest. "—you have a responsibility to your sister, to your...." The words caught in her throat. "To your father and your mother. You're all Clara's got now."

Adina placed her hand on Clara's head. "You're all each other's got, and I'm not letting either of you put that at risk."

Emalyne opened her mouth to protest, then looked at her sister, who was nearly in tears. Finally, Emalyne nodded and reached to embrace her sister. "I won't leave you, Clara."

Adina glanced over at me and wiped a tear from her cheek.

Emalyne turned. "My guess is the senator is heading toward the Capitol. All the senators will be there, but once they go inside, I don't know how you'll get in yourself."

Draben reached for the door handle. "I'm sure we'll figure something out." He yanked the door open and moved to step outside.

"Wait." Emalyne ran from her sister to Draben. She reached up and pulled his face to hers, and kissed him on the lips.

He wrapped an arm around her waist and squeezed her against him.

I glanced at Adina, who actually had a slight smile on her face.

Emalyne took a step back. "Come find me when this is all over."

"I will." Draben turned and strode into the night.

* * *

We peered out of a dark alley at Senator Billingsworth's apartment across the street. The quality of the surroundings had definitely changed in the few blocks since we left Emalyne and Clara's. The streets were clean, the smell of rotten garbage gone, and the buildings had tall windows and doors with ornate decoration in the stonework.

Thankfully, the Poligarchy presence was less noticeable here. Apparently, only the poorer neighborhoods needed "protection" by the police force.

"It's dark in his apartment," Adina said.

"He must've left already." Draben glanced around frantically. "What do we do now?"

Adina stepped out into the street and held her hand toward us. "Stay here." She flitted across the smooth pavement.

So graceful. She reminded me of a cat I had seen back on Earth, stalking a bird. Every muscle in her body moved with purpose.

She vanished into the shadow of a doorway, one apartment down from the senator's. Then she reappeared and crouched down by the edge of the street, touching her fingers to a small puddle that must have been left by a street sweeper. She glanced up the road and then dashed back over to where we hid.

"There was a fresh footprint on the pavement. Someone stepped into that puddle and then crossed over to this side. They headed up the street only minutes ago." She waved us out of the alley. "Let's go."

She led the way as we zigzagged through the streets and alleyways, always moving toward the center of the city. "It seems like he's trying not to be seen," she said.

I nodded. That would explain why he didn't just go straight down any of the main roads that headed toward the Capitol building.

Adina's movements reminded me of when she had tracked Haon across the barren wasteland outside the Yellowstone crater. Her ability to follow him with the barest of signs had boggled my mind. Here, in a city of concrete, stone, and steel, I was even more stunned. How she could see any kind of trail was beyond my understanding, but she did—a tiny thread of fabric stuck to a jagged corner of brick, or the scrape of a shoe in some fine dirt on a sidewalk. She even sniffed the air. I couldn't smell anything specific, but she moved with purpose after each time she took a smell.

She caught my puzzled look after sampling the air. "He wears a pungent cologne. Can't you smell it?"

I tried, but couldn't isolate any of the many scents in the city.

As we neared the Capitol, Adina put her finger to her lips and quickened her pace. She dashed around a corner, and then immediately ran back into sight and flattened herself against the wall.

We moved up beside her, and she whispered, "He's just up the street."

She peeked around the corner, then waved us on.

There was no one in sight, but as we neared an intersection with another alley, we heard a voice. Again we flattened against the wall.

"Can you believe this?"

The voice was familiar, but I couldn't place it.

"I know. Those Zarcs are insane."

That was Senator Billingsworth.

"They're saying it's a full-on invasion." The other man lowered his voice. "The Prime Senator's got to be furious."

Billingsworth chuckled. "I'm sure he is. Let's go watch the show."

We heard footsteps receding, and again Adina looked around the corner and waved us on.

The two men turned another corner ahead. The second man was Senator Kline, Billingsworth's underling.

The street the senators were on headed straight for the Capitol building. Billingsworth must have been more comfortable now that he wasn't alone, because they walked down the middle of the empty street.

Adina waved us on and we followed as quickly as we dared, sticking to the sidewalk. A few times we had to dart into doorways, or duck behind stone stairs, when one senator or the other glanced back.

They approached the Capitol from the front, but bypassed the huge stone stairs and turned to go around the right. At the same time, a column of about twenty soldiers marched down the stairs. With any luck, the Capitol building would be empty of all but a few soldiers soon.

We waited until the armed men marched off down the street, toward the battle outside. The senators had disappeared down a path between some small fruit trees, so we ran across the open square in front of the steps. I shook my head at the idea of trees on Mars. Somehow they'd transplanted enough for this small garden.

We moved down the walk between the trees. A flash of color appeared ahead, and we heard voices. Scrambling off the path, we hid in the trees.

Ahead, the two senators stood outside a small door to the Capitol. Billingsworth rapped twice and the door opened, and the senators moved to enter.

Draben let out a yelp and dashed forward. Before we could move, the door swung wide and two guards barreled out. Draben was taken by surprise but managed to take a swing at one of the guards, knocking him to the side. The other guard jammed something in Draben's side and an electrical hum sounded. Draben crumpled to the ground, and the two guards grabbed him by the ankles and dragged him inside.

The door slammed shut behind them. It all happened so fast, we didn't even have time to react.

Adina ran to the door and pressed her ear against it. "I hear shouting, but I can't make out the words." She tried the handle and shook her head. "Locked."

"How are we going to get in?"

"Wait, I think I hear—" Adina was knocked back, almost into my lap, as the door swung open.

A guard stepped out, dressed in white, wearing a helmet with face-mask, and with a rifle slung over his shoulder. Caught by surprise, he reached for a sidearm at his hip. Then his eyes flew wide and he slumped to the ground, his helmet clattering across the stone.

Memory Keeper stood behind him, his own gun held like a hammer in his hand.

"The door!" Adina yelled as she dove forward. She just managed to get her hand between the door and the jamb before it shut. She yelped out, but pulled the door open a crack.

I reached down to pull the guard's rifle from his shoulder and laid it across my lap.

Memory Keeper relieved him of his sidearm, and a set of keys, and handed the guard's gun to Adina, who was nursing her bruised hand by sucking on the fingers. She had her foot in the door, keeping it from closing. She stuck the gun in the back of her pants and peered inside.

"All clear," she whispered, and pulled the door open.

She stepped aside and allowed me to push through. Memory Keeper followed, and Adina closed the door quietly behind us.

My eyes adjusted to the dark corridor. We stood in a long hall lit by recessed lights in the ceiling.

Adina pattered down the hall ahead of us, stopped at an opening to the right, and waved us on. Another hall split off from the one we were in. At the end was a door with a glass window in it.

The hall ended in a large room up ahead, probably a lobby off the front entrance. Murmurs echoed around the large space.

Adina dashed over to a door just beyond the second hallway, and tried the handle. It was unlocked. She waved us over and shut the door behind us.

We were in pitch black.

"One second." She fumbled along the wall and, with a click, the lights came on.

We stood in a maintenance closet—a tight squeeze.

Memory Keeper said, "What now?"

"We have to figure out where the senators are," Adina said. "That's probably where they're keeping Draben."

I brought up a schematic of the Senate building on my wrist display. I'd made sure I had a local copy before we left the *ARC*. "I'm not sure this is going to help us much. Most likely they don't have everything in the public files, but this is what I've got."

Pushing my finger into the image projected above my wrist, I spun it around until our location came up. "Here we are. It looks like this hallway leads to the main lobby."

"What about this?" Adina pointed to the hall with the door at the end.

"Yeah, that's what I was thinking. It looks like it heads back to the Senate chambers. That's got to be where they're meeting."

"So what are we waiting for?" Memory Keeper grabbed the door handle.

"We can't. According to the diagram, that door's locked from the other side. I think it's an emergency exit from the Senate chambers."

"One of us needs to go open it," Adina said.

We all looked at each other.

I reached for the door. "I'll—"

Shouts filled the hall outside, and Adina quickly flipped the light switch, covering us in darkness. A sliver of light seeped under the door, and shadows passed across the light as footsteps pounded down the hall.

"They must have discovered our friend the guard," Memory Keeper whispered.

An alarm sounded down the hall, and soldiers ran back and forth just outside the door. It was beginning to look like we'd be here a while.

"How's it going out there, James?"

'It's pretty ugly. We're terribly out-gunned.'

CHAPTER TWENTY-NINE

It was easy to shove aside the blackness of the closet. Forgetting about Adina's hand that brushed against mine would be a harder matter. I reached out and held it, and she squeezed back. I could hear her breath. If Memory Keeper weren't around....

What am I thinking? We're in the middle of battle. I tried to push thoughts of Adina aside, at least a little, and brought up the view James was seeing.

Chaos reigned on the battlefield. The sun was rising and an orange glow bathed the plains below. General Roosevelt's orderly columns— what was left of them—now moved in disarray. It had been a very hard night for them.

James banked sharply left and dropped toward a group of horsemen that rallied around a mech, about to be surrounded by at least three times their number. Poligarchy troops marched forward, firing blasters into the ranks. The mech listed to the side and looked about to topple over, but still it fired, its pilot doing his best to protect the horses and riders around him.

James flew in low and strafed the enemy with his blasters. It was enough to cause them to retreat.

'We're not going to last much longer.' Even in my head, James sounded desperate and tired.

I also felt a deep sense of sadness.

He and I had played holo games our whole lives, enacting glorious battles across the stars, destroying legions of aliens and dark enemies. Yet nothing could prepare us for the real thing. I felt it first on Callisto when

I'd seen men die. I mean really die, not just to be respawned next time I booted up the game.

"I'm sorry, James." What more could I say?

'I know.' He pulled up to look for another target.

"Do you still have both ships?"

'Yes, but I'm getting tired.'

I couldn't stand the feeling of helplessness. *"I'm taking over this one."* It was *Annihilation.*

'No way. I told you –'

"I know what you told me, but I'll figure out a way. Take her up high and away from the action."

'Okay.' James swung the J-3500 around, headed out over an open plain, and climbed to several thousand kilometers. *'You sure about this? We really need this ship.'*

"How much longer do you think you'll be able to keep this up?" I knew the answer.

'You know I'm at my limit.'

"Then it's settled. Either you lose it and crash the ship, or I do. Let me take the fall."

He didn't like it, but relief flooded through him. *'Push into the controls. I may be able to help with the lag – just give you a little signal boost.'*

I felt my way into *Annihilation's* system. It was like pushing through pudding, or trying to do my geometry homework while tired; I had to think everything over more than once. The ship bucked and rolled as I gave it the same command a few times each.

'You've got to trust that the signal will get there. Just give it a moment.'

I calmed down and reined in my impatience. *Annihilation* had plummeted a couple thousand kilometers, so I gave it the command to level off. A few moments later, it did. It lagged only a second or two, but it felt like minutes. I turned her toward the battle, and she responded.

"I think I have it, James."

'Great. I'll pull into Lady's Revenge II. Obviously, keep the connection open, since you're flying this bird through me.'

"Will do." I pushed *Annihilation* forward, and she rocketed back to the battle.

There was no way we were going to win. It had already turned into a fight for survival for the general's troops. We were simply outgunned. Fallen horses, men, and women lined the field. Mechs lay on their side, burning.

One group of a couple dozen riders galloped in retreat from a mass of Poligarchy solders marching forward. Horses dropped along the rear flanks as the enemy opened fire.

I checked *Annihilation's* weapons systems. She only had a few missiles left, so I'd have to rely on blasters.

Diving toward the marching soldiers, I opened up the guns. Bolts of energy roared off both wings in rapid fire, and the front ranks of the attackers crumpled. I banked right and strafed along the line, but still they marched on.

The riders had almost reached a handful of mechs that guarded at least a hundred riders around them. A man stood in his stirrups, yelling orders — General Roosevelt. The horses around him parted and allowed the retreating riders to charge into their midst. The moment they were behind him, the general gave the signal and his cavalry charged forward. The mechs began firing at the same time.

A wall of riders firing blasters, backed by a half-dozen mechs, were enough to disrupt the Poligarchy charge. Several hundred soldiers dressed in white turned and fled.

But even with this small rout, the Poligarchy advanced. James's J-3500 took a few hits as he fired on a group of soldiers who had taken position on a hill overlooking the battlefield. It wouldn't be long until the ships were lost.

I dove down and fired on the retreating soldiers, who were already forming up for another attack.

Pulling back up, I inspected the battle. The noose was tightening, as Poligarchy troops marched forward in a circle, firing their blasters. It wouldn't be long now.

The *ARC* sat stationary a few kilometers away. The rising sun caused the ship to be nothing but a massive silhouette on the horizon. What would happen to my family when the Poligarchy won? Would all the animals on board ever get back to Earth where they belonged?

A glint of light caught my eye, then another, then two more. Four ships flew out of the shadow of the *ARC*. They were *DUV* class.

I opened up a channel. "What are you doing out here?"

Dad's voice came over the comm. "I should ask you the same thing."

"I, um—"

Mom cut me off. "We Zarcs have to stick together."

"Hamilton and Sam, too?" I asked.

"Yup," Hamilton said.

"Me too." Sam sounded excited. She'd change her mind when she saw the mess below.

"But the *DUVs*—"

"Hamilton worked his magic and retrofitted some blasters on them." I could hear the pride in Dad's voice. "Let's see what Team Zarc can accomplish with six ships instead of two."

I smiled. That was the first time I'd ever heard Dad say Team Zarc— typically a Mom-ism.

"But, Noah...." Dad's voice grew serious. "What about our primary mission?"

I couldn't say much because our transmission was most likely being intercepted. "We're on track. We just need a little more time."

"Then let's give it to you."

* * *

Keeping the battle in the forefront, I pulled slightly back into the janitor's closet.

"We've got to get moving," I whispered. "That battle isn't going well. They don't have much time."

"It's quieting down out there." Adina's voice quavered in the dark. "I think they finally decided we must still be outside."

Another set of footsteps pounded by outside the door.

"Okay, let's give it a few more minutes." I just hoped we could hold off the Poligarchy army long enough. Once they figured out they had our forces defeated, the soldiers that left the Capitol with only a few guards would be back.

***

Even with the added firepower of four more ships, the battle grew desperate. We basically flew in a huge circle, dodging and weaving fire from the enemy while strafing their front lines. It was the easiest way to keep from running into each other, but it was also a lot easier for the Poligarchy to hit us. They pretty much knew where we were going to be one moment to the next. They also brought in the bigger guns.

The Poligarchy brought tanks to the front. The armored and shielded vehicles resisted our blasters and could fire off much higher-powered charges. Already, Hamilton's ship had two holes clean through the wings. He seemed to list to the right a bit, but so far it hadn't caused any serious trouble.

I hated the fact that my family were putting themselves in actual danger. While I hid in a closet, flying remotely, they physically flew in the line of fire.

The Poligarchy adapted, learning how to counter our attacks. They'd concentrate all their fire to one area of the sky, forcing us to avoid it, then their troops would surge forward. In this way, they inched forward.

General Roosevelt's men continued to charge forward and fire, then retreat, but his numbers were dwindling. There couldn't have been more than a few hundred remaining of the original one thousand cavalry.

Thousands of Poligarchy troops surged toward the encircled cavalry, while several tanks fired into the air. If something wasn't done, they would reach the general's position.

I turned *Annihilation* toward the assault, but was too far off. One of the *DUVs* dropped toward the line and fired. Its blasters made a mess of the soldiers who charged forward, but didn't even scratch the tanks.

I checked my missiles: only two left. There were three tanks. My ship screamed over General Roosevelt's lines and targeted the front tanks. As they turned toward the *DUV* and powered up their guns, I shot off my missiles.

The first one hit and the tank erupted into a huge ball of fire and shrapnel. Then time seemed to slow. Moments before the second missile hit its target, the tank fired. Its bolt of super-heated energy lanced through the air between it and the *DUV*, and sliced through the ship's wing just as the missile destroyed the tank.

The wing of the DUV sheared off and spun off behind it.

"Noah!" Mom screamed over the comm.

It was Dad! His ship plummeted toward the ground. He fought with the controls, trying to bring her in soft, but he couldn't slow her descent.

The third tank was turning.

In that same moment, a rumble came from above us. I tore my eyes from the sight of Dad's *DUV* falling from the sky to see a fleet of beat-up old ships filling the skies around us. I recognized them at once: mining vessels, just like the ones on Callisto.

Annihilation rocketed toward Dad.

The final tank tracked him and fired, but barely missed.

I had no more missiles, so I did the only thing I could. Pushing the ship as fast as she would go, I shot over Dad and pointed her right at the tank. Just before impact, I heard a terrible grinding and tearing of metal behind me.

Annihilation smashed into the tank. My connection was severed.

CHAPTER THIRTY

"Dad!" I yelled out.

"Shhh!" Adina exclaimed in the dark next to me. Then quieter, "What's wrong?"

"Dad was shot down. I... lost my ship."

"Is he okay?" I heard her voice catch.

"I don't know, but we've got to get out there." I reached for the door handle, then felt a hand on my arm.

"The best thing we can do," Memory Keeper whispered, "is finish what we've started."

He was right, but I wanted desperately to get back to the battle. Then I thought of Prime Senator Sarx, and all my anger, all my hatred at what was happening out there, focused on that one man.

"James, can you see what happened to Dad's ship?"

'No. I'm trying to help out a group of riders pinned against a small canyon.'

"Let me know the moment you know anything."

"Sarx must pay!" I whispered through clenched teeth. "Let's go." I reached for the door handle again but before I turned it, the door was yanked open. I fumbled for the rifle on my lap as a guard, dressed in white, stood before us.

Adina whipped her gun out and raised it.

"Don't shoot."

I recognized the voice. "Draben?"

"Yeah, come on!" He was dressed as a Poligarchy soldier all the way down to.... He still wore his old sneakers. The guard he borrowed the uniform from must have had different-sized shoes.

"You're okay!" Adina wrapped him up in a huge hug.

For once it didn't bother me. I was just glad to see him.

"Of course I'm okay." He gave his best *how-could-you-doubt-my-extraordinary-skills* smile. "There'll be time to tell you what happened later. We gotta move."

We all nodded as he turned toward the side hall.

"But that door's locked," Adina said.

"Not if you have a key." He held up a ring of keys.

I remembered the ones we had lifted off the other guard. *Idiot!* I was just going to charge out of the closet with no plan. *Think, Noah! Stupid people die.* My mind flashed again to Dad's ship going down.

"Hurry!" Draben had the door open before I made it down the hall, and waved us on.

We were through the door and running down the hall. Our footsteps sounded so loud in my ears, I was sure we'd be heard, but no one came running. No soldiers jumped out to block our path.

The hallway dead-ended into another hall. Draben turned right, then pointed to the wall on the left. "The Senate chambers are in there. I think we're in luck. They locked the whole building down as soon as the alarm went off. Everyone is stuck inside."

He stopped in front of a rich faux-mahogany door. "Are we ready?" He knelt to examine the lock.

I glanced at Memory Keeper, who stood taller and squared his shoulders.

"We'll find a way so you don't have to do it," I said.

He nodded.

"Okay," I whispered to Draben.

"This lock's a bit tricky. I'm gonna have to blow it." He pulled out a small wrapped package and tore the paper off. He pulled out a putty-like material and pressed it into the lock mechanism. "Stand back."

We got out of the way as Draben shoved a tiny wire into the clay and tapped it twice. He stepped back as a red light flashed at the end of the wire, then a loud pop filled the hallway and the locking mechanism, along with part of the door, disintegrated in a puff of smoke.

Draben shoved against the door and it swung inward.

Senators looked up, stunned.

* * *

Prime Senator Sarx's eyes narrowed when he recognized me. "What a pleasure. Welcome, welcome, young Zarc."

Adina and Draben glanced at me, their eyebrows raised in surprise.

"I thought it was time you and I had a good talk." I looked around the senate chambers, a large, round room with a long table in the center. Great holo-displays covered the back wall, and the battle outside was projected on the screens. I was surprised to see the Poligarchy soldiers were driven back slightly by the assault from the Callisto miners, who remained woefully outnumbered.

The senators, both men and women, stood or sat where they were when we'd come in. They were frozen, waiting to see what the Prime Senator would do.

"It seems everyone is here," I said.

When it came down to it, all the anxiety and roiling in my stomach disappeared. Sarx was a bully, but surely when everyone else heard what I had to say —

"And you brought some friends." He glanced at Draben and Adina.

They both stood with their weapons out, but pointed at the floor.

Memory Keeper stayed behind us. Sarx didn't seem to pay him any mind.

I just nodded.

"And this *invasion*? What is your father thinking?" His voice dripped with disdain.

I could feel my face darken, but I kept my mouth shut.

"Does he really think he can go up against *my* army with...?" He leaned toward the senator next to him. "What did they say?"

"Horses, sir," the senator replied.

"Right," scoffed Sarx. "Your father comes at us with an army on horse-back. You do realize this is the thirty-first century?"

"My father will do whatever it takes to see you defeated."

Sarx laughed again. "Well, if this is the best he's got, I'm afraid his 'whatever' isn't going to cut it."

One of the younger senators edged toward the door we'd entered, and Draben waved his gun at him. "Don't even try it. Trust me, you won't make it two steps."

The senator stopped and glanced at Prime Senator Sarx.

Sarx shook his head, then turned back toward me and smiled. "So, young Mr. Zarc, you've obviously gone to a great deal of trouble to get here. What is this all about?"

"This is about holding you accountable."

Sarx raised his eyebrows. "For?"

"For...." I glanced around the room.

Some of the senators tried to look bored, while others were visibly nervous. A few, including Senator Billingsworth, leaned forward, curious to hear what I was going to say.

"For everything. For your attacks on your own people. For your brutality on Venus. For—"

"Yes, and I suppose for causing the Great Cataclysm?" He glanced at the senators around him and smiled. "We've heard this *story* before. No matter how many times you say it, it still won't make it true."

"Except this time, we have proof."

The Prime Senator raised his eyebrows again, but his expression was one of pure confidence. "Now you have proof? Well...." He looked at each of us. "Let's have it."

I stepped aside and motioned for Memory Keeper to come forward. "This man bears an eyewitness account of your deeds."

Sarx eyed Memory Keeper up and down. "This little man looks old, but old enough for my supposed deeds of a thousand years ago?" He laughed and looked at his fellow senators.

Some chuckled, but again Billingsworth looked genuinely interested in what Memory Keeper might say.

"The floor is yours, Mr...?" Sarx said.

The old man raised himself to his full height, which came to my chest. "I am Memory Keeper."

"And what does a *memory keeper* do?"

"Not *a* memory keeper. I *am* Memory Keeper. To that name I was born, and with that name I will die. I am here to bring charges and witness against you for all you have done to the human race. Memory Keeper was there the day you invaded my world." The old man stepped forward, his finger pointed at Sarx.

Sarx smiled but, almost imperceptibly, moved backward.

"Memory Keeper saw your ships land, and your troops spill out onto Martian soil. Men of peace, men of science, died at your hand. It was a bloodbath."

His voice was rising. He kept one finger pointed at the Prime Senator and put his other hand into the pocket of his jacket.

"Not only did you *slaughter* those men who came here to build a new, peaceful society, you wiped out entire families—to the smallest child." Memory Keeper's words were so powerful that he almost seemed to grow.

Sarx felt it too and took a step back, but bumped into the big table that spanned the length of the room.

"Once your rule was secure, you set up this *puppet government.*" Memory Keeper gestured at the rest of the senators. "And if anyone ever got in your way, they quickly disappeared."

Sarx attempted a confident stance, but he was visibly shaken. "This... this is quite entertaining."

"Your most recent crimes against *my* people cannot go unpunished." Memory Keeper took another step, and was now only a meter from Sarx. "I held my only grandchild in my arms as he died. You...." He jammed his finger in the Prime Senator's chest. "You killed my grandson, along with thousands of helpless men, women, and children."

Sarx looked around, trying to find a way to escape the tiny man's fury.

"And for that, you must pay!" Memory Keeper yanked his hand from his pocket.

I caught a flash of metal before I heard a loud bang.

At that very moment my head exploded in pain. '*Noah?*' My vision blurred and I nearly fell out of my chair. I heard shouting around me and heard the thud of a body hitting the floor, but it faded into the background.

'Noah, can you hear me?'

Even though I didn't really *hear* James's voice in my head when he and I communicated, I knew immediately this wasn't him. "*Who are you?*"

'It's your father – I mean – it's Haon.'

"Haon, but you're – "

'There's no time to explain. I'm sending you a key.'

"*A what?*"

'An encryption key. Sarx has a back door.'

"*Back door?*"

'Noah, please, just listen. When I programmed his robot, I left a way for me to gain access to his operating system, in case he double-crossed me. I never had a chance to use it, but the key I send you will allow you to connect. You can shut him down.'

"But I think he's already dead."

'A single gunshot most likely won't to do it.'

"How long have you been watching me?"

'It's not important. You have to act now. Get ready for the key.'

Before I could respond, a searing pain seemed to drill into my head right between my eyeballs. I heard a scream, but wasn't sure if it was me or someone else. Then, as quickly as the pain came, it was gone.

Shouting enveloped me and I opened my eyes. I'd slid out my chair and was lying on the floor.

The senators were all on their feet, shouting.

Adina and Draben struggled to break free of two Poligarchy soldiers who had them disarmed and in cuffs.

I pushed myself to a seated position, then saw a small body lying near my feet.

Memory Keeper's vacant gaze looked my direction. A small trickle of blood fell from his parted lips.

I twisted around.

Prime Senator Sarx stood with a small blaster pointed toward Memory Keeper. He turned the gun in my direction, his other hand reaching toward his own chest. His hand wasn't big enough to cover the hole that was blasted through his torso. The screens behind him shone through a mass of wires and dripping tubes.

He smiled grimly. "That's going to leave a mark."

The other senators stood with their mouths open. They didn't have the view I had, and probably didn't see that Sarx was a robot, but they knew he shouldn't be standing after taking a shot like that.

"So all of this...." Sarx waved his gun around the room. "The invasion, and your little visit to our chambers, was an assassination attempt? How clever. If I weren't the target, I would have been rooting for you to succeed."

He glanced at Draben and Adina, who had stopped struggling. "But now that you have failed, the question is, what to do with you?" He pretended to have a difficult decision, but his eyes indicated he'd already made up his mind.

"I'm sorry to say, but I think it's time we put an end to this... this *revolution* of yours." He gestured toward the screens behind him. "As you can see, your father's little army has been overrun. So that leaves you." He motioned with his gun for Draben and Adina to be brought over.

The soldiers pushed them toward me, then forced them to kneel. One soldier grabbed the rifle that had fallen next to me and pushed my magchair out of reach.

"You certainly have been entertaining." Sarx raised the blaster and pointed it at Adina.

"Stop!" Senator Billingsworth sprang forward. "These are children. You cannot do this!"

"Can't I?" Sarx glanced around the room. "We are the Poligarchy. Is it not our job to hold the nation together? These children are nothing less than usurpers of our authority."

I pushed with my mind through my neuro-processor, looking for Senator Sarx.

Senator Billingsworth looked around the room, trying to gain support from the other senators, but most turned away.

One of them stepped forward, and Senator Billingsworth's face brightened. It was Senator Kline, Billingsworth's biggest supporter. "I'm afraid I'm going to have to side with the Prime Senator."

Billingsworth's face went red.

"The Zarcs have done nothing but spew lies against the Prime Senator. Never once have they given any actual proof."

There it is! I could feel the Prime Senator's mind, but I couldn't get in. It was like shoving against a closed vault.

Senator Kline continued. "And without that proof, we must do the hard work of keeping our people together. Of course, I don't condone killing children." He glanced at Sarx. "We can take them into custody and then perhaps get their parents to—"

"No! This ends now." Sarx thrust his gun forward.

I shoved the key at Senator Sarx's mind with everything I had. A torrent of data rammed against the shield around his mind, and the barrier shattered.

The Prime Senator doubled over in pain. "No!" His gun clattered to the floor as he grabbed his head with both hands.

The simplest thing now would be to just shut him down. Like turning off my holo-pad, I could just flip a switch and Sarx would be no more.

'Do it!' Haon's voice sounded in my head.

I looked at Sarx standing there, rocking back and forth with his hands clamped around his skull.

After all he'd done, I had the right. I would be justified.

No! I would not do it. There was a better way.

Senator Kline moved toward Sarx, but stopped when the Prime Senator waved him off.

"You want proof?" Sarx stood straight and turned in an arc toward all those in the room, showing the gaping hole in his chest. "I will give you the proof you want."

The blackness that was the Prime Senator's mind enveloped me. A thousand years of hatred, greed, and lust for power surged through me. Surprisingly, so did self-loathing, doubt, and fear.

"It is all true," I said through Sarx.

Shocked senators looked up from the gaping hole in his chest to the Prime Senator's face.

"I was there, one thousand years ago."

I searched in his memory, like sorting through files, and found the ones I wanted. I glanced at the guards. A small image flashed on the inside of their visors. Tapping into the SolWeb, I pushed the holo up on the screens on the room's walls. I also found a link to the Poligarchy's network and hijacked the signal.

On the screen and, I hoped, the soldiers' visors, an image appeared.

It was the Capitol from the outside, but not the one we were in. Smoke poured from a huge hole in the roof as tanks surrounded it. It was the attack on Mars a millennia ago. A ship inside the dome was pushing its way out.

"These are my memories," I continued through Sarx. "I was there. I led an invasion that brought Mars under my control."

The image played on while I looked through his mind for another. Not sure I wanted to see it myself, I threw the holo up.

Sarx's voice came over the image. "Don't let a single one of them live."

He was running through a long corridor. Blasters could be heard, and screams. His hand reached for a door and it swung open, into the great room on Venus. Soldiers stepped over bodies, firing at anyone that moved, slaughtering helpless men, women, and children.

I pulled my focus away and looked for one final holo. I located some of the oldest data in his memory.

Again Sarx's voice. "So, this is completely effective?" He swirled a stoppered vial with amber liquid inside. "And there's no cure?" He glanced at a grizzled man in a white lab coat who watched the vial warily. Sweat rolled down his temple.

"That is correct," the scientist said. "It is highly contagious, with no cure, and is one hundred percent fatal."

"Excellent." The Prime Senator's voice expressed his glee.

"But, sir?" the scientist asked. "What's your plan for the virus?"

"To destroy Earth." Sarx raised an old revolver and pointed it at the man. "Of course, I can't have you blabbing about it before I've had a chance to release the virus." He pulled the trigger, and the scientist was knocked from his seat.

I pulled the holo off the screen and gazed around the room. The senators were stunned, their mouths all hanging open.

Senator Billingsworth was the first to recover. "Guards, place the *Prime Senator* under arrest."

The soldiers didn't hesitate. They strode over to Sarx and handcuffed his hands behind his back.

"You're going to need to do more than that," I said. "He's a robot with a great deal of strength. I'd bind him to a chair or something, including his feet, until you can move him somewhere more secure."

Everyone waited until the guards had Sarx bound tight, then a collective sigh filled the room.

I pulled from Sarx's mind and watched as his eyes came into focus.

He glanced around the room, then at his bound hands. A snarl escaped his lips. "What is the meaning of this?"

Senator Billingsworth stepped forward. "The meaning is you are going to spend the rest of your life locked away so you can contemplate the heinous crimes you've committed against humanity."

He glanced at the hole in Sarx's chest. "And since you're a robot, that could be a very, very long time."

I called my magchair over and pulled myself into it. "Do you mind releasing my friends?"

Billingsworth nodded, and one of the guards walked over and removed their handcuffs.

"You can't do this," Sarx yelled.

Then his voice echoed in my head. *'Please, Noah, just put an end to me. You know how.'*

I shook my head. *"It's not my place to decide whether you live or die."*

Several soldiers barged into the room. Billingsworth motioned toward Sarx. "Take him away."

The guards didn't hesitate. Four of them lifted the former Prime Senator, chair and all, and carried him from the room.

His voice screamed in my head until I severed the connection.

Haon was still there, though. *'Well done, Noah.'*

I turned toward the holo-displays. The Poligarchy troops had laid their weapons down after seeing Sarx's memories, which Hamilton had routed to their eye-screens. Everyone now knew the truth.

A ship flew across the screen—a *DUV* class.

"Dad!"

I turned to Draben and Adina. "We need to go."

Billingsworth stepped forward. "I'll send you an escort." Again he motioned to some guards.

They saluted and gestured for us to follow.

I glanced at the small body crumpled on the floor. "Can you—"

Senator Billingsworth nodded. "Memory Keeper will be handled with the dignity he deserves, until such a time he can be given a proper funeral."

I nodded thanks, turned my chair and left the room.

CHAPTER THIRTY-ONE

I chewed my fingernails down to nothing as we zipped along the Martian landscape. Draben and Adina looked equally stressed as we all peered anxiously out the front window of the hov-vee.

The soldier driving pushed the vehicle as fast as it could go.

"There!" I shouted, pointing to a column of smoke drifting into the thin Martian air.

The driver veered left and headed toward the smoke. I tried to keep my eyes off the landscape around us. From a distance it looked like the plain was covered in multi-colored rocks and boulders, but when we drew closer, I realized it was littered with bodies and destroyed equipment.

First we passed by men and women mostly dressed in the white uniforms of the Poligarchy, but within minutes we started passing the varied soldiers of the invasion force. Horses and riders alike lay scattered across the plain.

I tore my gaze back to the smoke ahead. We were nearly there.

We zipped past the remains of two tanks on either side of us, their bent steel carcasses covered in a thick layer of red dust. Then came a field of twisted metal that bore some resemblance to another tank, intermingled with the wreckage of *Annihilation*.

Up ahead, a *DUV IV* sat on the ground next to the shattered remains of another *DUV*-class ship.

Before the driver could bring the hov-vee to a stop, we were out and dashing across the debris field. Adina and Draben ran toward the ship, dodging still smoldering chunks of metal. I raised my chair up off the ground and pushed it in a straight line, passing them both.

I started yelling, "Dad? Mom? Anyone?"

A faint voice sounded from the wreckage, and I swung around to the far side of the crashed *DUV*. The ship had been ripped in two down its entire length. A red boulder, the size of an elephant, sat where the cockpit should have been. A figure dressed in white bent to the ground a few meters behind. At first I thought it was a Poligarchy soldier, but....

"Mom!"

She looked over her shoulder. Tears darkened the red dirt that coated her face. "Noah?"

"Yeah, it's me, Mom." I pushed over to her and there he lay.

Dad's left leg was bent up behind him, the small bars and pistons of his exoskeleton twisted and broken. His left arm was also mangled and wedged under his body.

Mom tried desperately to wipe away the grime that covered his face. "Is he...?"

She shook her head. "He's still alive, but barely."

Adina and Draben ran up behind me.

"We need to get some help!" I looked around, frantic for someone to make it all right.

"I called your brother. He's sending a medic, but...." Mom trailed off and continued to gently stroke Dad's forehead with her grimy cloth.

I dropped my chair down next to him, flung myself to the ground, and grabbed his hand. "Dad, you can't go."

He just lay there, unmoving.

"Please, don't go." I squeezed his hand and brought it to my tear-stained cheek.

His eyes fluttered open. "Noah?"

"Yes, it's me." I pulled myself forward so he could see my face.

"You... you did it?"

"Yeah, we did it, Dad. The war is over. Sarx won't hurt anyone again."

He nodded and closed his eyes for a moment, then looked up at me again. "Is everyone safe?"

I thought of the hundreds killed, of Memory Keeper's tiny body lying in a pool of blood, but I just nodded. "Everyone's safe, Dad."

Adina kneeled beside me, and Draben stood behind her.

She bent and kissed him on the cheek. "I love you, *Dad.*"

He smiled and patted her hand. "You've been a great addition to the family."

His eyes closed again as a coughing fit overcame him. Then he forced them open, and a serious look came over his face. "Be happy."

"We will," I said.

"No. Listen. We have it wrong." His voice gained strength and he locked eyes with Adina. "It's not about the *pursuit of happiness*, like the Declaration says." His eyes traveled to mine. "It's about being happy *in the pursuit.*"

He closed his eyes again. "No matter what life throws at you, *be happy*. Don't waste your time looking somewhere else." He coughed for several seconds, but when it cleared he said again, "Even in this, be happy."

"We will, Dad." I wiped the tears from my eyes. "We will."

His breathing became labored, and Mom moved around to the far side of his broken body. She bent over and gave him a long kiss on the lips.

When she sat back, his breathing had stopped.

CHAPTER THIRTY-TWO

The sun bathed the lush green valley below us. Mt. Rainier rose in the distance, her summit still painted white with the snows of a winter not long past. I had told Mom this is where Dad should be buried. It was where he'd felt most alive, and where my fondest memories of my father dwelt: just the two of us hiking through the forest, looking for that elusive great-horned owl.

The clearing Dad would lie beneath was filled with those he considered family, and those whom he sometimes wished weren't. Haon, back in his robot body, stood beside the open grave where they'd just lowered Dad's body. April clung to his arm. She had pleaded with my mom to allow Haon to come. It really hadn't taken that much convincing once she learned of his part in revealing Sarx to the Senate.

Dad's casket was lowered to its final resting place.

"We didn't always see eye to eye, but you were the best brother a man could have." Haon glanced at me then back at the coffin. "Thank you for being the father I couldn't be." He walked past me and smiled.

I still didn't know what to think of him, but I was ready to at least give him a shot.

Gramps couldn't make it. He was stuck on Deimos, and would be for the rest of his life, unless Mom could find away to remove the nano-virus in his blood that would kill him if he left the atmosphere of the prison. I'd promised we'd figure out a way to make him part of our lives, and I wouldn't let the solar system forget the hero he was.

From the moment he was taken to Deimos, Gramps had visited Haon on countless occasions. From appearances he was just a father reacquainting with his estranged son, but in secret, Gramps delivered the parts he'd scavenged so Haon could regain control of his neuro-implant. Even from an inescapable prison, the two of them were able to give me what I needed to defeat Sarx. Little did the former Prime Senator know that arresting Gramps would lead to his own downfall.

Draben smiled at Emalyne, who stood next to him along with her sister, Clara. Then he walked over beside me and tossed a flower on Dad's casket. "This one's for Memory Keeper, who kept the horror of the past with him his whole life. May that horror pass away with him, never to return."

He turned away, but spun back around. "And for Sastra, the best pilot in the solar system." He winked at me through tears, then went back to stand with Emalyne.

I looked down the line of my family standing in front of Dad's grave.

Mom stood tall, water in her eyes, but strong. She would be okay, I was sure of it.

Sam wasn't handling it nearly as well. Her eyes were puffy from crying. She'd hardly stopped since hearing the news. But even in her grief, she would be okay. There was nothing wrong with tears.

Hamilton tried to be a "man" and not cry, but he was in as much pain as the rest of us.

Then there was Adina. She stood stone-faced, staring at the casket as if by sheer force of will she could bring Dad back. My heart hurt more for her than my own loss. She'd been through so much.

I turned toward the small gathering. "Dad had a final few words for us before he died. At first I didn't understand why he chose those words to be his last, but I've had a chance to think about them a little more. He said, 'Be happy.' In everything we do, he said we should be happy."

I glanced down at my shriveled legs. "My whole life I've wanted nothing more than to walk. I've dreamed of the day I could stand on my own two legs, and always looked to the future when I could be truly happy."

I waved around me. "But it's not out there. Happiness isn't something in the future, something we pursue. It's the here and now." I glanced at

Sam. "Even with Dad's death, we can be happy — happy that he's not hurting anymore, happy that he's in a better place, happy that a large part of who we are is because of who he was."

Adina looked up at me, a tear running down her cheek.

"I know Dad believed there was a purpose in life, and that we were created to serve that purpose. As long as we work to do what is right, we should be happy no matter what. Today. Right now."

Turning toward the grave, I dropped the small flower I'd held in my hand. "So Dad, thank you. Thanks for everything you've given me. I'll miss you, but I won't be sad." Tears poured down my cheeks, and I laughed. "Even when I'm crying, I'll be happy. Thank you for that final gift."

CHAPTER THIRTY-THREE

I sat on the hill watching as the sun set behind Mt. Rainier. It was about time to head back to the ARC. I heard the soft pad of footsteps, and Adina sat down beside me.

"That was beautiful." She looked at the sunset with me. "What you said."

I nodded. "It was true. Real truth. You know what I mean?"

She nodded too. "I'm thinking about going back to Mars."

My heart sank, but I wasn't surprised. "I figured."

"It's just, with General Roosevelt being made Prime Senator, it made me think. I talked to Mom about going to study government and history. I want to be Prime Senator some day. I know it's silly, but if General Roosevelt can—"

"Of course it's not silly." I smiled and looked at her. "You'd be a great one."

Her cheeks turned red and she looked away.

"Everything's going to change," I said. "Mom needs me on the *ARC*. Oliver will be governor of Earth. Sam's going off to college. You and Draben are going to Mars. Dad's—" A lump in my throat cut me off.

Adina placed her hand on mine. "You'll be amazing. The *ARC* project must continue. Earth needs to be alive again. Really alive."

I looked down at her hand. Her dark skin was radiant in the last glow of the sun.

"What about...?" I couldn't bring myself to say it.

"Us?" She caressed my hand with her thumb. "You will always be the one for me. You saved my life back in the Ice Age. You saved me from Sarx. You've saved so many lives. The entire solar system is in your debt." She giggled. "How could a girl want anyone else?"

She bent forward. "You're my hero." Her lips met mine, and we kissed in the last rays of the setting sun.

I didn't want it to end. I just wanted to stay with her, on that hill, forever. But that wasn't how life worked.

She pulled back and looked me in the eyes. "Give me some time. Time to figure out my place in the universe. Time to learn who I am. But I'll come back, I promise."

I squeezed her hand and looked into her dark eyes. "Time is something I have plenty of."

THE END

ACKNOWLEDGEMENTS

There are so many people without whom this book wouldn't exist. First I want to thank Greg Scheetz, whose boundless creativity and vision was the original inspiration for Noah Zarc.

I'd also like to thank my beta readers who gave invaluable feedback: Jason Burdett, Abigail Pease, Samuel Pease, and Susan Quinn.

And to my wife, Beth, who puts up with me hiding away in my office, or at the coffee shop while I'm working on the stuff of writing, I can't offer enough thanks.

Finally, to my editors William Hampton and David Lane, it feels great to finally come to the end of the series knowing it is the best it can possibly be. Much of that is because of you. Thank you.

ABOUT THE **AUTHOR**

Epic adventures filled most of D. Robert Pease's childhood. Middle Earth, and the planets of Dune were his stomping grounds. It's not surprising he chose to write stories with worlds just beyond reach but familiar enough for readers to get lost in new lands with epic adventures all their own.

D. Robert lives in the grey-skied world of Northeast Ohio with his wife, son, daughter, dog, cat, and a back yard pond full of goldfish. When not writing, he loves travelling the country in an RV and riding his bike up and down the hills of Ohio.

Find out more at **www.drobertpease.com**

Also, sign up to be the first to hear about new releases at **http://bit.ly/11zTUEU**

WHAT'S NEXT FROM
D. ROBERT PEASE

CRIMSON SWARM
An Epic Fantasy Novel

Chapter 1 - Birth

Burning oil and cooked meats barely masked the acrid smell of death. His swollen tongue tasted thick dust on cracked lips. Rough stone dug into his back. Opening his eyes, he flung his hands up to shield his gaze. Dust billowed around nearly skeletal fingers, which glowed red against the searing light.

The reek of death grew stronger. He struggled to move, his legs stiff, his shoulders jammed between stone. Wedged in a cramped box, sweat poured from his brow. He kicked his legs and grappled toward the light.

Straining against the edges of the box, he pulled himself up toward the ruddy glow. Grey dots danced across his vision and he nearly fainted. His head spun.

At last, the room steadied.

He sat in a granite box on a raised platform at the end of a long narrow chamber. Stone sarcophagi lined both sides of the room. A chill prickled his skin. *I've awakened in a tomb.*

His mind raced as fresh sweat rolled down his grimy forehead into his eyes. Nightmarish visions of faces filled his mind — faces surrounding him, large pale eyes watching, always watching. A need to climb free of the coffin overpowered him.

Gathering his strength, he lifted his leg over the side and stepped to the floor. A dusty linen sheet fell from his body, and cool air tickled his bare flesh. He felt a touch upon his breast. A delicate amulet dangled on a thin gold strand: a dragon and a lion locked in mortal combat. Set between the beasts was a clear, flawless diamond.

Lamps on golden stands filled the chamber with warm light. Rows of columns on each wall supported a ceiling lost in darkness above. Sharp pain wrenched his hollow stomach. How long had it been since he'd eaten?

The aroma of food nearby drew him toward a bright alcove a few yards down the wall. His legs buckled as he lurched toward a coffin opposite his. Stone, intricately carved in the shape of robes and boot-shod feet, greeted his touch. The sarcophagus lid bore the likeness of a warrior with a sword crossed over his chest. A name came to him: *Vuzhex Mqueg*. He strained to remember.

A rich mural covered the wall above, in which Vuzhex Mqueg stood with a gleaming sword lifted toward a sky of red fire and black smoke.

I dub thee Loequazh Thabo, Bane of Death. Memories gnawed at the edge of his mind.

Columns on either side of the mural, carved in the likeness of majestic oaks, soared toward the ceiling and intertwined with branches from columns on the far wall. No frescos stood watch over his coffin. How did he come to be entombed with such as these? He looked at the richness beyond his drab, stone box. It was apparent he did not belong.

He stumbled toward the flickering light of the alcove. Fire smoldered on a hearth at the far end of a small chamber off the main. In the center, nearly filling the room, stood a polished cherrywood table surrounded by ten chairs, their backs carved to resemble the wings of dragons. Jewel-encrusted plates and goblets sat ready for unseen guests. Large platters and bowls contained soups, meats, cheeses, vegetables, and hard-crusted bread. His mind filled with wonder at the sumptuous meal, but his stomach called for action.

He moved to the nearest chair and sat. Fine utensils lay on each side of the dishes, but he tore into the fare without regard for manners, hoping whoever had prepared the banquet would not begrudge the sacrilege. He devoured the food, tearing off large chunks of meat and bread followed by frenetic gulps of a warm, sweet drink found in a finely etched silver pitcher.

When he could eat no more, he leaned back in his chair. His body shook as he gazed around. He was in a tomb, with no idea how he got there, nor any apparent way to leave. *Where am I? Am I dead? Am I doomed to spend all of eternity roaming this mausoleum, being fed by invisible beings?*

There were no doors in the paneled walls. Standing, he found he had a bit more strength and could walk with a higher confidence. To think his body had grown so weak. *Once I led legions in battle.* This thought stopped him, and he leaned his weight on a chair. He, too, was a warrior? He strained to remember, but fog enveloped his mind.

Shuffling from the alcove, he passed a stone basin with cool water. After splashing his face, he peered at the sarcophagus in front of him. Again, a kingly soldier lay in repose. The same sword, *Loequazh Thabo,* crossed his chest. No name for the warrior came to him, however. His gaze darted toward the fresco behind.

Dark reds and purples defined a scene drawn from the final moments of a grisly battle. A vast host arrayed in crimson surrounded a mounded hill. Fallen men lay in mangled heaps all around, as the vile army taunted their encircled prey. Fire filled the sky. At the summit, an ancient stone hand held aloft the broken body of a woman dressed in tattered white robes. In front of the woman, a shadow of a man grasped a bloodied sword; hope faded. Nevertheless, the figure stood, feet planted wide, blade held high.

He heard a voice as if through a great wind: "Desperation does not become you. Surrender now and sue for leniency."

He staggered back from the fresco. *I will not let you have her.* His eyes leapt to the figure of the woman, broken and bloodied on the stone hand, and tears blurred his vision. Why did she move him so? He clawed at his head trying to remember, but the fog did not lift. He slumped to the floor and cradled his face in his hands, and the voice faded. At the same time, his stomach began to murmur.

He should not have eaten so quickly. Within seconds, his insides twisted in pain, and he lurched to his feet and staggered toward the stone basin. Dousing his face with cool water did nothing to quench sweat that poured from his forehead, while his body quaked in the cold of the room. Bile rose in his throat, and he retched into the bowl. The room blurred around him as his limbs tingled and grew heavy. He collapsed to the floor, feeling cold stone before all went dark.

* * *

He awoke. Visions and voices flitted in and out of his thoughts. Then he realized he no longer shivered.

A soft pillow supported his head and a fragrant blanket covered him. Clothes of rich purple and forest green lay folded neatly near the water basin, along with a pair of supple, finely tooled leather shoes. He sat up, reached for the apparel, and once more caught a heavenly aroma—another meal? *Who has cared for me?*

He dressed, finding everything, including the shoes, fit his thin frame. He peered at the table. In place of dirtied dishes sat clean plates and bowls. A steaming meal drew him toward the room once more. This time the food consisted of fruits, eggs and meats, as well as toasted bread and juices.

He went to the table and ate—being more cautious, eating mainly fruit.

After his hunger subsided, he washed in the basin, now filled with clean water. Once more, he explored the hall and found no doors, no way for someone to get in or out of the mausoleum. *There must be a hidden entrance.* He ran his hands over each wall, searching for cracks or seams that would indicate an opening. He found none.

A raised dais, topped by a throne carved from the same granite as the sarcophagi, filled the far end of the mausoleum. Barren and forlorn it seemed, as if waiting for its owner to return and take rest.

Next to the throne stood a stone altar that held a glimmering, filigreed sword—*Loequazh Thabo*, the very sword depicted in several paintings and carved upon the breasts of many of the tomb's inhabitants. With care, he caressed the steel blade and intricately crafted pommel.

I have come to see your handiwork.

Echoes of some long-gone voice reverberated in his skull. He turned from the sword and gazed to the wall behind the throne.

A fresco of amazing beauty soared thirty feet into the air. It depicted a central figure, many times larger than life, against a star-filled sky overlooking a rich, green pastoral landscape. Animals cavorted in reverie while trees and plants, laden with fruit, made the world abundant and alive. Men and women of various races joined one another in discussion. All seemed at peace.

The portrait of a woman who gazed away from the others caught his eye. Fear filled her face. He followed the line of her stare. A boy-child of only three or four crouched in the lower left corner, his hand stretched toward a smoky darkness. At first, it appeared the painting had been damaged, but on further inspection it became apparent it was part of the work. Blackness boiled in the corner with tendrils reaching out to pull at the child's hand. Creatures with hatred on their faces gazed out from the darkness.

In his mind, he screamed at the child. *Flee! Why does the mother do nothing?* He lifted his eyes to the figure in the stars, whose gaze passed over all of creation toward the boy. A single tear ran down the giant figure's face.

No voices greeted him as he studied the painting, so he turned to regard the rows of sarcophagi. All tolled, there were nine, including his own. He stepped from the dais and moved between the stone coffins. All held men except one, whose lid portrayed a queenly figure carved with long flowing gowns. A mural was painted on the wall behind each one. After a while, a story began to emerge—a story of war that raged across generations. More than once, he found himself moved to tears as he beheld heroic deeds rewarded with blood and death.

Who were these people? What were their names? This thought caused him to pause. *What is my name?*

He stopped and seated himself on the floor with his back against a tree of stone. He closed his eyes and struggled in vain to remember. *Who am I? What is my name?* No voices spoke to him. He searched the room, desperate for clues to his identity.

Writings in multiple languages adorned everything—the sides of the sarcophagi, the walls, even the floors. To his surprise, he could read them all.

He gazed around the mausoleum, growing frantic for some answer to the riddles whispered in his head. Carved at the base of the sarcophagus in front of him, an inscription read:

> *Jafnethox defog adthaom mesgabasaeth thupo~ hegu-quosquauf~ eneafmiquo lomquegisquauf efle goviagol zhufuigo.*

> *Being king does not mean dominance and forced submission, but tenderness, compassion, and duty to protect at all cost the lowliest of the populace.*

Those enshrined in such magnificence must have been of royal blood, but surely not he. The fact of his plain coffin bore witness to that. *Then why am I here? Who am I?*

He stood and peered around. There must be an answer. At last he spied a name carved in small runes just over the head of the warrior nearest him — *Zhuquaif Mqueg.* He turned around and found another name on the coffin which held the woman — *Ellabeth Nauile.* He walked in the direction of his own coffin, past another sarcophagus — *Aerazhire Nauile.* He began to run. *Heulfryne Nauile.*

He reached his plain, stone coffin. Frantic, he searched the granite box, running his fingers over its surface. It was without mark.

He slumped to the floor, his head in his hands. *Who am I?* He pleaded with the voices, "Tell me something useful." The echo of his words faded into silence.

After a while, the effects of his exertion began to take their toll. He retrieved the blankets and pillow and lay down next to his coffin. Names danced in and out of his mind: *Ellabeth Nauile, Aerazhire Nauile, Heulfryne Nauile.* The last name tugged at his memory, but the more he wrestled with it, the less certain he felt the name held any more significance than the others.

At last, he drifted off to sleep, voices luring him from sanity.

* * *

The sound of soft shuffling awakened him. He slitted his eyes to try and catch a glimpse of who cared for him.

The hall had grown dark, and the shadow of a figure drew near and arranged a clean change of clothes on the floor. The rich smell of food told him a new meal had already been laid out on the table.

Down the row of coffins, light came from an open, previously hidden door near the throne. A strong desire overcame him to escape. It was not fear of the figure, but a desperate longing to discover what lay beyond the walls of the mausoleum. *Would I be stopped if I attempted to leave?*

The figure shuffled back toward the light. Within a few moments, the hall brightened as lamps were lit. The lamplighter appeared small, only two-thirds his size, and dressed in a coarse, black-hooded robe.

The figure's back was to him; the time had come to act. He got to his feet and dashed toward the open door.

He nearly reached the exit when he heard a gasp behind him. Not stopping, he ran through the door and into a dusty hallway.

A high-pitched plea sounded from the mausoleum. "Wait. You are not ready."

Nevertheless, he did not stop.

At the end of a short hall, a stair ascended in a spiral. Sputtering torches lined the walls every dozen steps or so.

"You do not understand. I am here to help." Again the voice yelled, insistent but not threatening.

He took the stairs two at a time as they wound upward. The frenzied sound of sandals flapping on stone came behind. After scores of steps, he came to a closed door. Barely slowing, he put his shoulder to the iron-clad wood and heaved. The door flew open, and he stumbled into a large hall filled with black-robed figures.

Every man, woman and child in the room swung their gaze toward him, and what had been boisterous chatter only a heartbeat earlier grew silent. He froze for a moment, his blood pounding in his ears. It was apparent a celebration was taking place. Tables laden with food lined the walls.

He glanced around and then walked toward the center of the room where a fire, with a roast animal on a spit, burned at the top of three steps. He turned when his pursuer entered the room behind him: a young girl, her faced flushed from running.

As he walked, the throng parted, and each in turn dropped their eyes with bowed heads.

He came to the steps around the fire, and stepped on the first. He turned and surveyed the room, and the crowd gaped at him with anticipation. Their faces beamed with wonder. Only the sound of his heavy breathing filled the hall.

At last, when he had breath to speak, he asked the question that haunted him. "What is my name?"

All in the room turned to one side and rested their gaze on a bent figure standing a few paces to his left. Those nearby stepped aside as an old man hobbled forward.

Surprise filled his eyes. "Do you not know?" Gaining his composure, the Elder drew a deep breath. "Your name was given you by your father on the steps outside these very halls in the *Year of Reckoning 3640*. Granted to your name is the highest honor among all men. At your name, nations rise to your aid and enemies tremble."

The old man smiled at the expectant crowd. "Rejoice, for he has come forth. Rejoice and give allegiance to your king: Aberthol Nauile, son of Heulfryne Nauile, rightful heir to the throne and Lord of all Nuadaim."

The black-robed figures fell prostrate to the floor.

RECOMMENDED FROM
EVOLVED PUBLISHING

CHILDREN'S PICTURE BOOKS

THE BIRD BRAIN BOOKS by Emlyn Chand:

    Courtney Saves Christmas

    Davey the Detective

    Honey the Hero

    Izzy the Inventor

    Larry the Lonely

    Poppy the Proud

    Ricky the Runt

    Tommy Goes Trick-or-Treating

    Vicky Finds a Valentine

Silent Words by Chantal Fournier

Thomas and the Tiger-Turtle by Jonathan Gould

I'd Rather Be Riding My Bike by Eric Pinder

VALENTINA'S SPOOKY ADVENTURES

by Majanka Verstraete:

    Valentina and the Haunted Mansion

    Valentina and the Masked Mummy

    Valentina and the Whackadoodle Witch

HISTORICAL FICTION

Circles by Ruby Standing Deer

Spirals by Ruby Standing Deer

Stones by Ruby Standing Deer

LITERARY FICTION

Torn Together by Emlyn Chand

Carry Me Away by Robb Grindstaff

Hannah's Voice by Robb Grindstaff

Turning Trixie by Robb Grindstaff

The Lone Wolf by E.D. Martin

Jellicle Girl by Stevie Mikayne
Weight of Earth by Stevie Mikayne
White Chalk by Pavarti K. Tyler

LOWER GRADE (Chapter Books)
THE THREE LOST KIDS by Kimberly Kinrade:
  The Death of the Sugar Fairy
  The Christmas Curse
  Cupid's Capture
TALES FROM UPON A. TIME by Falcon Storm
  Natalie the Not-So-Nasty
  The Perils of Petunia
  The Persnickety Princess
WEIRDVILLE by Majanka Verstraete
  Fright Train
  House of Horrors
  The Doll Maker

MEMOIR
And Then It Rained: Lessons for Life by Megan Morrison

MIDDLE GRADE
NOAH ZARC by D. Robert Pease:
  Mammoth Trouble (Book 1)
  Cataclysm (Book 2)
  Declaration (Book 3)

MYSTERY / CRIME / DETECTIVE
Hot Sinatra by Axel Howerton

NEW ADULT / CONTEMPORARY
Desert Flower by Angela Scott
Desert Rice by Angela Scott

ROMANCE / EROTICA
THE LOVING NATURE TRILOGY
by Darby Davenport:
    Melt My Heart (Loving Nature Trilogy #3)
    Skinny-Dipping at Dawn (Loving Nature Trilogy #2)
    Walk Away with Me (Loving Nature Trilogy #1)
Claire and J.T. by Amelia James
Secret Storm by Amelia James
Tell Me You Want Me by Amelia James
THE TWISTED MOSAIC by Amelia James
    Her Twisted Pleasures (Twisted Mosaic #1)
    His Twisted Choice (Twisted Mosaic #3)
    The Twisted Mosaic – Special Omnibus Edition
    Their Twisted Love (Twisted Mosaic #2)
The Devil Made Me Do It by Amelia James
Protecting Portia (Sugar House Novella #2) by Pavarti K. Tyler
Sugar & Salt (Sugar House Novella #1) by Pavarti K. Tyler
Two Moons of Sera by Pavarti K. Tyler

SCI-FI / FANTASY
Eulogy by D.T. Conklin

SHORT STORY ANTHOLOGIES
FROM THE EDITORS AT EVOLVED PUBLISHING:
    Evolution: Vol. 1 (A Short Story Collection)
    Evolution: Vol. 2 (A Short Story Collection)
    Pathways (A Young Adult Anthology)
All Tolkien No Action: Swords, Sorcery & Sci-Fi by Eric Pinder

SUSPENSE / THRILLER
Forgive Me, Alex by Lane Diamond
The Devil's Bane by Lane Diamond
Whispers of the Dead by C.L. Roberts-Huth
Whispers of the Serpent by C.L. Roberts-Huth

YOUNG ADULT

Farsighted by Emlyn Chand
Open Heart by Emlyn Chand
Pitch by Emlyn Chand
The Silver Sphere by Michael Dadich
The Sinister Kin by Michael Dadich
Dead Plains (Zombie West #3) by Angela Scott
Survivor Roundup (Zombie West #2) by Angela Scott
Wanted: Dead or Undead (Zombie West #1) by Angela Scott
Zombie West – Special Omnibus Edition by Angela Scott

CPSIA information can be obtained at www.ICGtesting.com
Printed in the USA
BVOW09s2006160415

396515BV00003B/6/P

9 781622 534081